The Rayner-Slade Amalgamation

By J. S. Fletcher

Originally published in 1922

The Rayner-Slade Amalgamation

© 2011 Resurrected Press
www.ResurrectedPress.com

Published by Intrepid Ink, LLC

Intrepid Ink, LLC provides full publishing services to authors of fiction and non-fiction books, eBooks and websites. From editing to formatting, to publishing, to marketing, Intrepid Ink gets your creative works into the hands of the people who want to read them.
Find out more at www.IntrepidInk.com.

ISBN 13: 978-1-937022-05-1

Printed in the United States of America

FOREWORD

In *The Rayner-Slade Amalgamation* J.S. Fletcher takes a somewhat unusual turn for him by dealing with a more conventional crime, that of a large scale jewel theft that results in the murder of his protagonist, the Yorkshire industrialist, Marshall Allerdyke. In many of his earlier mysteries, the locale had been more often been some small coastal town, and the participants more lower middle class, but in Rayner-Slade, Allerdyke is anything but poor, and the stakes are extraordinarily high, a quarter of a million pounds in jewels belonging to a Russian princess.

Allerdyke, however, proves at heart to be a typical Yorkshireman, hard-headed and practical, tenacious, and sharp as a tack. It's not surprising that he is given a flattering characterization as Fletcher, himself, came from Yorkshire and had written extensively of the area's history.

As in most of Fletcher's mysteries, the police play only a minor role in solving the crime, and the private detective makes only a brief appearance at the end. Detection, in the best British manner, is something best left to amateurs, in this case, Allerdyke, Appleyard, his London assistant and fellow Yorkshireman, and the American associate of Allerdyke's cousin, Franklin Fullaway, assisted by Allerdyke's Cockney chauffeur and his brother.

In typical fashion, clues lead first in one direction and then another, suspicion falls on each suspect in turn, and more murders follow the first. Friend and foe become indistinguishable, and only at the last moment are things resolved.

Though published in 1922, the mystery takes place in some vague time period before the First World War, a time when Russian nobility still held sway, only the wealthy could afford motor-cars, and first class travel on train and steamship was still something glamorous. But it was also a time when a man such as Marshall Allerdyke could rise to prominence manufacturing dress goods and American millionaires were staples of British detective fiction.

The Rayner-Slade Amalgamation is an interesting and entertaining novel from the period just before the "Golden Age" of British mysteries that took place in the twenties and thirties. J. S. Fletcher was a prolific writer during this period who's works have been too long neglected. For this reason, Resurrected Press is proud to present *The Rayner-Slade Amalgamation* to a new generation of readers.

About the Author

Joseph Smith Fletcher (1863-1935) was a journalist and the author of over 200 books. Born in Halifax, West Yorkshire, he studied law before turning to journalism. His earlier works were either histories or historical fiction, and he was made a fellow of the Royal Historical Society. He didn't start writing mysteries until 1914, though before he died he had written over 100 in the genre.

Greg Fowlkes
Editor-In-Chief
Resurrected Press
www.ResurrectedPress.com

TABLE OF CONTENTS

1. THE MIDNIGHT RIDE

About eleven o'clock on the night of Monday, May 12, 1914, Marshall Allerdyke, a bachelor of forty, a man of great mental and physical activity, well known in Bradford as a highly successful manufacturer of dress goods, alighted at the Central Station in that city from an express which had just arrived from Manchester, where he had spent the day on business. He had scarcely set foot on the platform when he was confronted by his chauffeur, a young man in a neat dark-green livery, who took his master's travelling rug in one hand, while with the other he held out an envelope.

"The housekeeper said I was to give you that as soon as you got in, sir," he announced. "There's a telegram in it that came at four o'clock this afternoon—she couldn't send it on, because she didn't know exactly where it would find you in Manchester."

Allerdyke took the envelope, tore it open, drew out the telegram, and stepped beneath the nearest lamp. He muttered the wording of the message—

"*On board SS. Perisco*
"*63 miles N.N.E. Spurn Point, 2.15 p.m., May 12th.*

"Expect to reach Hull this evening, and shall stop Station Hotel there for night on way to London. Will you come on at once and meet me? Want to see you on most important business—

"JAMES."

Allerdyke re-read this message, quietly and methodically folded it up, slipped it into his pocket, and with a swift glance at the station clock turned to his chauffeur.

"Gaffney," he said, "how long would it take us to run across to Hull?"

The chauffeur showed no surprise at this question; he had served Allerdyke for three years, and was well accustomed to his ways. "Hull?" he replied. "Let's see, sir—that 'ud be by way of Leeds, Selby, and Howden. About sixty miles in a straight line, but there's a good bit of in-and-out work after you get past Selby, sir. I should say about four hours."

"Plenty of petrol in the car?" asked Allerdyke, turning down the platform. "There is? What time did you have your supper?"

"Ten o'clock, sir," answered Gaffney, with promptitude.

"Bring the car round to the hotel door in the station yard," commanded Allerdyke. "You'll find a couple of Thermos flasks in the locker—bring them into the hotel lounge bar."

The chauffeur went off down the platform. Allerdyke turned up the covered way to the Great Northern Hotel. When the chauffeur joined him there a few minutes later he was giving orders for a supply of freshly-cut beef sandwiches and hard-boiled eggs; the Thermos flasks he handed over to be filled with hot coffee.

"Better get something to eat now, Gaffney," he said. "Get some sandwiches, or some bread and cheese, or something—it's a longish spin."

He himself, waiting while the chauffeur ate and drank, and the provisions were made ready, took a whisky and soda to a chair by the fire, and once more pulled out and read the telegram. And as he read he wondered why his cousin, its sender, wished so particularly to see him at once. James Allerdyke, a man somewhat younger than himself, like himself a bachelor of ample means and of a similar temperament, had of late years concerned himself greatly with various business speculations in Northern Europe, and especially in Russia. He had just been over to St. Petersburg in order to look after certain of his affairs in and near that city, and he was returning home by way of Stockholm and Christiania, in each of which towns he had other ventures to inspect. But Marshall Allerdyke was quite sure that his cousin did not wish to see him about any of these matters—anything connected with them would have kept until they met in the ordinary way, which would have happened within a day or two. No, if James had taken the trouble to send him a message by wireless from the North Sea, it meant that James was really anxious to see him at the first available moment, and would already have landed in Hull, expecting to find him there. However, with a good car, smooth roads, and a fine, moonlit night—

It was not yet twelve o'clock when Allerdyke wrapped himself up in a corner of his luxurious Rolls-Royce, saw that the box of eatables and the two Thermos flasks were safe in the locker, and told Gaffney to go ahead. He himself had the faculty of going to sleep whenever he pleased, and he went to sleep now. He was asleep as Gaffney went through Leeds and its suburbs; he slept all along the country roads which led to Selby and thence to Howden. But in the silent streets of Howden he woke with a start, to find that Gaffney had pulled up in answer to a question flung to him by the driver of another car, which had come alongside their own from the opposite direction. That car had also been pulled up; within it Allerdyke saw a woman, closely wrapped in furs.

"What is it, Gaffney?" he asked, letting down his own window and leaning out.

"Wants to know which is the best way to get across the Ouse, sir," answered Gaffney. "I tell him there's two ferries close by—one at Booh, the other at Langrick—but there'll be nobody to work them at this hour. Where do you want to get to?" he went on, turning to the driver of the other car.

"Want to strike the Great Northern main line somewhere," answered the driver. "This lady wants to catch a Scotch express. I thought of Doncaster, but—"

The window of the other car was let down, and its occupant looked out. The light of the full moon shone full on her, and Allerdyke lifted his cap to a pretty, alert-looking young woman of apparently twenty-five, who politely returned his salutation.

"Can I give you any advice?" asked Allerdyke. "I understand you want—"

"An express train to Scotland—Edinburgh," replied the lady. "I made out, on arrival at Hull, that if I motored across country I would get a train at some station on the Great Northern line—a morning express. Doncaster, Selby, York—which is nearest from wherever we are!"

"This is Howden," said Allerdyke, looking up at the great tower of the old church. "And your best plan is to follow this road to Selby, and then to York. All the London expresses stop there, but they don't all stop at Selby or at Doncaster. And there's no road bridge over the Ouse nearer than Selby in any case."

"Many thanks," responded the lady. "Then," she went on, looking at her driver, "you will go on to York—that is—how far?" she added, favouring Allerdyke with a gracious smile. "Very far?"

"Less than an hour's run," answered Gaffney for his master. "And a good road."

The lady bowed; Allerdyke once more raised his cap; the two cars parted company. And Allerdyke stopped Gaffney as he was driving off again, and produced the provisions.

"Half-past two," he remarked, pulling out his watch. "You've come along in good style, Gaffney. We'll have something to eat and drink. Queer thing, eh, for anybody to motor across from Hull to catch a Great Northern express on the main line!"

"Mayn't be any trains out of Hull during the night, sir," answered Gaffney, taking a handful of sandwiches. "They'll get one at York, anyway. Want to reach Hull at any particular time, sir?"

"No," answered Allerdyke. "Go along as you've come. You'll have a bit of uphill work over the edge of the Wolds, now. When we strike Hull, go to the Station Hotel."

He went to sleep again as soon as they moved out of Howden, and he only awoke when the car stopped at the hotel door in Hull. A night-porter, hearing the buzz of the engine, came out.

"Put the car in the garage, Gaffney, and then get yourself a bed and lie as long as you like," said Allerdyke. "I'll let you know when I want you." He turned to the night-porter. "You've a Mr. James Allerdyke stopping here I think?" he went on. "He'd come in last night from the Christiania steamer."

The night-porter led the way into the hotel, and towards the office.

"Mr. Marshall Allerdyke?" he asked of the new arrival. "The gentleman left a card for you; I was asked to give it to you as soon as you came."

Allerdyke took the visiting-card which the man produced from a letter rack, and read the lines hastily scribbled on the back—

If you land here during the night, come straight up to my room—263—and rouse me out. Want to see you at once.—J.A.

Allerdyke slipped the card into his pocket and turned to the night-porter.

"My cousin wants me to go up to his room at once," he said. "Just show me the way. Do you happen to know what time he got in last night?" he continued, as they went upstairs. "Was it late?"

"Passengers from the *Perisco*, sir?" answered the night-porter. "There were several of 'em came in last night—she got into the river about eight-thirty. It 'ud be a bit after nine o'clock when your friend came in."

Allerdyke's mind went back to the meeting at Howden.

"Did you have a lady set off from here in the middle of the night?" he asked, out of sheer curiosity. "A lady in a motor-car?"

"Oh! that lady," exclaimed the night-porter, with a grim laugh. "Ah! nice lot of bother she gave me, too. She was one of those *Perisco* passengers—she got in here with the rest, and booked a room, and went to it all right, and then at half-past twelve down she came and said she wanted to get on, and as there weren't no trains she'd have a motor-car and drive to catch an express at Selby, or Doncaster, or somewhere. Nice job I had to get her a car at that time o' night!—and me single-handed—there wasn't a soul in the office then. Meet her anywhere, sir?"

"Met her on the road," replied Allerdyke laconically. "Was she a foreigner, do you know?"

"I shouldn't wonder if she was something of that sort," answered the night-porter. "Sort that would have her own way at all events. Here's the room, sir."

He paused before the door of a room which stood halfway down a long corridor in the centre of the hotel, and on its panels he knocked gently.

"Every room's filled on this floor, sir," he remarked. "I hope your friend's a light sleeper, for there's some of 'em'll have words to say if they're roused at four o'clock in the morning."

"He's a very light sleeper as a rule," replied Allerdyke. He stood listening for the sound of some movement in the room: "Knock again," he said, when a minute had passed without response on the part of the occupant. "Make it a bit louder."

The night-porter, with evident unwillingness, repeated his summons, this time loud enough to wake any ordinary sound sleeper. But no sound came from within the room, and after a third and much louder thumping at the door, Allerdyke grew impatient and suspicious.

"This is queer!" he growled. "My cousin's one of the lightest sleepers I ever knew. If he's in there, there's something wrong. Look here! you'll have to open that door. Haven't you got a key?"

"Key'll be inside, sir," replied the night-porter. "But there's a master-key to all these doors in the office. Shall I fetch it, then?"

"Do!" said Allerdyke, curtly. He began to walk up and down the corridor when the man had hurried away, wondering what this soundness of sleep in his cousin meant. James Allerdyke was not a man who took either drink or drugs, and Marshall's experience of him was that the least sound awoke him.

"Queer!" he repeated as he marched up and down. "Perhaps he's not—"

The quiet opening of a door close by made him lift his eyes from the carpet. In the dim light he saw a man looking out upon him—a man of an unusually thick crop of hair and with a huge beard. He stared at Allerdyke half angrily, half sulkily; then he closed his door as quietly as he had opened it. And Allerdyke, turning back to his cousin's room, mechanically laid his hand on the knob and screwed it round.

The door was open.

Allerdyke drew a sharp breath as he crossed the threshold. He had stayed in that hotel often, and he knew where the switch of the electric light should be. He lifted a hand, found the switch, and turned the light on. And as it flooded the room, he pulled himself up to a tense rigidity. There, sitting fully dressed in an easy chair, against which his head was thrown back, was his cousin—unmistakably dead.

2. THE DEAD MAN

For a full minute Marshall Allerdyke stood fixed—staring at the set features before him. Then, with a quick catching of his breath, he made one step to his cousin's side and laid his hand on the unyielding shoulder. The affectionate, familiar terms in which they had always addressed each other sprang involuntarily to his lips.

"Why, James, my lad!" he exclaimed. "James, lad! James!"

Even as he spoke, he knew that James would never hear word or sound again in this world. It needed no more than one glance at the rigid features, one touch of the already fixed and statue-like body, to know that James Allerdyke was not only dead, but had been dead some time. And, with a shuddering sigh, Marshall Allerdyke drew himself up and looked round at his surroundings.

Nothing could have been more peaceful than that quiet hotel bedroom; nothing more orderly than its arrangements. Allerdyke had always known his cousin for a man of unusually tidy and methodical habits; the evidence of that orderliness was there, where he had pitched his camp for presumably a single night. His toilet articles were spread out on the dressing-table; his pyjamas were laid across his pillow; his open suit-case lay on a stand at the foot of the bed; by the bedside lay his slippers. An overcoat hung from one peg of the door; a dressing-gown from another; on a chair in a corner lay, neatly folded, a couple of travelling rugs. All these little details Allerdyke's sharp eyes took in at a glance; he turned from them to the things nearer the dead man.

James Allerdyke sat in a big easy chair, placed at the side of a round table set towards a corner of the room. He was fully dressed in a grey tweed suit, but he had taken off one boot—the left—and it lay at his feet on the hearthrug. He himself was thrown back against the high-padded hood of the chair; there was a little frown on his set features, a tiny puckering of the brows above his closed eyes. His hands were lying at his sides, unclasped, the fingers slightly stretched, the thumbs slightly turned inward; everything looked as if, in the very act of taking off his boots, some sudden spasm of pain had seized him, and he had sat up, leaned back, and died, as swiftly as the seizure had come. There was a slight blueness under the lower rims of the eyes, a corresponding tint on the clean-shaven upper lip, but neither that nor the pallor which had long since settled on the rigid features had given anything of ghastliness to the face. The dead man lay back in his chair in such an easy posture that but for his utter quietness, his intense immobility, he might have well been taken for one who was hard and fast asleep.

The sound of the night-porter's returning footsteps sent Allerdyke out into the corridor. Unconsciously he shook his head and raised a hand—as if to warn the man against noise.

"Sh!" he said, still acting and speaking mechanically. "Here's—I knew something was wrong. The fact is, my cousin's dead!"

In his surprise the night-porter dropped the key which he had been to fetch. When he straightened himself from picking it up, his ruddy face had paled.

"Dead!" he exclaimed in a whisper. "Him! Why, he looked the picture of health last night. I noticed that of him, anyway!"

"He's dead now," said Allerdyke. "He's lying there dead. Come in!"

The door along the corridor from which the man of the shock head and great beard had looked out, opened again, and the big head was protruded. Its owner, seeing the two standing there, came out.

"Anything wrong?" he asked, advancing towards them in his pyjamas. "If there's any illness, I'm a medical man. Can I be of use?"

Allerdyke turned sharply, looking the stranger well over. He was not sure whether the man was an Englishman or a foreigner; he fancied that he detected a slightly foreign accent. The tone was well-meaning, and even kindly.

"I'm obliged to you," replied Allerdyke, in his characteristically blunt fashion. "I'm afraid nobody can be of use. The truth is, I came to join my cousin here, and I find him dead. Seems to me he's been dead some time. As you're a doctor, you can tell, of course. Perhaps you'll come in?"

He led the way back into the bedroom, the other two following closely behind him. At sight of the dead man the bearded stranger uttered a sharp exclamation.

"Ah!" he said. "Mr. Allerdyke!"

"You knew him, then?" demanded Marshall. "You've met him?"

The other, who had stooped over the body, bestowing a light touch on face and hand, looked up and nodded.

"I came over with him from Christiania," he answered. "I met him there—at a hotel. I had several conversations with him. In fact, I warned him."

"Warned him? Of what!" asked Allerdyke.

"Over-exertion," replied the doctor quietly. "I saw symptoms of heart-strain. That was why I talked with him. I gathered from what he told me that he was a man who lived a very strenuous life, and I warned him against doing too much. He was not fitted for it."

"Good Lord!" exclaimed Allerdyke, with obvious impatience. "Why, I always considered him as one of the fittest men I ever knew!"

"Perhaps you did," said the doctor. "Laymen, sir, do not see what a trained eye sees. The proof in his case is— there!"

He pointed to the dead man, at whom the night-porter was staring with astonished eyes.

Allerdyke stared, too, or seemed to stare. In reality, he was gazing into space, wondering about what had just been said.

"Then you think he died a natural death?" he asked, suddenly turning on his companion. "You don't think there's—anything wrong?"

The doctor shook his head calmly.

"I think he died of precisely what I should have expected him to die of," he answered. "Heart failure. It came upon him quite suddenly. You see, he was in the act of taking off his boots. He is a little fleshy—stout. The exertion of bending over and down—that was too much. He felt a sharp spasm—he sat back—he died, there and then."

"There and then!" repeated Allerdyke mechanically. "Well—what's to be done!" he went on. "What is done in these cases—I suppose you know?"

"There will have to be an inquest later on," answered the doctor. "I can give evidence for you, if you like—I am staying in Hull for a few days—for I can certainly testify to what I had observed. But that comes later—at present you had better acquaint the manager of the hotel, and I should suggest sending for a local medical man—there are some eminent men of my profession in this town. And—the body should be laid out. I'll go and dress, and then do what I can for you."

"Much obliged," responded Allerdyke. "Very kind of you. What name, sir?"

"My name is Lydenberg," replied the stranger. "I will give you my card presently. I have the honour of addressing—?"

Allerdyke pulled out his own card-case.

"My name's Marshall Allerdyke," he answered. "I'm his cousin," he went on, with another glance at the still figure. "And, my conscience, I never thought to find him like this! I never heard of any weakness on his part—I always thought him a particularly strong man."

"You will send for another medical man?" asked Dr. Lydenberg. "It will be more satisfactory to you."

"Yes, I'll see to that," replied Allerdyke. He turned to look at the night-porter, who was still hanging about as if fascinated. "Look here!" he said. "We don't want any fuss. Just rouse the manager quietly, and ask him to come here. And find that chauffeur of mine, and tell him I want him. Now, then, what about a doctor? Do you know a real, first-class one?"

"There's several within ten minutes, sir," answered the night-porter. "There's Dr. Orwin, in Coltman Street— he's generally fetched here. I can get a man to go for him at once."

"Do!" commanded Allerdyke. "But send me my driver first—I want him. Tell him what's happened."

He waited, standing and staring at his dead cousin until Gaffney came hurrying along the corridor. Allerdyke beckoned him into the room and closed the door.

"Gaffney," he said. "You see how things are? Mr. James is dead—I found him sitting there, dead. He's been dead some time—hours. There's a doctor, a foreigner, I think, across the passage there, who says it's been heart failure. I've sent for another doctor. Now in the meantime, I want to see what my cousin's got on him, and I want you to help me. We'll take everything off him in the way of valuables, papers, and so on, and put 'em in that small hand-bag of his."

Master and man went methodically to work; and an observer of an unduly sentimental shade of mind might have said that there was something almost callous about their measured, business-like proceedings. But Marshall Allerdyke was a man of eminently thorough and practical habits, and he was doing what he did with an idea and a purpose. His cousin might have died from sudden heart failure; again, he might not, there might have been foul play; there might have been one of many reasons for his unexpected death—anyway, in Allerdyke's opinion it was necessary for him to know exactly what James was carrying about his person when death took place. There was a small hand-bag on the dressing-table; Allerdyke opened it and took out all its contents. They were few—a muffler, a travelling-cap, a book or two, some foreign newspapers, a Russian word-book, a flask, the various odds and ends, small unimportant things which a voyager by sea and land picks up. Allerdyke took all these out, and laying them aside on the table, directed Gaffney to take everything from the dead man's pockets. And Gaffney, solemn of face and tight of lip, set to his task in silence.

There was comparatively little to bring to light. A watch and chain—the small pocket articles which every man carries—keys, a monocle eyeglass, a purse full of gold, loose silver, a note-case containing a considerable sum in bank-notes, some English, some foreign, letters and papers, a pocket diary—these were all. Allerdyke took each as Gaffney produced them, and placed each in the bag with no more than a mere glance.

"Everything there is, sir," whispered the chauffeur at last. "I've been through every pocket."

Allerdyke found the key of the bag, locked it, and set it aside on the mantelpiece. Then he went over to the suit-case lying on the bench at the foot of the bed, closed and locked it, and dropped the bunch of keys in his pocket. And just then Dr. Lydenberg came back, dressed, and on his heels came the manager of the hotel, startled and anxious, and with him an elderly professional-looking man whom he introduced as Dr. Orwin.

When James Allerdyke's dead body had been lifted on to the bed, and the two medical men had begun a whispered conversation beside it, Allerdyke drew the hotel manager aside to a corner of the room.

"Did you see anything of my cousin when he arrived last night?" he asked.

"Not when he arrived—no," replied the manager. "But later—yes. I had some slight conversation with him after he had taken supper. It was nothing much—he merely wished to know if there was always a night-porter on duty. He said he expected a friend, who might turn up at any hour of the night, and he wanted to leave a card for him. That would be you, I suppose, sir?"

"Just so," replied Allerdyke. "Now, how did he seem at that time? And what time was that?"

"Ten o'clock," said the manager. "Seem? Well, sir, he seemed to be in the very best of health and spirits! I was astonished to hear that he was dead. I never saw a man look more like living. He was—"

The elderly doctor came away from the bed approaching Allerdyke.

"After hearing what Dr. Lydenberg tells me, and examining the body—a mere perfunctory examination as yet, you know—I have little doubt that this gentleman died of what is commonly called heart failure," he said. "There will have to be an inquest, of course, and it may be advisable to make a post-mortem examination. You are a relative?"

"Cousin," replied Allerdyke. He hesitated a moment, and then spoke bluntly. "You don't think it's been a case of poisoning, do you?" he said.

Dr. Orwin pursed his lips and regarded his questioner narrowly.

"Self-administered, do you mean?" he asked.

"Administered any way," answered Allerdyke. "Self or otherwise." He squared his shoulders and spoke determinedly. "I don't understand about this heart-failure notion," he went on. "I never heard him complain of his heart. He was a strong, active man—hearty and full of go. I want to know—everything."

"There should certainly be an autopsy," murmured Dr. Orwin. He turned and looked at his temporary colleague, who nodded as if in assent. Then he turned back to Allerdyke. "If you'll leave us for a while, we will just make a further examination—then we'll speak to you later."

Allerdyke signified his assent with a curt nod of the head. Accompanied by the manager and Gaffney he left the room, and with him he carried the small hand-bag in which he had placed the dead man's personal effects.

3. THE SHOE BUCKLE

Once outside the death-chamber, Allerdyke asked the manager to give him a bedroom with a sitting-room attached to it, and to put Gaffney in another room close by—he should be obliged, he said, to stay at the hotel until the inquest was over and arrangements had been made for his cousin's funeral. The manager at once took him to a suite of three rooms at the end of the corridor which they were then in. Allerdyke took it at once, sent Gaffney down to bring up certain things from the car, and detained the manager for a moment's conversation.

"I suppose you'd a fair lot of people come in last night from that Christiania boat?" he asked.

"Some fifteen or twenty," answered the manager.

"Did you happen to see my cousin in conversation with any of them?" inquired Allerdyke.

The manager shrugged his shoulders. He was not definitely sure about that; he had a notion that he had seen Mr. James Allerdyke talking with some of the *Perisco* passengers, but the notion was vague.

"You know how it is," he went on. "People come in— they stand about talking in the hall—groups, you know— they go from one to another. I think I saw him talking to that doctor who's in there now with Dr. Orwin—the man with the big beard—and to a lady who came at the same time. There were several ladies in the party—the passengers were all about in the hall, and in the coffee-room, and so on. There are a lot of other people in the house, too, of course."

"It's this way," said Allerdyke. "I'm not at all satisfied about what these doctors say, so far. They may be right, of course—probably are. Still I want to know all I can, and, naturally, I'd like to know who the people were that my cousin was last in company with. You never know what may have happened—there's often something that doesn't show at first."

"There was—nothing missing in his room, I hope?" asked the manager with professional anxiety.

"Nothing that I know of," answered Allerdyke. "My man and I have searched him, and taken possession of everything—all that he had on him is in that bag, and I'm going to examine it now. No—I don't think anything had been taken from him, judging by what I've seen."

"You wouldn't like me to send for the police?" suggested the manager.

"Not at present," replied Allerdyke. "Not, at any rate, until these doctors say something more definite—they'll know more presently, no doubt. Of course, you've a list of all the people who came in last night?"

"They would all register," answered the manager. "But then, you know, sir, many of them will be going this morning—most of them are only breaking their journey. You can look over the register whenever you like."

"Later on," said Allerdyke. "In the meantime, I'll examine these things. Send me up some coffee as soon as your people are stirring."

He unlocked the hand-bag when the manager had left him. It seemed to his practical and methodical mind that his first duty was to make himself thoroughly acquainted with the various personal effects which he and Gaffney had found on the dead man. Of the valuables he took little notice; it was very evident, in his opinion, that if James Allerdyke's death had been brought about by some sort of foul play—a suspicion which had instantly crossed his mind as soon as he discovered that his cousin was dead—the object of his destroyer had not been robbery. James had always been accustomed to carrying a considerable sum of money on him; Gaffney's search had brought a considerable sum to light. James also wore a very valuable watch and chain and two fine diamond rings; there they all were. Not robbery—no; at least, not robbery of the ordinary sort. But—had there been robbery of another, a bigger, a subtle, and deep-designed sort? James was a man of many affairs and schemes—he might have had valuable securities, papers relating to designs, papers containing secrets of great moment; he was interested, for example, in several patents—he might have had documents pertinent to some affair of such importance that ill-disposed folk, eager to seize them, might have murdered him in order to gain possession of them. There were many possibilities, and there was always—to Allerdyke's mind—the improbability that James had died through sudden illness.

Now that Marshall Allerdyke's mind was clearing, getting free of the first effects of the sudden shock of finding his cousin dead, doubt and uneasiness as to the whole episode were rising strongly within him. He and James had been brought up together; they had never been apart from each other for more than a few months at a time during thirty-five years, and he flattered himself that he knew James as well as any man of James's acquaintance. He could not remember that his cousin had ever made any complaint of illness or indisposition; he had certainly never had any serious sickness in his life. As to heart trouble, Allerdyke knew that a few years previous to his death, James had taken out a life-policy with a first-rate office, and had been passed as a first-class life: he remembered, as he sat there thinking over these things, the self-satisfied grin with which James had come and told him that the examining doctor had declared him to be as sound as a bell. It was true, of course, that disease might have set in after that—still, it was only six weeks since he had seen James and James was then looking in a fit, healthy, hearty state. He had gone off on one of his Russian journeys as full of life and spirits as a man could be—and had not the hotel manager just said that he seemed full of health, full of go, at ten o'clock last night? And yet, within a couple of hours or so—according to what the medical men thought from their hurried examination—this active vigorous man was dead—swiftly and mysteriously dead.

Allerdyke felt—felt intensely—that there was something deeply strange in all this, and yet it was beyond him, with his limited knowledge, to account for James's sudden death, except on the hypothesis suggested by the two doctors. All sorts of vague, half-formed thoughts were in his mind. Was there any person who desired James's death? Had any one tracked him to this place—got rid of him by some subtle means? Had—

"Pshaw!" he muttered, suddenly interrupting his train of thought, and recognizing how shapeless and futile it all was. "It just comes to this—I'm asking myself if the poor lad was murdered! And what have I to go on? Naught—naught at all!"

Nevertheless, there were papers before him which had been taken from James's pocket; there was the little journal or diary which he always carried, and in which, to Allerdyke's knowledge, he always jotted down a brief note of each day's proceedings wherever he went. He could examine these, at any rate—they might cast some light on his cousin's recent doings.

He began with the diary, turning over its pages until he came to the date on which James had left Bradford for St. Petersburg. That was on March 30th. He had travelled to the Russian capital overland—by way of Berlin and Vilna, at each of which places he had evidently broken his journey. From St. Petersburg he had gone on to Moscow, where he had spent the better part of a week. All his movements were clearly set out in the brief pencilled entries in the journal. From Moscow he had returned to St. Petersburg; there he had stayed a fortnight; thence he had journeyed to Revel, from Revel he had crossed the Baltic to Stockholm; from Stockholm he had gone across country to Christiania. And from Christiania he had sailed for Hull to meet his death in that adjacent room where the doctors were now busied with his body.

Marshall Allerdyke, though he had no actual monetary connection with them, had always possessed a fairly accurate knowledge of his cousin's business affairs—James was the sort of man who talked freely to his intimates about his doings. Therefore Allerdyke was able to make out from the journal what James had done during his stay at St. Petersburg, in Moscow, in Revel, and in Stockholm, in all of which places he had irons of one sort or another in the fire. He recognized the names of various firms upon which James had called—these names were as familiar to him as those of the big manufacturing concerns in his own town. James had been to see this man, this man had been to see James. He had dined with such an one; such an one had dined with him. Ordinarily innocent entries, all these; there was no subtle significance to be attached to any of them: they were just the sort of entries which the busy commercial man, engaged in operations of some magnitude, would make for his own convenience.

There was, in short, nothing in that tiny book—a mere, waistcoat-pocket sort of affair—which Allerdyke was at a loss to understand, or which excited any wonder or speculation in him: with one exception. That exception was in three entries: brief, bald, mere lines, all made during James's second stay—the fortnight period—in St. Petersburg. They were:—

April 18: Met Princess.

April 20: Lunched with Princess.

April 23: Princess dined with me.

These entries puzzled Allerdyke. His cousin had been going over to Russia at least twice a year for three years, but he had never heard him mention that he had formed the acquaintance of any person of princely rank. Who was this Princess with whom James had evidently become on such friendly terms that they had lunched and dined together? James had twice written to him during his absence—he had both letters in his pocket then, and one of them was dated from St. Petersburg on April 24th, but there was no mention of any Princess in either. Seeking for an explanation, he came to the conclusion that James, who had a slight weakness for the society of ladies connected with the stage, had made the acquaintance of some actress or other, ballet-dancer, singer, artiste, and had given her the nickname of Princess.

That was all there was to be got from the diary. It amounted to nothing. There were, however, the loose papers. He began to examine these methodically. They were few in number—James was the sort of man who never keeps anything which can be destroyed: Allerdyke knew from experience that he had a horror of accumulating what he called rubbish. These papers, fastened together with a band of india-rubber, were all business documents, with one exception—a letter from Allerdyke himself addressed to Stockholm, to wait James's arrival. There were some specifications relating to building property; there was a schedule of the timber then standing in a certain pine forest in Sweden in which James had a valuable share; there was a balance-sheet of a Moscow trading concern in which he had invested money; there were odds and ends of a similar nature—all financial. From these papers Allerdyke could only select one which he did not understand, which conveyed no meaning to him. This was a telegram, dispatched from London on April 21st, at eleven o'clock in the morning. He spread it out on the table and slowly read it:—

"To *James Allerdyke, Hotel Grand Monarch, St. Petersburg.*

"Your wire received. If Princess will confide goods to your care to personally bring over here have no doubt matter can be speedily and satisfactorily arranged. Have important client now in town until middle May who seems to be best man to approach and is likely to be a generous buyer.

"FRANKLIN FULLAWAY, Waldorf Hotel, London."

Here was another surprise: Allerdyke had never in his life heard James mention the name—Franklin Fullaway. Yet here Mr. Franklin Fullaway, whoever he might be, was wiring to James as only a business acquaintance of some standing would wire. And here again was the mention of a Princess—presumably, nay, evidently, the Princess to whom reference was made in the diary. And there was mention, too, of goods—probably valuable goods—to be confided to James's care for conveyance to England, to London, for sale to some prospective purchaser. If James had brought them, where were they? So far as Allerdyke had ascertained, James had no luggage beyond his big suitcase and the handbag which now stood on the table before his own eyes—he was a man for travelling light, James, and never encumbered himself with more than indispensable necessities. Where, then—

A tap at the door of the sitting-room prefaced the entry of the two medical men.

"We heard from the manager that you were in this room, Mr. Allerdyke," said Dr. Orwin. "Well, we made a further examination of your relative, and we still incline to the opinion expressed already. Now, if you approve it, I will arrange at once for communicating with the Coroner, removing the body, and having an autopsy performed. As Dr. Lydenberg has business in the town which will keep him here a few days, he will join me, and it will be more satisfactory to you, no doubt, if another doctor is called—I should advise the professional police surgeon. If you will leave it to me—"

"I'll leave everything of that sort to you, doctor," said Allerdyke. "I'm much obliged to both of you, gentlemen. You understand what I'm anxious about?—I want to be certain—certain, mind you!—of the cause of my cousin's death. Now you speak of removing him? Then I'll just go and take a look at him before that's done."

He presently locked up his rooms, leaving the hand-bag there, also locked, and went alone to the room in which James lay dead. Most folks who knew Marshall Allerdyke considered him a hard, unsentimental man, but there were tears in his eyes as he stooped over his cousin's body and laid his hand on the cold forehead. Once more he broke into familiar, muttered speech.

"If there's been aught wrong, lad," he said. "Aught foul or underhand, I'll right thee!—by God, I will!"

Then he stooped lower and kissed the dead man's cheek, and pressed the still hands. It was with an effort that he turned away and regained his self-command—and it was in that moment that his eyes, slightly blurred as they were, caught sight of an object which lay half-concealed by a corner of the hearth-rug—a glittering, shining object, which threw back the gleam of the still burning electric light. He strode across the room and picked it up—the gold buckle of a woman's shoe, studded with real, if tiny, diamonds.

4. Mr. Franklin Fullaway

Allerdyke carried his find away to his own room and carefully examined it. The buckle was of real gold; the stones set in it were real diamonds, small though they were. He deduced two ideas from these facts—one, that the owner was a woman who loved pretty and expensive things; the other, that she must have a certain natural carelessness about her not to have noticed that the buckle was loose on her shoe. But as he put the buckle safely away in his own travelling bag, he began to speculate on matters of deeper import—how did it come to be lying there in James Allerdyke's room? How long had it been lying there? Had its owner been into that room recently? Had she, in fact, been in the room since James Allerdyke took possession of it on his arrival at the hotel?

He realized the possibility of various answers to these questions. The buckle might have been dropped by a former occupant of the room. But was that likely? Would an object sparkling with diamonds have escaped the eyes of even a careless chambermaid? Would it have escaped the keener eyes of James Allerdyke? Anyhow, that question could easily be settled by finding out how long that particular room had been unoccupied before James was put into it. A much more important question was—had the owner of the buckle been in the room between nine o'clock of the previous evening and five o'clock that morning? Out of that, again, rose certain supplementary questions: What had she been doing there? And most important of all—who was she? That might possibly be solved by an inspection of the hotel register, and after he had drunk the coffee which was presently brought up to him, Allerdyke went down to the office to set about that necessary, yet problematic, task.

As he reached the big hall on the ground floor of the hotel, the manager came across to him, displaying a telegram.

"For your cousin, sir," he announced, handing it over to Allerdyke. "Just come in."

Allerdyke slowly opened the envelope, and as he unfolded the message, caught the name Franklin Fullaway at its foot—

"Let me know what time you arrive King's Cross today and I will meet you, highly important we should both see my prospective client at once."

This message bore the same address which Allerdyke had found in the telegram discovered in James's pocketbook—Waldorf Hotel—and he determined to wire Mr. Franklin Fullaway immediately. He sat down at a writing-table in the hall and drew a sheaf of telegraph forms towards him. But it was not easy to compose the message which he wished to send. He knew nothing of the man to whom he must address it, nothing of his business relations with James; he had no clear notion of what the present particular transaction was, nor how it might be connected with what had just happened. After considerable thought he wrote out a telegram of some length, and carried it himself to the telegraph office in the station outside:—

"To *Franklin Fullaway, Waldorf Hotel, London.*

"Your wire to James Allerdyke opened by undersigned, his cousin. James Allerdyke died suddenly here during night. Circumstances somewhat mysterious. Investigation proceeding. Have found on body your telegram to him of April 21. Glad if you can explain business referred to therein, or give any other information about his recent doings abroad.

"From MARSHALL ALLERDYKE, Station Hotel, Hull."

It was by that time eight o'clock, and the railway station and the hotel had started into the business of another day. There were signs that people who had stayed in the hotel over-night were about to take their departure by early trains, and Allerdyke hastened back to the office to look over the register—he was anxious to know who and what the folk were who had been near and about his cousin in his last hours. But a mere glance at the big pages showed him the uselessness of his task. There were some seventy or eighty entries, made during the previous twenty-four hours; it was impossible to go into the circumstances of each. He turned with a look of despair to the manager at his elbow.

"Nothing much to be made out of that!" he muttered. "Still—which are the people who came off the *Perisco* last night?"

The manager summoned a clerk; the clerk indicated a sequence of entries, amongst which Allerdyke at once noticed the name of Dr. Lydenberg. The rest were, of course, unfamiliar to him.

"There was a lady here last night, who, according to your night-porter, changed her mind about staying, and set off in a motor-car about midnight," observed Allerdyke. "Which is she, now, in this lot?"

The clerk instantly pointed to an entry, made in a big, dashing, artistic-looking handwriting.

"That," he answered. "Miss Celia Lennard—Number 265."

Two numbers away from James Allerdyke's room—Number 263! The inquirer pricked his ears.

"It was she who went off in the middle of the night," continued the clerk. "She pestered me with a lot of questions as to how she could get North—to Edinburgh. That would be about eleven o'clock. I told her she couldn't get a train until morning. I saw her going upstairs just before I went off duty—soon after eleven. It seems, according to the night-porter—"

"I know—he told me," said Allerdyke, interrupting him. "He got her a car, she wanted to be driven to some station on the Great Northern main line—I met her on the road at two-thirty. I suppose the driver of that car can be found?—he'll have returned by this, I should think."

"Oh, you can find him all right," answered the clerk. "The car was got from a garage close by."

Allerdyke jotted down the name of the garage in his pocket-book, and proceeded to make further inquiries about his cousin's movements on the previous night. He interviewed various hotel servants—waiters, chambermaids, porters, all could tell him something, and the sum total of what they could tell amounted, for all practical purposes, to next to nothing. James Allerdyke had come to the hotel just as several other people had come. He had been served with a light supper in the coffee-room; he had been seen chatting with one or two people in the lounge and in the smoking-room; a chambermaid had seen him in his own room—according to all these people there was nothing in his appearance or his behaviour that was out of the common, and all agreed that he looked very well.

The manager, who accompanied Allerdyke in his round of these inquiries, glanced at him with a puzzled expression when they came to an end.

"Of course, sir, if you would like the police to be summoned," he suggested for the second time. "Perhaps—"

"No—not yet!" answered Allerdyke. "I daresay they'll have to be called in; indeed, I suppose it's absolutely necessary, because of the inquest, but I'll wait until I hear what these doctors have to say, and, besides that, I want to get some news from London. It's a queer business altogether, and if there has been any foul play, why"—he paused and looked round at the people who were passing in and out of the hall, in a corner of which he and the manager were standing—"we can't hold up all these folk and ask 'em if they know anything, you know," he added, with a grim smile.

"That's the devil of it! If there has, as I say, been aught wrong—murder, to put it plainly—why, the criminal or criminals may already be off or going off now, amongst these people, and I can't stop them. In a few hours they may be where nobody can find them—don't you see?"

The manager did see, and shrugged his shoulders with a gesture of helplessness. Again he could only suggest expert help from the police—but this time he added to his suggestion the remark that he understood there was nothing for the police to take hold of—no clue, no signs of foul play.

"Not yet," agreed Allerdyke. "But—there may be. Well, I'm afraid that register is no good. It's meaningless. A list of names conveys nothing—except for future reference. For the present we must wait. But—in any way you can—keep your eyes open. There's one thing you can do—there was a lady in here last night who took Room 265 and left it at midnight to go away in a motor-car which your night-porter got for her. I particularly want to see the chambermaid who attended that lady. Let me see her privately—I've a question to ask her."

"She shall be sent up to your sitting-room as soon as I've found her," responded the manager. "This is the servants' breakfast-hour, but—"

"Send her up there after nine o'clock," said Allerdyke. "In the meantime I've another inquiry to make elsewhere."

He found Gaffney and sent him round to the garage from which Miss Celia Lennard had obtained her midnight car, with instructions to find the chauffeur who had driven her, and to get from him what information he could as to her movements subsequent to the rencontre at Howden.

"Don't excite his suspicions," said Allerdyke, "but pump him for any news he can give you. I want to know what became of her."

Gaffney speedily returned, fully informed of Miss Lennard's movements up to a certain point. The chauffeur had just got back, and was about to seek the bed from which he had been pulled at one o'clock in the morning. He had taken the lady to York—only to find that there was no train thence to Edinburgh until after nine o'clock. So she had turned into the Station Hotel at York, to wait, and there he had left her.

There was little of importance in this, but it seemed to indicate that Miss Lennard was certainly about to travel North, and that her hurried departure from the hotel was due to a genuine desire to reach her ultimate destination as speedily as possible. While Allerdyke was wondering if it would be worth while to follow her up, merely because she had been a fellow-passenger with his cousin, the manager came to him with another telegram.

"That lady we were talking about," he said, laying the telegram before Allerdyke, "has just sent me this. I thought you'd like to see it as you were asking about her."

Allerdyke saw that the message was addressed to the manager, and had been dispatched from York railway station three-quarters of an hour previously.

"Please ask chambermaid to search for diamond shoe-buckle which I believe I lost in your hotel last night. If found send by registered post to Miss Lennard, 503*a*, Bedford Court Mansions, London."

Allerdyke memorized that address while he secretly wondered whether he should or should not tell the manager that the missing property was in his possession. Finally he determined to keep silence for the moment, and he handed back the message with an assumption of indifference.

"I should think a thing of that sort will soon be found," he observed. "Look here—never mind about sending that chambermaid to me just now; I'll see her later. I'm going to breakfast."

He wondered as he sat in the coffee-room, eating and drinking, if any of the folk about him knew anything about the dead man whose body had been quietly taken away by the doctors while the hotel routine went on in its usual fashion. It seemed odd, strange, almost weird, to think that any one of these people, eating fish or chops, chatting, reading their propped-up newspapers, might be in possession of some knowledge which he would give a good deal to appropriate.

Of one fact, however, he was certain—that diamond buckle belonged to Miss Celia Lennard, and she lived at an address in London which he had by that time written down in his pocket-book. And now arose the big (and, in view of what had happened, the most important and serious) question—how had Miss Celia Lennard's diamond buckle come to be in Room Number 263? That question had got to be answered, and he foresaw that he and Miss Lennard must very quickly meet again.

But there were many matters to be dealt with first, and they began to arise and to demand attention at once. Before he had finished breakfast came a wire from Mr. Franklin Fullaway, answering his own:—

"Deeply grieved and astonished by your news. Am coming down at once, and shall arrive Hull two o'clock. In meantime keep strict guard on your cousin's effects, especially on any sealed package. Most important this should be done."

This message only added to the mass of mystery which had been thickening ever since the early hours of the morning. Strict guard on James's effects—any sealed package—what did that mean? But a very little reflection made Allerdyke come to the conclusion that all these vague references and hints bore relation to the possible transaction mentioned in the various telegrams already exchanged between James Allerdyke and Franklin Fullaway, and that James had on him or in his possession when he left Russia something which was certainly not discovered when Gaffney searched the dead man.

There was nothing to do but to wait: to wait for two things—the result of the medical investigation, and the arrival of Mr. Franklin Fullaway. The second came first.

At ten minutes past two a bustling, quick-mannered American strode into Marshall Allerdyke's private sitting-room, and at the instant that the door was closed behind him asked a question which seemed to burst from every fibre of his being—

"My dear sir! Are they safe?"

5. THE NASTIRSEVITCH JEWELS

Allerdyke, like all true Yorkshiremen, had been born into the world with a double portion of caution and a triple one of reserve, and instead of answering the question he took a leisurely look at the questioner. He saw before him a tall, good-looking, irreproachably attired man of from thirty to thirty-five years of age, whose dark eyes were ablaze with excitement, whose equally dark, carefully trimmed moustache did not conceal the agitation of the lips beneath. Mr. Franklin Fullaway, in spite of his broad shoulders and excellent muscular development, was evidently a highly strung, nervous, sensitive gentleman; nothing could be plainer than that he had travelled from town in a state of great mental activity which was just arriving at boiling-point. Everything about his movements and gestures denoted it—the way in which he removed his hat, laid aside his stick and gloves, ran his fingers through his dark, curly hair, and—more than anything—looked at Marshall Allerdyke. But Allerdyke had a habit of becoming cool and quiet when other men grew excited and emotional, and he glanced at his visitor with seeming indifference.

"Mr. Fullaway, I suppose?" he said, phlegmatically. "Aye, to be sure! Sit you down, Mr. Fullaway. Will you take anything?—it's a longish ride from London, and I daresay you'd do with a drink, what?"

"Nothing, nothing, thank you, Mr. Allerdyke," answered Fullaway, obviously surprised by the other's coolness. "I had lunch on the train."

"Very convenient, that," observed Allerdyke. "I can remember when there wasn't a chance of it. Aye—and what might this be that you're asking about, now, Mr. Fullaway? What do you refer to?"

Fullaway, after a moment's surprised look at the Yorkshireman's stolid face, elevated his well-marked eyebrows and shook his head. Then he edged his chair nearer to the table at which Allerdyke sat.

"You don't know, then, that your cousin had valuables on him?" he asked in an altered tone.

"I know exactly what my cousin had on him, and what was in his baggage, when I found him dead in his room," replied Allerdyke drily. "And what that was—was just what I should have expected to find. But—nothing more."

Fullaway almost leapt in his chair.

"Nothing more!" he exclaimed. "Nothing more than you would have expected to find! Nothing?"

Allerdyke bent across the table, giving his visitor a keen look.

"What would you have expected to find if you'd found him as I found him?" he asked. "Come—what, now?"

He was watching the American narrowly, and he saw that Fullaway's excitement was passing off, was being changed into an attentive eagerness. He himself thrust his hand into his breast pocket and drew out the papers which had been accumulating there since his arrival and discovery.

"We'd best be plain, Mr. Fullaway," he said. "I don't know you, but I gather that you knew James, and that you'd done business together."

"I knew Mr. James Allerdyke very well, and I've done business with him for the last two years," replied Fullaway.

"Just so," assented Allerdyke. "And your business—"

"That of a general agent—an intermediary, if you like," answered Fullaway. "I arrange private sales a good deal between European sellers and American buyers— pictures, curiosities, jewels, antiques, and so on. I'm pretty well known, Mr. Allerdyke, on both sides the Atlantic."

"Quite so," said Allerdyke. "I'm not in that line, however, and I don't know you. But I'll tell you all I do know and you'll tell me all you know. When I searched my cousin for papers, I found this wire from you—sent to James at St. Petersburg. Now then, what does it refer to? Those valuables you hinted at just now?"

"Exactly!" answered Fullaway. "Nothing less!"

"What valuables are they?" asked Allerdyke.

"Jewels! Worth a quarter of a million," replied Fullaway.

"What? Dollars?"

Fullaway laughed derisively.

"Dollars! No, pounds! Two hundred and fifty thousand pounds, my dear sir!" he answered.

"You think he had them on him?"

"I'm sure he had them on him!" asserted Fullaway. He, in his turn, began to produce papers. "At any rate, he had them on him when he was in Christiania the other day. He was bringing them over here—to me."

"On whose behalf?" asked Allerdyke.

"On behalf of a Russian lady, a Princess, who wished to find a purchaser for them," replied the American promptly.

"In that case—to come to the point," said Allerdyke, "if my cousin James had that property on him when he landed here last night and it wasn't—as it certainly wasn't—on him when I found him this morning—-he's been robbed?"

"Robbed—and murdered that he might be robbed!" answered Fullaway.

The two men looked steadily at each other for a while. Then Allerdyke laid his papers on the table between them.

"You'd better tell me all you know about it," he said quietly. "Let's hear it all—then we shall be getting towards knowing what to do."

"Willingly!" exclaimed the American. He produced and spread out a couple of cablegrams on which he laid a hand while he talked. "As I have already said, I have had several deals in business with Mr. James Allerdyke. I last saw him towards the end of March, in town, and he then mentioned to me that he was just about setting out for Russia. On April 20th I received this cable from him—sent, you see, from St. Petersburg. Allow me to read it to you. He says. 'The Princess Nastirsevitch is anxious to find purchaser for her jewels, valued more than once at about a quarter of million pounds. Wants money to clear off mortgages on her son's estate, and set him going again. Do you know of any one likely to buy in one lot? Can arrange to bring over myself for buyers' inspection if chance of immediate good sale. James Allerdyke.' Now, as soon as I received that from your cousin I immediately thought of a possible and very likely purchaser—Mr. Delkin, a Chicago man, whose only daughter is just about to marry an English nobleman. I knew that Mr. Delkin had a mind to give his daughter a really fine collection of jewels, and I went at once to him regarding the matter. In consequence of my interview with Mr. Delkin, I cabled to James Allerdyke on April 21st, saying—"

"This is it, no doubt," said Allerdyke, producing the message of the date mentioned.

"That is it," assented Fullaway, glancing across the table. "Very well, you see what I said. He replied to that at once—here is his reply. It is, you see, very brief. It merely says, 'All right—shall wire details later—keep possible buyer on.' I heard no more until last Thursday, May 8th, when I received this cablegram, sent, you see, from Christiania. In it he says: 'Expect reach Hull Monday night next. Shall come London next day. Arrange meeting with your man. Have got all goods.' Now those last four words, Mr. Allerdyke, if they mean anything at all, mean that your cousin was bringing these valuable jewels with him; had them on him when he cabled from Christiania. And if you did not find them when you searched him—where are they? Two hundred and fifty thousand pounds' worth!"

Allerdyke took the three cablegrams from his visitor and carefully read them through, comparing them with the dates already known to him, and with Fullaway's messages in reply. Eventually he put all the papers together, arranging them in sequence. He laid them on the table between Fullaway and himself, and for a moment or two sat reflectively drumming the tips of his fingers on them.

"Who is this Princess Nastirsevitch?" he asked suddenly looking up. "Royalty, eh?"

"No," answered Fullaway, with a smile. "I don't know much about these European titles and dignities, but I don't think the title of Prince means in Russia what it does in England. A Prince there, I think, is some sort of nobleman, like your dukes and earls, and so on, here. But, anyway, the Princess Nastirsevitch isn't a Russian at all, except by marriage—she's a countryman of my own. I guess you've heard of her—she was Helen Hamilton, the famous dancer."

Allerdyke shook his head.

"Not my line at all," he said. "It was a bit in James's, though. Dancer, eh? And married a Prince?"

"Twenty-five years ago," replied Fullaway. "Ancient history, that. But I know a good deal about her. She made a big fortune with her dancing, and she invested largely in pearls and diamonds—I know that. I also happen to know that she'd one son by her marriage, of whom she's passionately fond. And I read this thing in this way: I guess the old Prince's estates (he's dead, a year or two ago) were heavily mortgaged, and she hit on the notion of clearing all off by selling her jewels, so that her son might start clear—no encumbrances on the property, you know."

Allerdyke pursed his lips and rubbed his chin.

"What I don't understand is that she confided a quarter of a million's worth of goods of that sort to a man whom she couldn't know so very well," he observed. "I never heard James speak of her."

"That may be." replied Fullaway. "But he may have
known her very well for all that. However, there are the
facts. And," he added, with emphasis, "there, Mr.
Allerdyke, are those four words, sent from Christiania,
'Have got all goods!' Now, we can be reasonably sure of
what he meant. He'd got the Princess's jewels. Very well!
Where are they?"

Allerdyke got to his feet, and, thrusting his hands in
his pockets, began to stride about the room. All this was
not merely puzzling, but, in a way which he could not
understand, distasteful to him. Somehow—he did not
know why, nor at that moment try to think why—he
resented the fact that any one knew more about his dead
cousin than he did. And he began to wonder as he strode
about the room how much this Mr. Franklin Fullaway
knew.

"Did my cousin James ever mention this Princess to
you?" he suddenly asked, stopping in his walk to and fro.
"I mean—before he went over to Russia this last time?"

"He just mentioned that he knew her—mentioned it
in casual conversation," answered Fullaway. "She and I
being fellow Americans, the subject interested me, of
course. But—he only said that he had met her in Russia."

"Aye, well," said Allerdyke musingly, "it's true he did
go across to Russia a good deal, and no doubt he knew
folk there that he never told me about."

"Well," he went on, throwing himself into his chair
again, "what's to be done? Do you honestly think that he
had those things on him when he came here last night?
You do? Very well, then, he's been murdered by some
devil or devils who's got 'em! But how? And who are
they—or who's he—or—good Lord! it might be who's
she?"

"Poisoned," said Fullaway. "That's my answer to your
question of—how? As to your other question—is there no
clue to anything? you forget—I don't know any details. I
only know that he was found dead. Under what
circumstances?"

Allerdyke pulled his chair nearer to his visitor.

"I'd forgotten," he said. "I'll tell you the lot. See if you can make aught out of it—they always say you Yankees have sharp brains. Try to see a bit of daylight! So far it licks me."

He gave the American a brief yet full account of all that had happened since his receipt of James Allerdyke's wireless message. And Fullaway listened in silence, taking everything in, making no interruption, and at the end he spoke quietly and with decision.

"We must find that woman—Miss Celia Lennard—and at once," he said. "That's absolutely necessary."

"Just so," agreed Allerdyke. "But look here—I've been thinking that over. Is it very likely that a woman who'd stolen two hundred and fifty thousand pounds' worth of stuff from an hotel would wire back to its manager, giving her address, for the sake of a shoe-buckle, even one set with diamonds?"

"I'm not—for the moment—supposing that she is the thief," answered Fullaway. "Why I want—and must—find her at once is to ask her a simple question. What was she doing in James Allerdyke's room? For—I've an idea."

"What?" demanded Allerdyke.

"This," replied Fullaway. "They were fellow-passengers on the *Perisco*. Your cousin—as I daresay you know—was the sort of man who readily makes friends, especially with women. My idea is that if this Miss Lennard went into his room last night it was to be shown the Princess Nastirsevitch's jewels. Your cousin was just the sort of man who knew how a woman would appreciate an exhibition of such things. And—"

At that moment a waiter tapped at the sitting-room door and announced Dr. Orwin.

6. THE PRIMA DONNA'S PORTRAIT

Marshall Allerdyke's sharp eyes were quick to see that his new visitor had something of importance to communicate and wished to give his news in private. Dr. Orwin glanced inquiringly at the American as he took the seat which Allerdyke drew forward, and the cock of his eyes indicated a strong desire to know who the stranger was.

"Friend of my late cousin," said Allerdyke brusquely. "Mr. Franklin Fullaway, of London—just as anxious as I am to hear what you have to tell us, doctor. You've come to tell something, of course?"

The doctor inclined his head towards Fullaway, and added a grave bow in answer to Allerdyke's question.

"The autopsy has been made," he replied. "By Dr. Lydenberg, Dr. Quillet, who is one of the police-surgeons here, and myself. We made a very careful and particular examination."

"And—the result?" asked Allerdyke eagerly. "Is it what you anticipated from your first glance at him—here?"

The doctor's face became a shade graver; his voice assumed an oracular tone.

"My two colleagues," he said, "agreed that your cousin's death resulted from heart failure which arose from what we may call ordinary causes. There is no need for me to go into details—it is quite sufficient to say that they are abundantly justified in coming to the conclusion at which they have arrived: it is quite certain that your cousin's heart had recently become seriously affected. But as regards myself"—here he paused, and looking narrowly from one to the other of his two hearers, he sank his voice to a lower, more confidential tone—"as

regards myself, I am not quite so certain as Dr.
Lydenberg and Dr. Quillet appear to be. The fact of the
case is, I think it very possible that Mr. James Allerdyke
was—poisoned."

Neither of the two who listened so intently made any
reply to this significant announcement. Instead they kept
their eyes intently fixed on the doctor's grave face; then
they slowly turned from him to each other, exchanging
glances. And after a pause the doctor went on, speaking
in measured and solemn accents.

"There is no need, either, at present—only at
present—that I should tell you why I think that," he
continued. "I may be wrong—my two colleagues are
inclined to think I am wrong. But they quite agree with
me that it will be proper to preserve certain organs—you
understand?—for further examination by, say, the Home
Office analyst, who is always, of course, a famous
pathological expert. That will be done—in fact, we have
already sealed up what we wish to be further examined.
But"—he paused again, shaking his head more solemnly
than ever—"the truth is, gentlemen," he went on at last,
"I am doubtful if even that analysis and examination will
reveal anything. If my suspicions are correct—and
perhaps I ought to call them mere notions, theories,
ideas, rather than suspicions—but, at any rate, if there is
anything in the vague thoughts which I have, no trace of
any poison will be found—and yet your cousin may have
been poisoned, all the same."

"Secretly!" exclaimed Fullaway.

Dr. Orwin gave the American a sharp glance which
indicated that he realized Fullaway's understanding of
what he had just said.

"Precisely," he answered. "There are poisons—known
to experts—which will destroy life almost to a given
minute, and of which the most skilful pathologist and
expert will not be able to find a single trace. Now, please,
understand my position—I say, it is quite possible, quite
likely, quite in accordance with what I have seen, that

this unfortunate gentleman died of heart failure brought about by even such an ordinary exertion as his stooping forward to untie his shoe-lace, but—I also think it likely that his death resulted from poison, subtly and cunningly administered, probably not very long before his death took place. And if I only knew—"

He paused at that, and looked searchingly and meaningly at Marshall Allerdyke before he continued. And Allerdyke looked back with the same intentness and nodded.

"Yes—yes!" he said. "If you only knew—? Say it, doctor!"

"If I only knew if there was any reason why any person wished to take this man's life," responded Dr. Orwin, slowly and deliberately. "If I knew that somebody wanted to get him out of the way, for instance—"

Allerdyke jumped to his feet and tapped Fullaway on the shoulder.

"Come in here a minute," he said, motioning towards the door of his bedroom. "Excuse us, doctor—I want to have a word with this gentleman. Look here," he continued, when he had led the American into the bedroom and had closed the door. "You hear what he says? Shall we tell him? Or shall we keep it all dark for a while? Which—what?"

"Tell him under promise of secrecy," replied Fullaway after a moment's consideration. "Medical men are all right—yes, tell him. He may suggest something. And I'm inclined to think his theory is correct, eh?"

"Correct!" exclaimed Allerdyke, with a grim laugh. "You bet it's correct! Come on, then—we'll tell him all. Now, doctor," he went on, leading the way back into the sitting-room, "we're going to give you our confidence. You'll treat it as a strict confidence, a secret between us, for the present. The truth is that when my cousin came to this hotel last night he was in possession—that is, we have the very strongest grounds for believing him to have been in possession—of certain extremely valuable property—-jewels worth a large amount—which he was carrying, safeguarding, from a lady in Russia to this gentleman in London. When I searched his body and luggage, these valuables were missing. Mr. Fullaway and myself haven't the least doubt that he was robbed. So your theory—eh?"

Dr. Orwin had listened to this with deep attention, and he now put two quick questions.

"The value of these things was great?"

"Relatively, very great," answered Allerdyke.

"Enough to engage, the attention of a clever gang of thieves?"

"Quite!"

"Then," said the doctor, "I am quite of opinion that my ideas are correct. These, people probably tracked your cousin to this place, contrived to administer a subtle and deadly poison to him last night, and entered his room after the time at which they knew it would take effect. Have you any clue—even a slight one?"

"Only this," answered Allerdyke, and proceeded to narrate the story of the shoe-buckle, adding Fullaway's theory to it. "That's not much, eh?"

"You must find that woman and produce her at the inquest," said the doctor. "I take it that Mr. Fullaway's idea is a correct one. Your cousin probably did invite Miss Lennard into his room to show her these jewels—that, of course, would prove that he had them in his possession at some certain hour last night. Now, about that inquest. It is fixed for ten o'clock to-morrow morning. Let me advise you as to your own course of procedure, having an eye on what you have told me. Your object should be to make the proceedings to-morrow merely formal, so that the Coroner can issue his order for interment, and then adjourn for further evidence. It will be sufficient if you give evidence identifying the body, if evidence is given of the autopsy, and an adjournment asked for until a further examination of the reserved organs and viscera can be made. For the present, I should keep back the matter of the supposed robbery until you can find this Miss Lennard. At the adjourned inquest—say in a week or ten days hence—everything pertinent can be brought out. But you will need legal help—I am rather trespassing on legal preserves in telling you so much."

"Deeply obliged to you, doctor—and you can add to our obigations by giving us the name of a good man to go to," said Allerdyke. "We'll see him at once and fix things up for to-morrow morning."

Dr. Orwin wrote down the name and address of a well-known solicitor, and presently went away. When he had gone, Allerdyke turned to Fullaway.

"Now, then," he said, "you and I'll do one or two things. We'll call on this lawyer. Then we'll cable to the Princess. But how shall we get her address!"

"There's sure to be a Russian Consul in the town," suggested Fullaway.

"Good idea! And I'm going to telephone to this Miss Lennard's address in London," continued Allerdyke. "She evidently set off from here to Edinburgh; but, anyway, the address she gave in that wire to the manager is a London one, and I'm going to try it. Now let's get out and be at work."

The ensuing conversation between these two and a deeply interested and much-impressed solicitor resulted in the dispatch of a lengthy cablegram to St. Petersburg, a conversation over the telephone with the housekeeper of Miss Celia Lennard's London flat, and the interviewing of the captain and stewards of the steamship on which James Allerdyke had crossed from Christiania. The net result of this varied inquiry was small, and produced little that could throw additional light on the matter in question. The *Perisco* officials had not seen anything suspicious in the conduct or personality of any of their passengers. They had observed James Allerdyke in casual conversation with some of them—they had seen him talking to Miss Lennard, to Dr. Lydenberg, to others, ladies and gentlemen who subsequently put up at the Station Hotel for the night. Nothing that they could tell suggested anything out of the common. Miss Lennard's housekeeper gave no other information than that her mistress was at present in Edinburgh, and was expected to remain there for at least a week. And towards night came a message from the Princess Nastirsevitch confirming Fullaway's conviction that James Allerdyke was in possession of her jewels and announcing that she was leaving for England at once, and should travel straight, via Berlin and Calais, to meet Mr. Franklin Fullaway at his hotel in London.

The solicitor agreed with Dr. Orwin's suggestions as to the course to be followed with regard to the inquest; it would be wise, he said, to keep matters quiet for at any rate a few days, until they were in a position to bring forward more facts. Consequently, the few people who were present at the Coroner's court next morning gained no idea of the real importance of the inquiry which was then opened. Even the solitary reporter who took a perfunctory note of the proceedings for his newspaper gathered no more from what he heard than that a gentleman had died suddenly at the Station Hotel, that it had been necessary to hold an inquest, that there was some little doubt as to the precise cause of his death, and that the inquest was accordingly adjourned until the medical men could tell something of a more definite nature. Nothing sensational crept out into the town; no bold-lettered headlines ornamented the afternoon editions. An hour before noon Marshall Allerdyke entrusted his cousin's body to the care of certain kinsfolk who had come over from Bradford to take charge of it; by noon he and Fullaway were slipping out of Hull on their way to Edinburgh—to search for a witness, who, if and when they found her, might be able to tell them—what?

"Seems something like a wild-goose chase," said Allerdyke as the train steamed on across country towards

York and the North. "How do we know where to find this woman in Edinburgh? Her housekeeper didn't know what hotel she was at—I suppose we'll have to try every one in the place till we come across her!"

"Edinburgh is not a very big town," remarked Fullaway. "I reckon to run her down—if she's still there— within a couple of hours. It's our first duty, anyway. If she—as I guess she did—saw those jewels, then we know that James Allerdyke had them on him when he reached Hull, dead sure."

"And supposing she can tell that?" said Allerdyke. "What then? How does that help? The devils who got 'em have already had thirty-six hours' start of us!"

The American produced a bulky cigar-case, found a green cigar, and lighted it with a deliberation which was in marked contrast to his usual nervous movements.

"Seems to me," he said presently, "seems very much to me that this has been a great thing! I figure it out like this—somehow, somebody has got to know of what the Princess and your cousin were up to—that he was going to carry those valuable jewels with him to England. He must have been tracked all the way, unless—does any unless strike you, now?"

"Not at the moment," replied Allerdyke. "So unless what?"

"Unless the thieves—and murderers—were waiting there in Hull for his arrival," said Fullaway quietly. "That's possible!"

"Strikes me a good many possibilities are knocking around," remarked Allerdyke, with more than his usual dryness. "As for me, I'll want to know a lot about these valuables and their consignment before I make up my mind in any way. I tell you frankly. I'm not running after them—I'm wanting to find the folk who killed my cousin, and I only hope this young woman'll be able to give me a hand. And the sooner we get to the bottle of hay and begin prospecting for the needle the better!"

But the search for Miss Celia Lennard to which Allerdyke alluded so gloomily was not destined to be either difficult or lengthy. As he and his companion walked along one of the platforms in the Waverley Station in Edinburgh that evening, on their way to a cab, Allerdyke suddenly uttered a sharp exclamation and seized the American by the elbow, twisting him round in front of a big poster which displayed the portrait of a very beautiful woman.

"Good Lord!" he exclaimed. "There she is! See? That's the woman. Man alive, we've hit it at once! Look!"

Fullaway turned and stared, not so much at the portrait as at the big lettering above and beneath it:

ZELIE DE LONGARDE,
THE WORLD-FAMED SOPRANO.
RECENTLY RETURNED FROM MOSCOW
AND ST. PETERSBURG.
Only Visit to Edinburgh this Year.
TO-NIGHT AT 8.

7. The Frantic Impresario

Fullaway slowly read this announcement aloud. When he had made an end of it he laughed.

"So your mysterious lady of the midnight motor, your Miss Celia Lennard of the Hull hotel, is the great and only Zelie de Longarde, eh?" he said. "Well, I guess that makes matters a lot easier and clearer. But you're sure it isn't a case of striking resemblance?"

"I only saw that woman for a minute or two, by moonlight, when she stuck her face out of her car to ask the way," replied Allerdyke, "but I'll lay all I'm worth to a penny-piece that the woman I then saw is the woman whose picture we're staring at. Great Scott! So she's a famous singer, is she? You know of her, of course? That sort of thing's not in my line—never was—I don't go to a concert or a musical party once in five years."

"Oh, she's great—sure!" responded Fullaway. "Beautiful voice—divine! And, as I say, things are going to be easy. I've met this lady more than once, though I didn't know that she'd any other name than that, which is presumably her professional one, and I've also had one or two business deals with her. So all we've got to do is to find out which hotel she's stopping at in this city, and then we'll go round there, and I'll send in my card. But I say—do you see, this affair's to-night, this very evening, and at eight o'clock, and it's past seven now. She'll be arraying herself for the platform. We'd better wait until—"

Allerdyke's practical mind asserted itself. He twisted the American round in another direction, and called to a porter who had picked up their bags.

"All that's easy," he said. "We'll stick these things in the left-luggage spot, dine here in the station, and go straight to the concert. There, perhaps, during an interval, we might get in a word with this lady who sports two names. Come on, now."

He hurried his companion from the cloak-room to the dining-room, gave a quick order on his own behalf to the waiter, left Fullaway to give his own, and began to eat and drink with the vigour of a man who means to waste no time.

"There's one thing jolly certain, my lad!" he said presently, leaning confidentially across the table after he had munched in silence for a while. "This Miss Lennard, or Mamselle, or Signora de Longarde, or whatever her real label is, hasn't got those jewels—confound 'em! Folks who steal things like that don't behave as she's doing."

"I never thought she had stolen the jewels," answered Fullaway. "What I want to know is—has she seen them, and when, and where, and under what circumstances? You've got her shoe-buckle all safe?"

"Waistcoat-pocket just now," replied Allerdyke laconically.

"That'll be an extra passport," observed Fullaway. "Not that it's needed, because, as I said, I've done business for her. Oddly enough, that was in the jewel line—I negotiated the sale of Pinkie Pell's famous pearl necklace with Mademoiselle de Longarde. You've heard of that, of course?"

"Never a whisper!" answered Allerdyke. "Not in my line, those affairs. Who was Pinkie Pell, anyhow!"

"Pinkie Pell was a well-known music-hall artiste, my dear sir, once a great favourite, who came down in the world, and had to sell her valuables," replied the American. "To the last she stuck to a pearl necklace, which was said to have been given to her by the Duke of Bendlecombe—Pinkie, they said, attached a sentimental value to it. However, it had to be sold, and I sold it for Pinkie to the lady we're going to see to-night. Seven thousand five hundred—it's well worth ten. Mademoiselle will be wearing it, no doubt—she generally does, anyway—so you'll see it."

"Not unless we get a front pew," said Allerdyke. "Hurry up, and let's be off! Our best plan," he went on as they made for a cab, "will be to get as near the platform as possible, so that I can make certain sure this is the woman I saw at Howden yesterday morning—when I positively identify her, I'll leave it to you to work the interview with her, either at this concert place or at her hotel afterwards. If it can be done at once, all the more to my taste—I want to be knowing things."

"Oh, we're going well ahead!" said Fullaway. "I'll work it all right. I noticed on that poster that this affair is being run by the Concert-Director Ernest Weiss. I know Weiss—he'll get us an interview with the great lady after she's appeared the first time."

"It's a fortunate thing for me to have a man who seems to know everybody," remarked Allerdyke. "I suppose it's living in London gives you so much acquaintance?"

"It's my business to know a lot of people," answered Fullaway. "The more the better—for my purposes. I'll tell you how I came to know your cousin later that's rather interesting. Well, here's the place, and it's five to eight now. We've struck it very well, and the only trouble'll be about getting good seats, especially as we're in morning dress."

Allerdyke smiled at that—in his opinion, money would carry a man anywhere, and there was always plenty of that useful commodity in his pockets. He insisted on buying the seats himself, and after some parleying and explaining at the box-office, he and his companion were duly escorted to seats immediately in front of a flower-decked platform, where they were set down amidst a highly select company of correctly attired folk, who glanced a little questioningly at their tweed suits, both conspicuous amidst silks, satins, broadcloths, and glazed linen. Allerdyke laughed as he thrust a program into Fullaway's hand.

"I worked that all right," he whispered. "Told the chap in that receipt of custom that you were a foreigner of great distinction travelling incognito in Scotland, and I your travelling companion, and that our luggage hadn't arrived from Aberdeen, so we couldn't dress, but we must hear this singing lady at all cost and in any case. Then I slapped down the brass and got the tickets—naught like brass in ready form, my lad! Now, then, when does the desired party appear?"

Fullaway unfolded his program and glanced over the items. The Concert-Direction of Ernest Weiss was famous for the fare which it put before its patrons, and here was certainly enough variety of talent to please the most critical—a famous tenor, a popular violinist, a contralto much in favour for her singing of tender and sentimental songs, a notable performer on the violincello, a local vocalist whose speciality was the singing of ancient Scottish melodies, and—item of vast interest to a certain section of the audience—a youthful prodigy who was fondly believed to have it in her power to become a female Paderewski. These performers were duly announced on the program in terms of varying importance; outstanding from all of them, of course, was the great star of the evening, the one and only Zelie de Longarde, acknowledged Queen of Song in Milan and Moscow, Paris and London, New York and Melbourne.

"Comes on fifth, I see," observed Allerdyke, glancing over his program unconcernedly. "Well, I suppose we've got to stick out the other four. I'm not great on music, Fullaway—don't know one tune from another. However, I reckon I can stand a bit of noise until my lady shows herself."

He listened with good-natured interest, which was not far removed from indifference, to the contralto, the 'cellist, the violinist, only waking up to something like enthusiasm when the infant prodigy, a quaint, painfully shy little creature, who bobbed a side curtsey at the audience, and looked much too small to tackle the grand piano, appeared and proceeded to execute wonderful things with her small fingers.

"That's a bit of all right!" murmured Allerdyke, when the child had finished her first contribution. "That's a clever little party! But she's too big in the eye, and too small in the bone—wants plenty of new milk, and new-laid eggs, and fresh air, and not so much piano-thumping, does that. Clever—clever—but unnatural, Fullaway!—they mustn't let her do too much at that. Well, now I suppose we shall see the shoe-buckle lady."

The packed audience evidently supposed the same thing. Over it—the infant prodigy having received her meed of applause and bobbed herself awkwardly out of sight—had come that atmosphere of expectancy which invariably heralds the appearance of the great figure on any similar occasion. It needed no special intuition on Allerdyke's part to know that all these people were itching to show their fondness for Zelie de Longarde by clapping their hands, waving their program, and otherwise manifesting their delight at once more seeing a prime favourite. All eyes were fixed on the wing of the platform, all hands were ready to give welcome. But a minute passed—two minutes—three minutes—and Zelie de Longarde did not appear. Another minute—and then, endeavouring to smile bravely and reassuringly, and not succeeding particularly well in the attempt, a tall, elaborately attired, carefully polished-up man, unmistakably German, blonde, heavy, suave, suddenly walked on to the platform and did obeisance to the audience.

"Weiss!" whispered Fullaway. "Something's wrong! Look at his face—he's in big trouble."

The concert-director straightened himself from that semi-military bow, and looked at the faces in front of him with a mute appeal.

"Ladies and gentlemen," he said, "I have to entreat the high favour of your kind indulgence. Mademoiselle de Longarde is not yet arrived from her hotel. I hope—I think—she is now on her way. In the meantime I propose, with your gracious consent, to continue, our program with the next item, at the conclusion of which, I hope, Mademoiselle will appear."

The audience was sympathetic—the audience was ready to be placated. It gave cordial hearing and warm favour to the singer of Scottish melodies—it even played into Mr. Concert-Director Weiss's hands by according the local singer an encore. But when he had finally retired there was another wait, a longer one which lengthened unduly, a note of impatience sounded from the gallery; it was taken up elsewhere. And suddenly Weiss came again upon the platform—this time with no affectation of suave entreaty. He was plainly much upset; his elegant waistcoat seemed to have assumed careworn creases, his mop of blonde hair was palpably rumpled as if he had been endeavouring to tear some of its wavy locks out by force. And when he spoke his fat voice shook with a mixture of chagrin and anger.

"Ladies and gentlemen," he said, "I crave ten thousand—a million—pardons for this so-unheard-of state of affairs! The—the truth is, Mademoiselle de Longarde is not yet here. What is more—I have to tell you the truth—Mademoiselle refuses to come—refuses to fulfil her honourable engagement. We are—have been for some time—on the telephone with her. Mademoiselle is at her hotel. She declares she has been robbed—her jewels have all been stolen from their case in her apartments. She is—how shall I say?—turning the hotel upside down! She refuses to budge one inch until her jewels are restored to her. How then?—I cannot restore her jewels. I say to her—my colleagues say to her—it is not your jewels we desire—it is your so beautiful, so incomparable voice. She reply—I cannot tell you what she reply! In effect—no jewels, no song! Ladies and gentlemen, once more!—your most kind, most considerate indulgence! I go there just now—I fly; swift, to the hotel, to entreat Mademoiselle on my knees to return with me! In the meantime—"

As Weiss retired from the platform, and the longhaired 'cellist came upon it, Fullaway sprang up, dragging Allerdyke after him. He led the way to a sidedoor, whispered something to an attendant, and was quickly ushered through another door to an ante-room behind the wings, where Weiss, livid with anger, was struggling into an opera-cloak. The concert-director gasped as he caught sight of the American.

"Ah, my dear Mr. Fullaway!" he exclaimed. "You here! You have heard?—you have been in front. You hear, then—she will not come to sing because her jewels are missing, eh? She—"

"What hotel is Mademoiselle de Longarde stopping at, Weiss?" asked Fullaway quietly.

"The North British and Caledonian—I go there just now!" answered Weiss. "I am ruined if she will not appear—ruined, disgraced! Jewels! Ah—!"

"Come on—we're going with you," said Fullaway. "Quick now!"

Allerdyke got some vivid impressions during the next few minutes, impressions various, startling. They began with a swift whirl through the lighted streets of the smoky old city, of a dash upstairs at a big hotel; they ended with a picture of a beautiful, highly enraged woman, who was freely speaking her mind to a dismayed hotel manager and a couple of men who were obviously members of the detective force.

8. THE JEWEL BOX

Mademoiselle Zelie de Longarde, utterly careless of the fact that her toilette was but half complete, that she wore no gown, and that the kimono which she had hastily assumed on discovering her loss had slipped away from her graceful figure to fall in folds about her feet, interrupted the torrent of her eloquence to stare at the three men whom a startled waiter ushered into her sitting-room. Her first glance fell on the concert-director, and she shook her fist at him.

"Go away, Weiss!" she commanded, accompanying the vigorous action of her hand with an equally emphatic stamp of a shapely foot. "Go away at once—go and play on the French horn; go and do anything you like to satisfy your audience! Not one note do I sing until somebody finds me my jewels! Edinburgh's stole them, and Edinburgh'll have to give them back. It's no use your waiting here—I won't budge an inch. I—"

She paused abruptly, suddenly catching sight of Fullaway, who at once moved towards her with a confidential and reassuring smile.

"You!" she exclaimed. "What brings you here? And who's that with you—surely the gentleman of whom I asked my way in some wild place the other night! What—"

"Mademoiselle," said Fullaway, with a deep bow, "let me suggest to you that the finest thing in this mundane state of ours is—reason. Suppose, now, that you complete your toilet, tell us what it is you have lost; leave us—your devoted servants—to begin the task of finding it, and while we are so engaged, hasten with Mr. Weiss to the hall to fulfil your engagement? A packed audience awaits you—palpitating with sympathy and—"

"And curiosity," interjected the aggrieved prima donna, as she threw a hasty glance at her deshabille and snatched up the kimono. "Pretty talk, Fullaway—very, and all intended to benefit Weiss there. Lost, indeed!— I've lost all my jewels, and up to now nobody"—here she flashed a wrathful glance at the hotel manager and the two detectives—"nobody has made a single suggestion about finding them!"

Fullaway exchanged looks with the other men. Once more he assumed the office of spokesman.

"Perhaps you have not told them precisely what it is they're to find," he suggested. "What is it now, Mademoiselle? The Pinkie Pell necklace for instance!"

The prima donna, who was already retreating through the door of the bedroom on whose threshold she had been standing, flashed a scornful look at her questioner over the point of her white shoulder.

"Pinkie Pell necklace!" she exclaimed. "Everything's gone! The whole lot! Look at that—not so much as a ring left in it!"

She pointed a slender, quivering finger to a box which stood, lid thrown open, on a table in the sitting-room, by which the detectives were standing, open-mouthed, and obviously puzzled. Allerdyke, following the pointing finger, noted that the box was a very ordinary-looking affair—a tiny square chest of polished wood, fitted with a brass swing handle. It might have held a small type-writing machine; it might have been a medicine chest; it certainly did not look the sort of thing in which one would carry priceless jewels. But Mademoiselle de Longarde was speaking again.

"That's what I always carried my jewels in—in their cases," she said. "And they were all in there when I left Christiania a few days ago, and that box has never been out of my sight—so to speak—since. And when I opened it here to-night, wanting the things, it was as empty as it is now. And if I behave handsomely, and go with Weiss there, to fulfil this engagement, it'll only be on condition that you stop here, Fullaway, and do your level best to get me my jewels back. I've done all I can—I've told the manager there, and I've told those two policemen, and not a man of them seems able to suggest anything! Perhaps you can."

With that she disappeared and slammed the door of the bedroom, and the six men, left in a bunch, looked at each other. Then one of the detectives spoke, shaking his head and smiling grimly.

"It's all very well to say we suggest nothing," he said. "We want some facts to go on first. Up to now, all the lady's done is to storm at us and at everybody—she seems to think all Edinburgh's in a conspiracy to rob her! We don't know any circumstances yet, except that she says she's been robbed. Perhaps—"

"Wait a bit," interrupted Fullaway. "Let us get her off to her engagement. Then we can talk. I suppose," he continued, turning to the manager, "she first announced her loss to you?"

"She announced her loss to the whole world, in a way of speaking," answered the manager, with a dry laugh.

"She screamed it out over the main staircase into the hall! Everybody in the place knows it by this time—she took good care they should. I don't know how she can have been robbed—so far as I can learn she's scarcely been out of these rooms since she came into them yesterday afternoon. The grand piano had been put in for her before she arrived, and she's spent all her time singing and playing—I don't believe she's ever left the hotel. And as I pointed out to her when she fetched me up, she found this box locked when she went to it—why didn't the thieves carry it bodily away? Why—"

"Just so—just so!" broke in Fullaway. "I quite appreciate your points. But there is more in this than meets the first glance. Let us get Mademoiselle off to her engagement, I say—that's the first thing. Then we can do business. Weiss," he continued, drawing the concert-

director aside, "you must arrange to let her appear as
soon as possible after you get back to the hall, and to put
forward her appearance in the second half of your
program, so that she can return here as soon as
possible—she'll only be in irrepressible fidgets until she
knows what's been done. And—you know what she is!—
you ought to be very thankful that she's allowed herself to
be persuaded to go with you. Mademoiselle," he went on,
as the prima donna, fully attired, but innocent of jewelled
ornament, swept into the room, "you are doing the right
thing—bravely! Go, sing—sing your best, your divinest—
let your admiring audience recognize that you have a soul
above even serious misfortune. Meanwhile, allow me to
order your supper to be served in this room, for eleven
o'clock, and permit me and my friend, Mr. Allerdyke, to
invite ourselves to share it with you. Then—we will give
you some news that will interest and astonish you."

"That only makes me all the more frantic to get back,"
exclaimed the prima donna. "Come along, now, Weiss—
you've got a car outside, I suppose? Hurry, then, and let
me get it over."

When the vastly relieved concert-director had led his
bundle of silks and laces safely out, Fullaway laughed
and turned to the other men.

"Now, gentlemen," he said, "perhaps we can have a
little quiet talk about this affair." He flung himself into a
seat and nodded at the hotel-manager. "Just tell us
exactly what's happened since Mademoiselle arrived
here," he said. "Let's get an accurate notion of all her
doings. She came—when?"

"She got here about the beginning of yesterday
afternoon," answered the manager, who did not appear to
be too well pleased about this disturbance of his usual
proceedings. "She has always had this suite of rooms
whenever she has sung in Edinburgh before, and it was
understood that whenever she wrote or wired for them we
were to arrange for a grand piano, properly tuned to
concert-pitch, to be put in for her. She wrote for the suite

over a fortnight ago from Russia, and, of course, we had everything in readiness for her. She turned up, as I say, yesterday, alone—she explained something about her maid having been obliged to leave her on arrival in England, and since she came she's had the services of one of our smartest chambermaids, whom she herself picked out after carefully inspecting a whole dozen of them. That chambermaid can tell you that Mademoiselle's scarcely left her rooms since then, and it's an absolute mystery to me that any person could get in here, open this box, and abstract its contents. As I say—if anybody wanted to steal her jewels, why didn't he pick up this box and carry it bodily off instead of hanging about to pick the lock? I don't believe—"

"Ah, quite so!" interrupted Fullaway. "I quite agree with you. Now, at what time did Mademoiselle announce the loss of her jewels?"

"Oh, about—say, an hour ago. This chambermaid— she's there in the bedroom now—was helping her to dress for the concert. She—Mademoiselle—went to this box to get out what ornaments she wanted. According to the girl, she let out an awful scream, and, just as she was, rushed to the head of the main stairs—these rooms, as you see, are on our first floor—and began to shout for me, for anybody, for everybody. The hall below was just then full of people—coming in and out of the dining-room and so on. She set the whole place going with the noise she made," added the manager, visibly annoyed. "It would have been far better if she'd shown some reserve—"

"Reserve is certainly an admirable quality," commented Fullaway, "but it is foreign to young ladies of Mademoiselle's temperament. Well—and then?"

"Oh, then, of course, I came up to her suite. She showed me this box. It had stood, she declared, on a table by her bedside, close to her pillows, from the moment she entered her rooms yesterday. She swore that it ought to have been full of her jewels—in cases. When she had opened it—just before this—it was empty. Of course, she demanded the instant presence of the police. Also, she insisted that I should at once, that minute, lock every door in the hotel, and arrest every person in it until their effects and themselves could be rigorously searched and examined. Ridiculous!"

"As you doubtless said," remarked Fullaway.

"No—I said nothing. Instead I telephoned for police assistance. These two officers came. And," concluded the manager, with a sympathetic glance at the detectives, "since they came Mademoiselle has done nothing but insist on arresting every soul within these walls—she seems to think there's a universal conspiracy against her."

"Exactly," said Fullaway. "It is precisely what she would think—under the circumstances. Now let us see this chambermaid."

The manager opened the door of the bedroom, and called in a pretty, somewhat shy, Scotch damsel, who betrayed a becoming confusion at the sight of so many strangers. But she gave a plain and straightforward account of her relations with Mademoiselle since the arrival of yesterday. She had been in almost constant attendance on Mademoiselle ever since her election to the post of temporary maid—had never left her save at meal-times. The little chest had stood at Mademoiselle's bed-head always—she had never seen it moved, or opened. There was a door leading into the bedroom from the corridor. Mademoiselle had never left the suite of rooms since her arrival. She had talked that morning of going for a drive, but rain had begun to fall, and she had stayed in. Mademoiselle had seemed utterly horrified when she discovered her loss. For a moment she had sunk on her bed as if she were going to faint; then she had rushed out into the corridor, just as she was, screaming for the manager and the police.

When the pretty chambermaid had retired, Fullaway took up the box from which the missing property was believed to have been abstracted. He examined it with seeming indifference, yet he announced its particulars and specifications with business-like accuracy.

"Well—this chest, cabinet, or box," he observed carelessly. "Let us look at it. Here, gentlemen, we have a piece of well-made work. It is—yes, eighteen inches square all ways. It is made of—yes, rosewood. Its corners, you see, are clamped with brass. It has a swing handle, fitted into this brass plate which is sunk into the lid. It has also three brass letters sunk into that lid—Z. D. L. Its lock does not appear to be of anything but an ordinary nature. Taking it altogether, I don't think this is the sort of thing in which you would believe a lady was carrying several thousand pounds' worth of pearls and diamonds. Eh?"

One of the detectives stirred uneasily—he did not quite understand the American's light and easy manner, and he seemed to suspect him of persiflage.

"We ought to be furnished with a list of the missing articles," he said. "That's the first thing."

"By no means," replied Fullaway. "That, my dear sir, is neither the first, nor the second, nor the third thing. There is much to do before we get to that stage. At present, you, gentlemen, cannot do anything. To-morrow morning, perhaps, when I have consulted with Mademoiselle de Longarde, I may call you in again—or call upon you. In the meantime, there's no need to detain you. Now," he continued, turning to the manager, when the detectives, somewhat puzzled and bewildered, had left the room, "will you see that your nicest supper is served—for three—in this room at eleven o'clock, against Mademoiselle's return? Send up your best champagne. And do not allow yourself to dwell on Mademoiselle's agitation on discovering her loss. That agitation was natural. If it is any consolation to you, I will give you a conclusion which may be satisfactory to your peace of mind as manager. What is it? Merely this—that though

Mademoiselle de Longarde has undoubtedly lost her jewels, they were certainly not stolen from her in this hotel!"

9. The Lady's Maid's Mother

When the manager, much appeased and relieved in mind, had gone, Fullaway tapped at the door of the bedroom, summoned the pretty chambermaid, and handed her the rosewood box.

"Put this back exactly where Mademoiselle has kept it since she came here," he commanded. "Now you yourself—you're going to stay in the rooms until she comes back from the concert? That's right—if she returns before my friend and I come up again, tell her that we shall present ourselves at five minutes to eleven. Come downstairs, Allerdyke," he proceeded, leading the way from the room. "We must book rooms for the night here, so we'll send to the station for our things and make our arrangements, after which we'll smoke a cigar and talk—I am beginning to see chinks of daylight."

He led Allerdyke down to the office, completed the necessary arrangements, and went on to the smoking-room, in a quiet corner of which he pulled out his cigar-case.

"Well?" he said. "What do you think now?"

"I think you're a smart chap," answered Allerdyke bluntly. "You did all that very well. I said naught, but I kept an eye and an ear open. You'll do."

"Very complimentary!—but I wasn't asking you what you thought about me," said Fullaway, with a laugh. "I'm asking you what you think of the situation, as illuminated by this last episode?"

"Well, I'm still reflecting on what you said to that manager chap," answered Allerdyke. "You really think this young woman has lost her jewels?"

"Oh, no doubt, no doubt at all," replied Fullaway. "Mademoiselle is impetuous, impulsive, demonstrative, much given to insisting on her own way, but she's absolutely honest and truthful, and I've no doubt whatever—none!—that she's been robbed. But—not here. She never brought those jewels here. They were not in that box when she came here. Mademoiselle, my dear sir, was relieved of those jewels either on the steamer, as she crossed from, Christiania to Hull, or during the few hours she spent at the Hull hotel. The whole thing—the robbery from your cousin, the robbery from Mademoiselle de Longarde—is all the work of a particularly clever and brilliant gang of international thieves; and, by the holy smoke, sir, we've got our hands full! For there isn't a clue to the identity of the operators, so far, unless the lady with whom we are going to sup can help us to one."

Allerdyke ruminated over this for a moment or two. Then, after lighting the cigar which Fullaway had offered him, he shook his head—in grim affirmation.

"I shouldn't wonder," he said. "Certainly, it seems a big thing. You're figuring on its having been a carefully concocted scheme? No mere chance affair, eh?"

"This sort of thing's never done by chance," responded the American. "This is the work of very clever and accomplished thieves who somehow became aware of two facts. One, that your cousin was bringing with him to England the jewels of the Princess Nastirsevitch. The other, that Mademoiselle Zelie de Longarde carried her pearls and diamonds in an innocent-looking rosewood box. My dear sir! you observed that I examined that box with seeming carelessness—in reality, I was looking at it with the eye of a trained observer. I am one of those people who, from having knocked about the world a lot, engaging in a multifarious variety of occupations, have picked up a queer scrap-heap of knowledge, and I will lay you any odds you like that I am absolutely correct in affirming that the box which I just now handed to Maggie, the chambermaid, was newly made by a Russian cabinet-maker within the last four weeks!"

"For a purpose?" suggested Allerdyke.

"Just so—for a purpose," assented Fullaway. "That purpose being, of course, its substitution for the real original article. You did not handle the box which is now upstairs—it is carefully weighted, though it is empty. I believe—nay, I am sure, it contains a sheet of lead under its delicate lining of satin. That, of course, was to deceive Mademoiselle. You heard her say that the jewels were in her box at Christiania, and that she never opened the box until this evening here in Edinburgh? Very good—between here and Christiania somebody substituted the imitation box for the real one. Ah!—in all these great criminal operations there is nothing like sticking to the old, well-worn, tried-and-proved tricks of the trade!—they are like well-oiled, well-practised machinery. And now we come back to the real, great, anxious question—Who did it? And there, Allerdyke, we are at present—only at present, mind!—up against a very big, blank wall."

"On the other side of which, my lad, lies the secret of the murder of my cousin," said Allerdyke grimly. "Mind you that! That's what I'm after, Fullaway. Damn all these jewels and things, in comparison with that!—it's that I'm after, I tell you again, and a thousand times again. And I'm considering if I'm doing any good hanging round here after this singing woman when the probable sphere of action lies yonder away at Hull, eh?"

"The proper—not probable—sphere of action, my dear sir, is the supper-table to which we're presently going," answered Fullaway, with supreme assurance. "What the singing woman, as you call her, can tell us will most likely make all the difference in the world to our investigations. Remember the shoe-buckle! Have it ready to exhibit when I lead up to it. Then—we shall see."

The prima donna, back for her engagement at eleven o'clock, came in flushed and smiling—the extraordinary warmth and fervour of her reception by the audience which she had at first been so inclined to treat with scant courtesy had restored her to good humour, and when she had eaten a few mouthfuls of delicate food and drunk her first glass of champagne she began to laugh almost light-heartedly.

"Well, I suppose you've been doing your best, Fullaway," she said, with easy familiarity. "I declare you turned up at the very moment, for that fat Weiss would have been no good. But I'm still wondering how you came to be here, and what this gentleman—Mr. Allerdyke, is it?—is doing here with you. Allerdyke, now—well, that's the same name as that of a man I came across from Christiania with, and left at Hull."

Fullaway kicked Allerdyke under the table.

"You haven't heard of that Mr. Allerdyke since you left him at Hull, then?" he asked, gazing intently at their hostess.

"Heard? How should I hear?" asked the prima donna. "He was just a travelling acquaintance. All the same, I had certainly fixed up to see him in London on a business matter."

"You don't read the newspapers, then?" suggested Fullaway.

"Not unless there's something about myself in them," she answered, with an arch smile at Allerdyke.

"If you'd read this morning's papers, you'd have seen that the Mr. Allerdyke with whom you travelled—this gentleman's cousin, by the by—was found dead in his room at the hotel in Hull not so long after you quitted it," said Fullaway coolly. "In fact, he must have been dead when you passed his door on your way out."

The prima donna was genuinely shocked. She set down the glass which she was just lifting to her lips; her large, handsome eyes dilated, her lips quivered a little. She turned a look of sympathy on Allerdyke, who, at that moment, realized that she was a very beautiful woman.

"You don't say so!" she exclaimed. "Well, I'm really grieved to hear that—I am! Dead?—and when I left! Why, I was in his room that very night we reached Hull, having a talk on the business matter I mentioned just now—he was well enough and lively enough then, I'll swear. Dead!—why, what did he die of?"

The two men looked at each other. There was a brief pause; then Allerdyke slowly produced a small packet, wrapped in tissue-paper, from his waistcoat pocket. He laid it on the table at his side and looked at his hostess.

"I knew you had been in my cousin's room," he said. "You left or dropped your shoe-buckle there. I found it when I searched his room. Then the hotel manager showed me your wire. Here's the buckle."

He was watching her narrowly as he spoke, and his glance deepened in intensity as he handed over the little packet and watched her unwrap the paper. But there was not a sign of anything but a little surprised satisfaction in the prima donna's face as she recognized her lost property, and her eyes were ingenuous enough as she turned them on him.

"Why, of course, that's mine!" she exclaimed. "I'm ever so much obliged to you, Mr. Allerdyke. Yes, I wired to the hotel, in my proper name, you know—Zelie de Longarde is only my professional name. I didn't want to lose that buckle—it was part of a birthday present from my mother. But you don't mean to say that you travelled all the way to Edinburgh to hand me that! Surely not?"

"No!" replied Allerdyke. He wanted to take a direct share in the talking, and went resolutely ahead now that the chance had come. "No—not at all. I knew you'd come to Edinburgh—found it out from that chauffeur who was driving you when you and I met at Howden the night before last, and so I came on to find you. I want to ask you some questions about my cousin, and maybe to get you to come and give evidence at the inquest on him."

"Inquest!" she exclaimed. "I know what that means, of course. Why—you don't say there's been anything wrong?"

"I believe my cousin was murdered that night," answered Allerdyke. "So, too, does Fullaway there. And you were probably the last person who ever spoke to him alive. Now, you see, I'm a plain, blunt-spoken sort of chap—I ask people straight questions. What did you go into his room to talk to him about?"

"Business!" she replied, with a directness which impressed both men. "Mere business. He and I had several conversations on board the *Perisco*—I made out he was a clever business man. I want to invest some money—he advised me to put it into a development company in Norway, which is doing big things in fir and pine. I went into his room to look at some plans and papers—he gave me some prospectuses which are in that bag there just now—-I was reading them over again only this evening. That's all. I wasn't there many minutes— and, as I told you, he was very well, very brisk and lively then."

"Did he show you any valuables that he had with him—jewels?" asked Allerdyke brusquely.

"Jewels! Valuables!" she answered. "No—certainly not."

"Nor when you were on the steamer?"

"No—nor at any time," she said. "Jewels?—why— what makes you ask such a question?"

"Because my cousin had in his possession a consignment of such things, of great value, and we believe that he was murdered for them—that's why," replied Allerdyke. "He had them when he left Christiania—he had them when he entered the Hull hotel—"

Fullaway, who had been listening intently, leant forward with a shake of his head.

"Stop at that, Allerdyke," he said. "We don't know, now, that he did have them when he entered the hotel at Hull! He mayn't have had. Miss Lennard—we'll drop the professional name and turn to the real one," he said, with a bow to the prima donna—"Miss Lennard here thinks she had her jewels in her little box when she entered the Hull hotel, and also when she came to this hotel, here in Edinburgh, but—"

"Do you mean to say that I hadn't?" she exclaimed. "Do you mean—"

"I mean," replied Fullaway, "that, knowing what I now know, I believe that both you and the dead man, James Allerdyke, were robbed on the *Perisco*. And I want to ask you a question at once. Where is your maid!"

Celia Lennard dropped her knife and fork and sat back, suddenly turning pale.

"My maid!" she said faintly. "Good heavens! you don't think—oh, you aren't suggesting that she's the thief? Because—oh, this is dreadful! You see—I never thought of it before—when she and I arrived at Hull that night she was met by a man who described himself as her brother. He was in a great state of agitation—he said he'd rushed up to Hull to meet her, to beg her to go straight with him to their mother, who was dying in London. Of course, I let her go at once—they drove straight from the riverside at Hull to the station to catch the train. What else could I do? I never suspected anything. Oh!"

Fullaway leaned across the table and filled his hostess's glass.

"Now," he said, motioning her to drink, "you know your maid's name and address, don't you? Let me have them at once, and within a couple of hours we'll know if the story about the dying mother was true."

10.. THE SECOND MURDER

It had been very evident to Allerdyke that ever since Fullaway had mentioned the matter of the missing maid, Celia Lennard had become a victim to doubt, suspicion, and uncertainty. Her colour came and went; her eyes began to show signs of tears; her voice shook. And now, at the American's direct question, she wrung her hands with an almost despairing gesture.

"But I can't!" she exclaimed. "I don't know her address—how should I? It's somewhere in London—Bloomsbury, I think—but even then I don't know if that's where her mother lives, to whom she said she was going. I did know her address—I mean I remembered it for a while, at the time I engaged her—a year ago, but I've forgotten it. Oh! do you really think she's robbed me, or helped to rob me?"

"Never mind opinions," answered Fullaway curtly. "They're no good. Is this the maid you brought with you once or twice when you called at my office some time ago, over the Pinkie Pell deal?"

"Yes—yes, the same!" she answered.

"A Frenchwoman?" said Fullaway.

"Yes—Lisette. Of course she went with me to your office—that was eight or nine months ago, and I've had her a year. And I had excellent testimonials with her, too. Oh, I can't think that—"

"Can't you make an effort to remember her address?" urged Fullaway. "What can we do until we know that?"

Celia drew her fine eyebrows together in a palpable effort to think.

"I've got it somewhere," she said at last. "I must have it somewhere—most likely in an address-book at my flat—I should be sure to put it down at the time."

"Who is there at your flat?" asked Fullaway.

"My housekeeper and a maid," answered Celia. "They're always there, whether I'm at home or not. But they couldn't get at what you want—all my papers and things are locked up—and in a hopeless state of confusion, too."

Fullaway pushed aside his plate.

"Then there's only one thing to be done," he said, with an accent of finality. "We must go up to town at once."

Allerdyke, still quietly eating his supper, looked up.

"That's just what I was going to suggest," he said. "There's no good to be done hanging about here. Let's get on to the scene of operations. If Miss Lennard's maid has stolen her jewels, she's probably had some hand in the theft from my cousin. We must find her. Now, then, let me come in. I'll look up the train, settle up with these hotel folk, and we'll be off. You give your attention to your packing, Miss Lennard, and leave the rest to me—you won't mind travelling the night?"

Celia shook her head.

"I don't mind travelling all night for half a dozen nights if I can track my lost property," she said lugubriously. "You're dead sure it's no use stopping here?—that the robbery didn't take place here?"

"Sure!" answered Fullaway. "We must get off. That French damsel's got to be found—somehow."

The supper-party came to an end—the prima donna and her temporary maid began to bustle with garments and trunks, the two men attended to all other necessary matters, and at two o'clock in the morning the three sped out of Edinburgh for the South, each secretly wondering what was going to come of their journey. Allerdyke, preparing to go to sleep in the compartment which he and Fullaway occupied by themselves, dropped one grim remark to his companion as he settled himself.

"Seems like a wild-goose chase this, my lad, but it's one we've got to go through with! What'll the next stage be?"

The next stage was an arrival in London in the middle of a lovely May morning, a swift drive to Celia Lennard's flat in Bedford Court Mansions, the hurried rummaging of its owner amongst an extraordinary mass of papers, books, and documents, and the ultimate discovery of the French maid's address. Celia held it up with a sigh of vast relief, which changed into a groan of despairing doubt.

"There it is!" she exclaimed. "Lisette Beaurepaire, 911 Bernard Street, Bloomsbury—I knew it was Bloomsbury. That's where she lived when I engaged her, anyhow—but then her sick mother mayn't live there! The man who met her at Hull, who said he was her brother, didn't say where the mother lived, except that it was in London."

"We must go to Bernard Street, anyway, at once," said Fullaway. "We may get some information there."

But such information as they got on the door-step of 911 Bernard Street was scanty and useless. The house was a typical Bloomsbury lodging-place, let off in floors and rooms. Its proprietor, summoned from a neighbouring house, recollected, with considerable difficulty and after consultation of a penny pocket-book, that he had certainly let a top-floor room to a young Frenchwoman about a year ago, but he had never caught her name properly, and simply had her noted down as Mamselle. She had paid her rent regularly, and had remained in the house five weeks—that was all he knew about her. Had he ever seen her since? Not that he knew of—in fact, he shouldn't know her if he saw her—they were all pretty much alike, these young Frenchwomen. Did he know where she came from to his house—where she went from his house? Not he! he knew no more than what he had just told.

"What now?" asked Allerdyke as the three searchers paced dejectedly up the street. "This is doing no good—it's worse than the Hull affair. However, there's one thing suggests itself to me. Didn't you say," he went on, turning to Celia, "that you had some very good testimonials with this young woman? If so, and you've still got them, we might trace her in that way."

"I had some, and I may have them still, but you saw just now what an awful mess all my letters and papers are in," replied Celia, almost tearfully. "I always do get things like that into hopeless confusion—I never know what to destroy and what to keep, and they accumulate so. It would take hours upon hours to look for those letters, and in the meantime—"

"In the meantime," remarked Fullaway as he signalled to a taxi-cab, "there's only one thing to be done. We must go to the police. Get in, both of you, and let's make haste to New Scotland Yard."

Once more Allerdyke received an impression of the American's usefulness and practical acquaintance with things. Fullaway seemed to know exactly what to do, whom to approach, how to go about the business in hand; within a few minutes all three were closeted with a high official of the Criminal Investigation Department, a man who might have been a barrister, a medical specialist, or a scientist of distinction, and who maintained an unmoved countenance and a perfect silence while Fullaway unfolded the story. He and Allerdyke had held a brief consultation as they drove from Bloomsbury to Whitehall, and they had decided that as things had now reached a critical stage it would be best to tell the authorities everything. Therefore the American narrated the entire sequence of events as they related not only to Mademoiselle de Longarde's loss but to the death of James Allerdyke and the disappearance of the Nastirsevitch valuables. And the official heard, and made mental notes, soaking everything into some proper cell of his brain, and he said nothing until Fullaway had come to an end, and at that end he turned to Celia Lennard.

"You can, of course, describe your maid?" he asked.

"Certainly!" answered Celia. "To every detail."

"Do so, if you please," continued the official, producing a pile of papers from a drawer and turning them over until he came to one which he drew from the rest.

"A Frenchwoman," said Celia. "Aged, I should say, about twenty-six. Tall. Slender—but not thin. Of a very good figure. Black hair—a quantity of it. Black eyes— very penetrating. Fresh colour. Not exactly pretty, but attractive—in the real Parisian way—she is a Parisian. Dressed—when she left me at Hull—in a black tailor-made coat and skirt, and carrying a travelling coat of black, lined with fur—one I gave her in Russia."

"Her luggage?" asked the official.

"She had a suit-case: a medium-sized one."

"Large enough, I presume, to conceal the jewel-box your friend has told me about just now?"

"Oh, yes—certainly!"

The official put his papers back in the drawer and turned to his visitors with a business-like look which finally settled itself on Celia's face.

"You must be prepared to hear some serious news," he said. "I mean about this woman. I have no doubt from what you have just told me that I know where she is."

"Where?" demanded Celia excitedly. "You know? Where, then?"

"Lying in the mortuary at Paddington," answered the official quietly.

In spite of Celia's strong nerves she half rose in her seat—only to drop back with a sharp exclamation.

"Dead! Probably murdered. And I should say," continued the official, with a glance at the two men, "murdered in the same way as the gentleman you have told me of was murdered at Hull—by some subtle, strange, and secret poison."

No one spoke for a minute or two. When the silence was broken it was by Allerdyke.

"I should like to know about this," he said in a hard, keen voice. "I'm getting about sick of delay in this affair of my cousin's, and if this murder of the young woman is all of a piece with his, why, then, the sooner we all get to work the better. I'm not going to spare time, labour, nor expense in running that lot down, d'you understand? Money's naught to me—I'm willing—"

"We are already at work, Mr. Allerdyke," said the official, interrupting him quietly. "We've been at work in the affair of the young woman for twenty-four hours, and although you didn't know of it, we've heard of the affair of your cousin at Hull, and the two cases are so similar that when you came in I was wondering if there was any connection between them. Now, as regards the young woman. You may or may not be aware that in Eastbourne Terrace, Paddington, a street of houses which runs alongside the departure platform of the Great Western Railway, there are a number of small private hotels, which are largely used by railway passengers. To one of these hotels, about nine o'clock on the evening of May 13th (just about twenty-four hours after you, Miss Lennard, landed at Hull), there came a man and a woman, who represented themselves as brother and sister, and took two rooms for the night. The woman answers the description of your maid—as to the man, I will give you a description of him later. These two, who had for luggage such a medium-sized suit-case as that Miss Lennard has spoken of, partook of some supper and retired. There was nothing noticeable about them—they seemed to be quiet, respectable people—foreigners who spoke English very well. Nothing was heard of them until next morning at eight o'clock, when the man rang his bell and asked for tea to be brought up for both. This was done—he took it in at his door, and was seen to hand a cup in at his sister's door, close by. An hour later he came downstairs and gave instructions that his sister was not to be disturbed—she was tired and wanted to rest, he said, and she would ring when she wanted attendance. He then booked the two rooms again for the succeeding night, and, going into the coffee-room, ate a very good breakfast, taking his time over it. That done, he lounged about a little, smoking, and eventually crossed the road towards the station—since when he has not been seen. The day passed on—the woman neither rang her bell nor came down. When evening arrived, as the man had not returned, and no response could be got to repeated knocks at the door, the landlady opened it with a master-key, and entered the room. She found the woman dead—and according to the medical evidence she had been dead since ten or eleven o'clock in the morning. Then, of course, the police were called in. There was nothing in the room or in the suit-case to establish or suggest identity. The body was removed, and an autopsy has been held. And the conclusion of the medical men is that this woman has been secretly and subtly poisoned."

Here the official paused, rang a bell, and remained silent until a quiet-looking, middle-aged man who might have been a highly respectable butler entered the room: then he turned again to his visitors.

"I want you, Miss Lennard, to accompany this man— one of my officers—to the mortuary, to see if you can identify the body I have told you of. Perhaps you gentlemen will accompany Miss Lennard? Then," he continued, rising, "if you will all return here, we will go into this matter further, and see if we can throw more light on it."

Allerdyke's next impressions were of a swift drive across London to a quiet retreat in Paddington, where, in a red-brick building set amidst trees, official-faced men conducted him and his two companions into a sort of annex, one side of which was covered with sheet glass. On the other side of that glass he became aware of a still figure, shrouded and arranged in formal lines, of a white face, set amidst dark hair ... then as in a dream he heard Celia Lennard's frightened whisper—

"That's she—that's Lisette! Oh, for God's sake, take me out!"

11. THE RUSSIAN BANK-NOTES

The three searchers into what was rapidly becoming a most complicated mystery drove back to New Scotland Yard in a silence which lasted until they were set down at the door of the department whereat they had interviewed the high official. Celia Lennard was thoroughly upset; the sight of the dead woman had disturbed her even more than she let her companions see; she remained dumb and rigid, staring straight before her as if she still gazed on the white face set in its frame of dark hair. Allerdyke, too, stared at the crowds in the streets as if they were abstract visions—his keen brain felt dazed and mystified by this accumulation of strange events. And Fullaway, active and mercurial though he was, made no attempt at conversation—he sat with knitted forehead, trying to think, to account, to surmise, only conscious that he was up against a bigger mystery than life had ever shown him up to then.

The detective who had accompanied them to the mortuary conducted the three straight back to his chief's office—the chief, noticing the effect of the visit on Celia, hastened to give her a chair at the side of his desk, and looked at her with a lessening of his official manner. He signed to the other two to sit down, and motioned the detective to remain. Then he turned to Celia.

"You recognized the woman?" he said softly. "Just so. I thought you would, and I was sorry to ask you to perform such an unpleasant task but it was absolutely necessary. Now," he continued, taking up his bundle of papers again, "I want you to describe the man who met you and your maid on your arrival at Hull the other night. Of course you saw him?"

"Certainly I saw him," replied Celia. "And I should know him again anywhere—the scoundrel!"

The high official smiled and glanced at Fullaway.

"You are thinking, Miss Lennard, that the man you then saw is the man who accompanied your maid to the hotel in which she was found dead," he said. "Well, that may be so—but it mayn't. That is why I want you to give us an accurate description of the man you saw. You described the maid very well indeed. Now describe the man."

"I can do that quite well," said Celia, with assurance. "And I can tell you the circumstances. The steamer—the *Perisco*—got into the river at Hull about a quarter to nine and anchored off the Victoria Pier. We understood that she couldn't get into dock just then because of the tide, and that we must go on shore by tender. A tender came off—some of the people on board it came on our deck. There was a good deal of bustle. I went down to my cabin to see after something or other. Lisette came to me there, evidently much agitated, saying that her brother had come off on the tender to fetch her at once to their mother who was ill in London—dying. She begged to be allowed to go with him. Of course I said she might. She immediately picked up her suit-case and travelling coat out of our pile of luggage, and I went up with her on deck. She and the man—her brother, as I understood—got into a small boat which was alongside and went straight off to the pier: the tender was not leaving for shore for some time. And—that was the last I saw of her. It was all done in a minute or two."

"Now—the man," suggested the chief softly.

"A young man—about Lisette's age, I should say— twenty-seven to thirty anyway. Tallish. Dark hair, moustache, eyes, and complexion. Good-looking—in a foreign way. I had no doubt he was her brother—he looked French, though he spoke English quite well and without accent. Very respectably dressed in dark clothes and overcoat. He would have passed for a well-to-do clerk—that type. I spoke to him—a few words. He spoke well—had very polite, almost polished manners. Of course he was hurried—wanting to get Lisette away—he said they could just catch the last train to London."

The chief shook his head.

"Not the man who accompanied her to the Paddington Hotel," he said. "Listen—this is the description of that man, as given to the police by the landlady and her servants: 'Age, presumably between forty and forty-five years, medium height. Brown hair. Clean-shaven. Dressed in grey tweed suit, over which he wore a fawn-coloured overcoat. Deerstalker hat—light brown. Brown brogue shoes.' That, you see," continued the chief, "describes a quite different person. You do not recognize the description as that of any man you have ever seen in company with your late maid, Miss Lennard?"

"I never saw my maid in any man's company," replied Celia. "Since I first engaged her we have not been much in London. I was in New York and Chicago for a time last year; then in Paris; then in Milan and Turin; lately in Moscow and St. Petersburg. When we were at home, here in London, she certainly had time of her own—her evenings out, you know—but of course I don't know with whom she spent them. No—I don't know any man answering that description."

The chief folded up his papers and restored them to his desk.

"Now that you are here," he said, "you may as well give me a few particulars about your doings on the *Perisco*, especially as they relate to Mr. James Allerdyke. When and where did you make his acquaintance?"

"On the steamer—a few hours after we left Christiania," replied Celia.

"Just as fellow-passengers, I suppose?"

"Quite so—just that. We sat next to each other at meals."

"Do you know where his cabin was on the steamer?"

"Yes, exactly opposite my own. He and I, I believe, were the only passengers who had cabins all to ourselves."

"Did he ever mention to you these valuables which Mr. Fullaway tells us he was carrying to England!"

"No—never at any time."

"Did you see him leave the *Perisco* for the shore?"

"Why, yes, certainly! As a matter of fact, he and I came ashore at Hull together, ahead of any other passengers. After Lisette had left the steamer with her brother, I happened to come across Mr. James Allerdyke. I told him what had just occurred, and asked him if he would help me about my things, as my maid had gone. He immediately suggested that we shouldn't wait for the tender, but should get a boat of our own—there were several lying around. He said he was in a great hurry to get ashore, because he'd a friend awaiting him at the Station Hotel. So he got a boat, and his things and mine were put into it, and we left the steamer, and were rowed to the landing-stage, just opposite."

"And you, of course, carried your jewel-case—or what you believed to be your jewel-case—the duplicate chest which you subsequently carried to Edinburgh?"

"Yes, of course—I had it in my hand when Lisette left, and, I never left hold of it until I got into the hotel."

"Do you remember if Mr. James Allerdyke carried anything in his hand?"

"Yes, he carried a hand-bag. He had that bag in his hand when I met him on deck; he kept it on his knee in the boat, and in the cab in which we drove to the hotel from the landing-stage; I saw him carrying it upstairs after we got to the hotel. What is more, I saw him bring it into the coffee-room later on, and place it on the table at which he had some supper. I saw it again in his room when I went in there to look at the plans of the Norwegian estate which he had told me about. He didn't take those plans out of that hand-bag; he took them out of a side flap-pocket in a suit-case."

"Did you have supper with him that night?"

"No—I was sitting at another table, talking to a lady who had been with us on the *Perisco*. A lot of *Perisco* passengers—twenty, at least—had come to the hotel by that time."

"Did any of them join Mr. James Allerdyke—at his table, I mean?"

"I don't remember—no, I think not. He sat at a table, one end of which adjoined the wall—he put the hand-bag at that end. I remember wondering why he carried his bag about with him. But then I, of course, was carrying what I believed to be my jewel-case."

"Did you see him talking to any of your fellow-passengers that night?"

"Oh, yes—to two or three of them—in the hall of the hotel. I didn't know who they were, particularly—except the doctor with the big beard. I saw him talking to Mr. Allerdyke at the door of the smoking-room."

"Had you taken any special notice of your fellow passengers on board the *Perisco*?"

"No—not at all. They were just the usual sort of passengers—I wasn't interested in them. Of course, I talked to some of them, in the ordinary way, as one does talk on board ship. But I don't remember anything particular about them, nor any of their names, even if I ever knew their names. Of course I remember Mr. James Allerdyke's name, because of the business talk."

The chief, who had been making shorthand notes of this conversation, paused for a moment, evidently considering matters, and then turned to Celia with a smile.

"Why did you leave the hotel at Hull so suddenly?" he asked. "I daresay you had good reasons, but I should just like to know what they were, if you don't mind."

"I'd no reason at all," replied Celia, with almost blunt directness. "At least, if I had, they were only a woman's reasons. I was a bit upset at being left alone. I didn't like the hotel. I knew I shouldn't sleep. It was a most beautiful moonlight night, and I suddenly thought I'd like to go motoring. I knew enough of the geography of those parts to know if I motored across country I should strike the Great Northern main line somewhere and catch a train to Edinburgh in the early morning. So—I just cleared out."

"Ah—you see you had quite a number of reasons!" said the chief, smiling again. "Very well. Now then, before you go, Miss Lennard, I want you to do just one thing more which may be useful to us in our work." He turned to the detective. "Get those things," he said quietly. "Bring the lot in here."

Celia made a little sound of distaste as the detective presently returned to the room carrying in one hand a brown leather suit-case, and in the other a cardboard dress-box, to which was strapped a travelling-coat, lined with fur. Her face, which had regained its colour, paled again.

"Lisette's things!" she muttered. "Oh—I don't—don't like to see them! What is it you want?"

"We want you to identify them—and, if you will, to look them over," replied the chief. "The cardboard box contains everything she was wearing when she went to the hotel in Eastbourne Terrace; the suit-case and coat are what she took in with her. Spread the things out on that side table," he continued, turning to the detective.

"Let Miss Lennard look them over."

Celia performed the task required of her with dislike—it seemed somehow as if she were inspecting the dead woman afresh. She hurried over the task.

"All these things are hers, of course," she said. "That's the suit-case she had with her when she left me at Hull, and that's the coat I gave her—and the other things are hers, too. Oh—I don't like looking at them. Can't we go, please?"

"One moment," said the chief. "I wanted to tell you that amongst all these things there is nothing that establishes the woman's identity—I mean in the way of papers or anything of that sort. There were no letters in this case—not a scrap of paper. There is money in that purse—two or three pounds in gold, some silver. There is her watch—a good gold watch—and there are two or three rings she was wearing. Now we have only made a superficial examination of all these personal belongings—can you, as her mistress, suggest if she was likely to hide anything in her clothing, and if so, in what article? You might save us some trouble, Miss Lennard."

Allerdyke, who was more interested in Celia than in what was going on, saw a sudden gleam come into her eyes—her feminine spirit of curiosity was aroused. She hesitated, turned back to the side-table, paused before the various articles laid out there, took up and fingered two or three, and suddenly wheeled round on the men, exhibiting a quilted handkerchief case.

"There's something been sewn into the padding of this!" she said. "I can feel it. Can any one lend me pocket-scissors or a penknife?"

The men gathered round as Celia's deft fingers ripped open the satin covering: a moment later she drew out a wad of folded paper and handed it to the chief. Fullaway and Allerdyke craned their necks over his shoulders as he unwrapped and spread the bits of paper out before them. And it was Fullaway who broke the silence with a sharp exclamation.

"Bank-notes!" he said. "Russian bank-notes! And new ones!"

12. The Third Murder

Fullaway's exclamation was followed by a murmur of astonishment from Celia, and by a low growl which meant many things from Allerdyke. The chief turned the banknotes over silently, moved to his desk, and picked up a reference book.

"I'm not very familiar with Russian money—paper or otherwise," he remarked. "How much does this represent in ours, now?"

"I can tell you that," said Fullaway, taking the wad of notes and rapidly counting them. "Five hundred pounds English," he announced. "And you see that all the notes are new—don't forget to note that."

"Yes?—what do you argue from it?" asked the chief, with obvious interest. "It proves—what?"

"That these notes were given to this woman in Russia, recently—most likely in St. Petersburg," replied the American. "And, in my opinion, their presence—their discovery—proves more. It suggests at any rate that this woman, the dead maid, was a tool in the conspiracy to rob Miss Lennard and Mr. James Allerdyke, that this money is her reward, or part of it, and that the whole scheme was hatched and engineered in Russia."

"Good!" muttered Allerdyke. "Now we're getting to business."

"We shall have to get some evidence from Russia," observed the chief meditatively. "That's very evident. If the thing began there, or was put into active shape there—"

"The Princess Nastirsevitch is on her way now," said Fullaway. He pulled out his pocket-book, and began searching amongst its papers. "Here you are," he continued producing a cablegram. "That's from the

Princess—you see she says she's leaving for London at once, via Berlin and Calais, and will call upon me at my hotel as soon as she arrives. Now, that was sent off two days ago—she'd leave St. Petersburg that night. It's seventy-two hours' journey—three days. She'll be in London tomorrow evening."

The chief sat down at his desk and picked up a pen.

"Give me your addresses please, all of you," he said. "Then I can communicate with you at any moment. Miss Lennard, you mentioned Bedford Court Mansions. What number? Right.—yours, Mr. Fullaway, is the Waldorf Hotel—permanently there? Very good. You, Mr. Allerdyke, live in Bradford? It will be advisable, if you really want to clear up the mystery of your cousin's death, to remain in town for a few days, at any rate—now that we've got all this in hand, you'd better be close to the centre of things. Can you give me an address here?"

"I've a London office," answered Allerdyke. "I can always be heard of there when I'm in town. Allerdyke and Partners, Limited, Gresham Street—ask for Mr. Marshall Allerdyke. But as I'll have to put up here, I'll go to the Waldorf, with Mr. Fullaway, so if you want me you'll find me there. And look here," he went on, as the chief noted these particulars, "I want to know, to have some idea, you know, of what's going to be done. I tell you, I'll spare no time, labour, or expense in getting at the bottom of this! If it's a question of money, say the word, and—"

"All right, Mr. Allerdyke, leave it to us—for the present," said the chief, with an understanding smile. "I know what you mean. We're only beginning. This affair is doubtless a big thing, as Mr. Fullaway has suggested, and it will need some clever work. Now, at present, this case—the joint case of the Hull affair and the Eastbourne Terrace affair, for they're without doubt both parts of one serious whole—is in the hands of two of my best men. This is one of them: Detective-Sergeant Blindway. If and when Blindway wants any of you, he'll come to you. Miss Lennard, you'll be wanted at the inquest on your late maid—the Coroner's officer will let you know when. You two gentlemen will doubtless go with Miss Lennard. You'll all three certainly be wanted at that adjourned inquest at Hull. Now, that's all—except that when you, Miss Lennard, return home, you must at once begin searching for the references you had with your maid—let me have them as soon as they're found—and that you, Mr. Fullaway, must bring the Princess Nastirsevitch here as soon as you can after her arrival."

Outside New Scotland Yard Celia Lennard relieved her feelings with a fervent exclamation.

"I wish I'd never spent a penny on pearls or diamonds in my life!" she said vehemently. "Insane folly! What good have they done? Leading to all this bother, and to murder. What fools women are! All that money thrown away!—for of course I shall never see a sign of them again!"

"That's a rather hopeless way of looking at it," observed Fullaway. "You've got the cleverest police in Europe on the search for them; also you've got our friend Allerdyke and myself on the run, and we're neither of us exactly brainless. So hasten home in this taxi-cab, get some lunch, have an hour's nap, and then begin putting your papers straight and looking for those references. Search well!—you don't know what depends on it."

He and Allerdyke strolled up Whitehall when Celia had gone—in silence at first, both wrapped in meditation.

"There's only one thing one can say with any certainty about this affair, Allerdyke," remarked the American at last, "and that is precisely what the man we've been talking to said—it's a big do. The folk at the back of it are smart and clever and daring. We'll need all our wits. Well, come along to the Waldorf and let's lunch—then we'll talk some more. There's little to be done till the Princess turns up tomorrow."

"There's one thing I want to do at once," said Allerdyke. "If I'm going to stop in town I must wire to my housekeeper to send me clothes and linen, and to the manager at my mill. Then I'm with you—and I wish to Heaven we'd something to do! What I can't stand is this forced inaction, this hanging about, waiting, wondering, speculating—and doing naught!"

"We may be in action before you know it's at hand," said Fullaway. "In these cases you never know what a minute may bring forth. All we can do is to be ready."

He led the way to the nearest telegraph office and waited while Allerdyke sent off his messages. The performance of even this small task seemed to restore the Yorkshireman's spirits—he came away smiling.

"I've told my housekeeper to pack a couple of trunks with what I want, and to send my chauffeur, Gaffney, up with them, by the next express," he said. "I feel better after doing that. He's a smart chap, Gaffney—the sort that might be useful at a pinch. If any one wanted anything ferreted out, now!—he's the sense of an Airedale terrier, that chap!"

"High praise," laughed Fullaway. "And original too. Well, let's fix up and get some food, and then we'll go into my private rooms and have a talk over the situation."

Mr. Franklin Fullaway, following a certain modern fashion, introduced into life by twentieth-century company promoters and magnates of the high finance, had established his business quarters at his hotel. It was a wise and pleasant thing to do, he explained to Allerdyke; you had the advantage of living over the shop, as it were; of being able to go out of your private sitting-room into your business office; you had the bright and pleasant surroundings; you had, moreover, all the various rooms and saloons of a first-rate hotel wherein to entertain your clients if need be. Certainly you had to pay for these advantages and luxuries, but no more than you would have to lay out in the rents, rates, and taxes of palatial offices in a first-class business quarter.

"And my line of business demands luxurious fittings," remarked the American, as he installed Allerdyke in a sybaritic armchair and handed him a box of big cigars of a famous brand. "You're not the first millionaire that's come to anchor in that chair, you know!"

"If they're millionaires in penny-pieces, maybe not," answered Allerdyke. He lighted a cigar and glanced appraisingly at his surroundings—at the thick velvet pile of the carpets, the fine furniture, the bookcases filled with beautiful bindings, the choice bits of statuary, the two or three unmistakably good pictures. "Doing good business, I reckon?" he said, with true Yorkshire curiosity. "What's it run to, now?"

Fullaway showed his fine white teeth in a genial laugh.

"Oh, I've turned over two and three millions in a year in this little den!" he answered cheerily. "Varies, you know, according to what people have got to sell, and what good buyers there are knocking around."

"You keep a bit of sealing wax, of course?" suggested Allerdyke. "Take care that some of the brass sticks when you handle it, no doubt?"

"Commission and percentage, of course," responded Fullaway.

"Ah, well, you've an advantage over chaps like me," said Allerdyke. "Now, you shall take my case. We've made a pile of money in our firm, grandfather, father, and myself; but, Lord, man, you wouldn't believe what our expenses have been! Building mills, fitting machinery— and then, wages! Why, I pay wages to six hundred workpeople every Friday afternoon! Our wages bill runs to well over fourteen hundred pound a week. You've naught of that sort, of course—no great staff to keep up?"

"No," answered Fullaway. He nodded his head towards the door of a room through which they had just passed on their way into the agent's private apartments. "All the staff I have is the young lady you just saw—Mrs. Marlow. Invaluable!"

"Married woman?" inquired Allerdyke laconically.

"Young widow," answered Fullaway just as tersely. "Excellent business woman—been with me ever since I came here—three years. Speaks and writes several languages—well educated, good knowledge of my particular line of business. American—I knew her people very well. Of course, I don't require much assistance— merely clerical help, but it's got to be of a highly intelligent and specialized sort."

"Leave your business in her hands if need be, I reckon?" suggested Allerdyke, with a sidelong nod at the closed door.

"In ordinary matters, yes—comfortably," answered Fullaway. "She's a bit a specialist in two things that I'm mainly concerned in—pictures and diamonds. She can tell a genuine Old Master at a glance, and she knows a lot about diamonds—her father was in that trade at one time, out in South Africa."

"Clever woman to have," observed Allerdyke; "knows all your business, of course?"

"All the surface business," said Fullaway, "naturally! Anything but a confidential secretary would be useless to me, you know."

"Just so," agreed Allerdyke. "Told her about this affair yet?"

"I've had no chance so far," replied Fullaway. "I shall take her advice about it—she's a cute woman."

"Smart-looking, sure enough," said Allerdyke. He let his mind dwell for a moment on the picture which Mrs. Marlow had made as Fullaway led him through the office—a very well-gowned, pretty, alert, piquant little woman, still on the sunny side of thirty, who had given him a sharp glance out of unusually wide-awake eyes. "Aye, women are clever nowadays, no doubt—they'd show their grandmothers how to suck eggs in a good many new fashions. Well, now," he went on, stretching his long legs over Fullaway's beautiful Persian rug, "what do you make of this affair, Fullaway, in its present situation? There's no doubt that everything's considerably altered by what we've heard of this morning. Do you really think that this French maid affair is all of a piece, as one may term it, with the affair of my cousin James?"

"Yes—without doubt," replied Fullaway. "I believe the two affairs all spring from the same plot. That plot, in my opinion, has originated from a clever gang who, somehow or other, got to know that Mr. James Allerdyke was bringing over the Princess Nastirsevitch's jewels, and who also turned their eyes on Zelie de Longarde's valuables. The French maid, Lisette, was probably nothing but a tool, a cat's paw, and she, having done her work, has been cleverly removed so that she could never split. Further—"

A quiet knock at the door just then prefaced the entrance of Mrs. Marlow, who gave her employer an inquiring glance.

"Mr. Blindway to see you," she announced. "Shall I show him in?"

"At once!" replied Fullaway. He leapt from his chair, and going to the door called to the detective to enter. "News?" he asked excitedly, when Mrs. Marlow had retired, closing the door again. "What is it—important?"

The detective, who looked very solemn, drew a letter-case from his pocket, and slowly produced a telegram.

"Important enough," he answered. "This case is assuming a very strange complexion, gentlemen. This arrived from Hull half an hour ago, and the chief thought I'd better bring it on to you at once. You see what it is—"

He held the telegram out to both men, and they read it together, Fullaway muttering the words as he read—

From *Chief Constable, Hull, to Superintendent C.I.D., New Scotland Yard.*

Dr. Lydenberg, concerned in Allerdyke case, was shot dead in High Street here this morning by unseen person, who is up to now unarrested and to whose identity we have no clue.

13. Ambler Appleyard

Fullaway laid the telegram down on his table and looked from it to the detective.

"Shot dead—High Street—this morning?" he said wonderingly. "Why!—that means, of course, in broad daylight—in a busy street, I suppose? And yet—no clue. How could a man be shot dead under such circumstances without the murderer being seen and followed?"

"You don't know Hull very well," remarked Allerdyke, who had been pulling his moustache and frowning over the telegram, "else you'd know how that could be done easy enough in High Street. High Street," he went on, turning to the detective, "is the oldest street in the town. It's the old merchant street. Half of it—lower end—is more or less in ruins. There are old houses there which aren't tenanted. Back of these houses are courts and alleys and queer entries, leading on one side to the river, and on the other to side streets. A man could be lured into one of those places and put out of the way easily and quietly enough. Or he could be shot by anybody lurking in one of those houses, and the murderer could be got away unobserved with the greatest ease. That's probably what's happened—I know that street as well as I know my own house—I'm not surprised by that! What I'm surprised about is to hear that Lydenberg has been shot at all. And the question is—is his murder of a piece with all the rest of this damnable mystery, or is it clean apart from it? Understand, Fullaway?"

"I'm thinking," answered the American. "It takes a lot of thinking, too."

"You see," continued Allerdyke, turning to Blindway again, "we're all in a hole—in a regular fog. We know naught! literally naught. This Lydenberg was a

foreigner—Swede, Norwegian, Dane, or something. We
know nothing of him, except that he said he'd come to
Hull on business. He may have been shot for all sorts of
reasons—private, political. We don't know. But—mark
me!—if his murder's connected with the others, if it's all
of a piece with my cousin's murder, and that French
girl's, why then—"

He paused, shaking his head emphatically, and the
other two, impressed by his earnestness, waited until he
spoke again.

"Then," he continued at last, after a space of silence,
during which he seemed to be reflecting with added
strenuousness—"then, by Heaven! we're up against
something that's going to take it out of us before we get at
the truth. That's a dead certainty. If this is all conspiracy,
it's a big 'un—a colossal thing! What say, Fullaway?"

"I should say you're right," replied Fullaway. "I've
been trying to figure things up while you talked, though I
gave you both ears. It looks as if this Lydenberg had been
shot in order to keep his tongue quiet forever. Maybe he
knew something, and was likely to split. What are your
people going to do about this?" he asked turning to the
detective. "I suppose you'll go down to Hull at once?"

"I shan't," answered Blindway. "I've enough to do
here. One of our men has already gone—he's on his way.
We shall have to wait for news. I'm inclined to agree with
Mr. Allerdyke—it's a big thing, a very big thing. If Mr.
Allerdyke's cousin was really murdered, and if the
Frenchwoman's death arose out of that, and now
Lydenberg's, there's a clever combination at work. And—
where's the least clue to it?"

Allerdyke helped himself to a fresh cigar out of a box
which lay on Fullaway's table, lighted it, and smoked in
silence for a minute or two. The other men, feeling
instinctively that he was thinking, waited.

"Look you here!" he exclaimed suddenly. "Clue? Yes,
that's what we want. Where's that clue likely to be found?
Why, in this, and this only—who knew, person or

persons, that my cousin was bringing those jewels from the Princess Nastirsevitch to this country? Get to know that, and it narrows the field, d'ye see?"

"There's the question of Miss Lennard's jewels, too," remarked Fullaway.

"That may be—perhaps was—a side-issue," said Allerdyke. "It may have come into the big scheme as an after-thought. But, anyway, that's what we want—a first clue. And I don't see how that's to be got at until this Princess arrives here. You see, she may have talked, she may have let it out in confidence—to somebody who abused her confidence. What is certain is that somebody must have got to know of this proposed deal between the Princess and your man, Fullaway, and have laid plans accordingly to rob the Princess's messenger—my cousin James. D'ye see, the deal was known of at two ends—to you here, to this Princess, through James, over there, in Russia. Now, then, where did the secret get out? Did it get out there, or here?"

"Not here, of course!" answered Fullaway, with emphasis. "That's dead sure. Over there, of a certainty. The robbery was engineered from there."

"Then, in that case, there's naught to do but wait the arrival of the Princess," said Allerdyke. "And you say she'll be here to-morrow night. In the meantime no doubt you police gentlemen'll get more news about this last affair at Hull, and perhaps Miss Lennard'll find those references about the Frenchwoman, and maybe we shall mop things up bit by bit—for mopped up they'll have to be, or my name isn't what it is! Fullaway," he went on, rising from his chair, "I'll have to leave you—yon man o' mine'll be arriving from Yorkshire with my things before long, and I must go down to the hotel office and make arrangements about him. See you later—at dinner to-night, here, eh?"

He lounged away through the outer office, giving the smart lady secretary a keen glance as he passed her and getting an equally scrutinizing, if swift, look in return.

"Clever!" mused Allerdyke as he closed the door behind him. "Deuced clever, that young woman. Um— well, it's a pretty coil, to be sure!"

He went down to the office, made full and precise arrangements about Gaffney, who was to be given a room close to his own, left some instructions as to what was to be done with him on arrival, and then, hands in pockets, strolled out into Aldwych and walked towards the Strand, his eyes bent on the ground as if he strove to find in those hard pavements some solution of all these difficulties. And suddenly he lifted his head and muttered a few emphatic words half aloud, regardless of whoever might overhear them.

"I wish to Heaven I'd a right good, hard-headed Yorkshireman to talk to!" he said. "A chap with some gumption about him! These Cockneys and Americans are all very well in their way, but—"

Then he pulled himself up sharply. An idea, a name, had flashed into his mental field of vision as if sent in answer to his prayer. And still regardless of bystanders he slapped his thigh delightedly.

"Ambler Appleyard!" he exclaimed. "The very man! Here, you!"

The last two words were addressed to a taxi-cab driver whose car stood at the head of the line by the Gaiety Theatre. Allerdyke crossed from the pavement and jumped in.

"Run down to this end of Gresham Street," he said. "Go quick as you can."

He wondered as he sped along the crowded London streets why he had not thought of Ambler Appleyard before. Ambler Appleyard was the manager of his own London warehouse, a smart, clever, pushing young Bradford man who had been in charge of the London business of Allerdyke and Partners, Limited, for the last three years. He had come to London with his brains already sharpened—three years of business life in the Metropolis had made them all the sharper. Allerdyke rubbed his hands with satisfaction. Exchange of confidence with a fellow-Yorkshireman was the very thing he wanted.

He got out of his cab at the Aldersgate end of Gresham Street, and walked quickly along until he came to a highly polished brass plate on which his own name was deeply engraven. Running up a few steps into a warehouse stored with neat packages of dress goods, he encountered a couple of warehousemen engaged in sorting and classifying a consignment of fabrics just arrived from Bradford. Allerdyke, whose visits to his London warehouse were fairly frequent, and usually without notice, nodded affably to both and walked across the floor to an inner office. He opened the door without ceremony, closed it carefully behind him, and stepping forward to the occupant of the room, who sat busily writing at a desk, with his back to the entrant, and continued to write without moving or looking round, gave him a resounding smack on the shoulder.

"The very man I want, Ambler, my lad!" he said. "Sit up!"

Ambler Appleyard raised his head, slowly twisted in his revolving chair, and looked quietly at his employer. And Allerdyke, dropping into an easy-chair by the fireplace, over which hung a fine steel engraving of himself, flanked by photographs of the Bradford mills and the Bradford warehouse, looked at his London manager, secretly admiring the shrewdness and self-possession evidenced in the young man's face. Appleyard was certainly no beauty; his outstanding features were sandy-coloured hair, freckled cheeks, a snub nose, and a decidedly wide mouth; moreover, his ears, unusually large, stood out from the sides of his head in very prominent fashion, and gave a beholder the impression that they were perpetually stretched to attention. But he was the owner of a well-shaped forehead, a pair of steady and honest blue eyes, and a firmly cut square chin, and his entire atmosphere conveyed the idea of capacity, resource, and energy. It pleased Allerdyke, too, to see that the young man was attentive to his own personal appearance—his well-cut garments bore the undoubted stamp of the Savile Row tailor; the silk hat which covered his crop of sandy hair was the latest thing in Sackville Street headgear; from top to toe he was the smart man-about-town. And that was the sort of man Marshall Allerdyke liked to have about him, and to see as heads of his departments—not fops, nor dandies, but men who knew the commercial value of good appearance and smart finish.

"I didn't know you were in town, Mr. Allerdyke," said the London manager quietly. "Still, one never knows where you are these days."

"I've scarcely known that myself, my lad, these last seventy-two hours," replied Allerdyke. "You mightn't think it, but at this time yesterday I was going full tilt up to Edinburgh. I want to tell you about that, Ambler—I want some advice. But business first—aught new?"

"I've brought that South American contract off," replied Appleyard. "Fixed it this morning."

"Good!" said Allerdyke. "What's it run to, like?"

"Seventy-five thousand," answered Appleyard. "Nice bit of profit on that, Mr. Allerdyke."

"Good—good!" repeated Allerdyke. "Aught else?"

"Naught—at present. Naught out of the usual, anyway," said the manager.

He took off his hat, laid aside the papers he had been busy with on Allerdyke's entrance, and twisted his chair round to the hearth. "This advice, then?" he asked quietly. "I'm free now."

"Aye!" said Allerdyke. He sat reflecting for a moment, and then turned to his manager with a sudden question.

"Have you heard all this about my cousin James?" he asked with sharp directness.

Appleyard lifted a couple of newspapers from his desk.

"No more than what's in these," he answered. "One tells of his sudden death at Hull; the other begins to hint that there was something queer about it."

"Queer!" exclaimed Allerdyke. "Aye, and more than queer, my lad. Our James was murdered! Now, then, Ambler, I've come here to tell you all the story—you must listen to every detail. I know your brains—keep 'em fixed on what I'm going to tell; hear it all; weigh it up, and then tell me what you make of it; for I'm damned if I can make either head or tail, back, side, or front of the whole thing—so far. Happen you can see a bit of light. Listen, now."

Allerdyke, from long training in business habits, was a good teller of a plain and straightforward tale: Appleyard, for the same reason, was a good listener. So one man talked, in low, earnest tones, checking off his points as he made them, taking care that he emphasized the principal items of his news and dwelt lightly on the connecting links, and the other listened in silence, keeping a concentrated attention and storing away the facts in his memory as they were duly marshalled before him. For a good hour one brain gave out, and the other took in, and without waste of words.

It came to an end at last, and master looked at man.

"Well?" said Allerdyke, after a silence that was full of meaning—"well?"

"Take some thinking about," answered Appleyard tersely. "It's a big thing—a devilish clever thing, too. There's one fact strikes me at once, though. The news about the Nastirsevitch jewels leaked out somewhere, Mr. Allerdyke. That's certain. Either here in London, or over there in Russia, it leaked out. Now until this Princess comes you've no means of knowing if the leakage was over yonder. But there's one thing you do know now—at this very minute. There were three people here in England who knew that the jewels were on the way from Russia, in Mr. James Allerdyke's charge. Those three were this man Fullaway, his lady secretary, and Delkin, the Chicago millionaire! Now, then, Mr. Allerdyke—how much, or what, do you know about any one of 'em?"

14. Fifty Thousand Pounds Reward

Allerdyke encountered this direct question with a long, fixed stare of growing comprehension; his silence showed that he was gradually taking in its significance.

"Aye, just so!" he said at last. "Just so! How much do I know of any of 'em? Well, of Fullaway no more than I've seen. Of his secretary no more than what I've seen and heard. Of Delkin no more than that such a man exists. Sum total—what!"

"Next to naught," said Appleyard. "In a case like this you ought to know more. Fullaway may be all right. Fullaway may be all wrong. His lady secretary may be as right as he is, or as wrong as he is. As to Delkin—he might be a creature of Fullaway's imagination. Put it all to yourself now, Mr. Allerdyke—on the face of what you've told me, these three people—two of 'em, at any rate, for a certainty—knew about these valuables coming over in Mr. James's charge. So far as you know, your cousin had 'em when he left Christiania and reached Hull. There they disappear. So far as you're aware, nobody but these people knew of their coming—no other people in England knew, at any rate, so far, I repeat, as your knowledge goes. I should want to know something about these three, if I were in your place, Mr. Allerdyke."

"Aye—aye!" replied Allerdyke. "I see your point. Well, I've been in Fullaway's company now for two days— there's no denying he's a smart chap, a clever chap, and he seems to be doing good business. Moreover, Ambler, my lad, James knew him and James wasn't the sort to take up with wrong 'uns. As to the secretary, I can't say. Besides, Fullaway said this afternoon that he hadn't told her all about it yet."

"All about the Hull affair and the Lennard affair, I took that to mean from your account," remarked Appleyard. "If she's his confidential secretary, with access to his papers and business, she'd know all about the Princess transaction. Now, of course, an inquiry or two of the usual sort would satisfy you about Fullaway—I mean as a business man. An inquiry or two would tell you all about Delkin. But you can't get to know all about Mrs. Marlow from any inquiry. And you can't find out all about Fullaway from any inquiry. He may be the straightest business man in all London—and yet have a finger in this pie, and his secretary with him. Two hundred and fifty thousand pounds' worth of jewels, Mr. Allerdyke, is—a temptation! And—these folks knew the jewels were on the way. What's more, they'd time to intercept their bearer—Mr. James."

Allerdyke rubbed his chin and knitted his brows in obvious bewilderment. "There must ha' been more than them in at it," he said musingly. "A regular gang of 'em, judging by results."

"Every gang has its ganger," replied Appleyard, with a knowing smile. "There's no doubt this is a big thing—but there must be a central point, a head, a controlling authority in it. We come back, you see, after all, to where we started—these people were the only people in England who knew about these jewels, so far as we know."

"Aye, but only so far as we know," said Allerdyke. "There may have been others. There may have been folks who got to know about them over there in Russia and who communicated their knowledge to some folks here. And there's always this to be borne in mind—the affair, the plot, may have been originated there, and worked from there. Remember that!"

"Quite so—and you can't decide on anything relating to that until this Princess comes," agreed Appleyard. "It'll have to rest till you've heard all she has to say, and then you'll know where you are. But in the meantime you can find out a bit about Fullaway and this millionaire man—I can find out for you, if you like, in a few hours."

"Do, my lad!" said Allerdyke. "It's always well to know who you're dealing with. Aye—make an inquiry or two."

"But remember that all I can inquire about will be in the ordinary business way," continued Appleyard. "I can ascertain if there is a Delkin in town, who's a Chicago millionaire, and if Fullaway's a reputable business man— but that'll be all. As to the secretary, I can't do anything."

"I'll keep an eye on her myself," said Allerdyke. "Well, do this, then, and let me know the results. I've put up at the Waldorf, and there I shall stop while all this is being investigated here in London, but I shall pop in and out here, of course. And now I'll go back there and find out if there's any fresh news from the police or from Hull. I reckon there'll be some fine reading in the newspapers in a day or two, Ambler—it'll all have to come out now."

In this supposition Allerdyke was right. The police authorities, finding that the affair had assumed dimensions of an astonishing magnitude, decided to seek the aid of the Press, and to publish the entire story in the fullest possible fashion. And Allerdyke and all London woke next morning to find the newspapers alive with a new sensation, and every other man asking his neighbour what it all meant. Three mysterious murders—two big thefts—together—the newspaper world had known nothing like it for years, and the only regrets in Fleet Street were those of the men who would have sacrificed their very noses to have got the story exclusively to themselves. But the police authorities had exercised a wise generosity, and no one newspaper knew more than another at that stage—they all, as Fullaway said to Allerdyke at breakfast, got a fair start, and from that one could run their own race.

"We shall be to these Pressmen as a pot of honey to flies," he observed. "Take my advice, Allerdyke—see none of them, and if you should—as you will—get buttonholed and held up, refuse to say a word."

"You can leave that to me," answered Allerdyke, with a twitch of his determined jaw. "It 'ud be a clever newspaper chap that would get aught out of me. I've other fish to fry than to talk to these gentry. And what good will all this newspaper stuff do?"

"Lots!" replied Fullaway. "It will draw attention. There'll already be a few thousand amateur detectives looking out for the man who left the French maid dead in Eastbourne Terrace, and a few hundred amateur criminologists racking their brains for a plausible theory of the whole thing. Oh, yes, it's a good thing to arouse public interest, Allerdyke. All that's wanted now is a rousing reward. Have you thought of that?"

"Didn't I mention it to the man at Scotland Yard yesterday?" said Allerdyke. "I'm game to find aught reasonable in the way of brass. But," he added, with a touch of true Yorkshire caution, "I've been thinking that over during the night, and it seems to me that there are two other parties who ought to come in at it, with me, of course. Miss Lennard and the Princess, d'ye see? If they're willing, I am."

"You mean a joint reward for the detection of the murderer and the recovery of the jewels?" suggested Fullaway.

"Well, you can be pretty certain, by now, that the murders and the thefts are all the work of one gang," replied Allerdyke. "So it's long as it's short. These two women want their pearls and their diamonds back—I want to know who killed my cousin James. We're all three in the same boat, really; so if we make up a good, substantial purse between us—what?"

"Good!" agreed Fullaway. "We'll hear what the Princess says when she arrives to-night. I guess we shall all know better where we exactly are when we've heard what she has to say."

"If she's like most women that's lost aught in the way of finery," remarked Allerdyke drily, "she'll have plenty to say."

That night he had abundant opportunity of hearing the Princess Nastirsevitch's views on the situation, freely expressed. He himself fetched Celia Lennard to the conference at New Scotland Yard; they found Fullaway and the Princess already there, in full blast of debate. Allerdyke inspected the new arrival with keen interest and found her a well-preserved, handsome woman of middle-age, sharp, smart, and American to the finger-tips. The official whom they had met before was already questioning her, and for Allerdyke's benefit he repeated what had already transpired.

"The Princess affirms, Mr. Allerdyke, that not a soul but herself and your cousin, Mr. James Allerdyke, knew of this affair," he said. "I am right, am I not, madame," he went on, turning to the Princess, "in saying that not one word of this transaction, or proposed transaction, was ever mentioned by you to any person but Mr. James Allerdyke?"

"To no other person than Mr. James Allerdyke," assented the Princess firmly. "It would have been strange conduct on my part, I think, if I had told anybody else anything about it!—my object, of course, being secrecy. From the moment I first mentioned it to Mr. James Allerdyke until I arrived here just now and met Mr. Fullaway there, I never spoke of the matter to any one!"

The official looked at Allerdyke as if inviting him to ask any question that occurred to him, and Allerdyke immediately brought up that which had been in his mind ever since his discovery of James Allerdyke's pocket-diary.

"How came you to repose such confidence in my cousin, ma'am?" he asked brusquely. "I always thought I was pretty deep in his counsels, but I never heard him mention your name. Did he know you well?"

"I had known Mr. James Allerdyke for a little over a year," replied the Princess. "I met him first in Paris—then on the Riviera—then in Russia. The fact is, he did some business for me. I had every confidence in him—the fullest confidence. I knew he was a thoroughly straight man. And just as I had decided to sell these jewels'—all my own property, mind—in order to clear off the whole lot of the mortgages on my son's estate, so's he could come into them quite unencumbered, I happened to meet Mr. James Allerdyke in St. Petersburg—that's of course, a few weeks ago—and I immediately took him into my confidence and asked his help. With the result," added the Princess, "that he cabled to Mr. Fullaway there and that all this has come about! I tell you in the most emphatic manner at my command," she went on, turning to the official, and tapping the edge of his desk as if to accentuate her words, "it's impossible that anybody over there in Russia could have known of my arrangements with Mr. James Allerdyke—utterly impossible. For I never spoke of them to any one there, and I'm sure he would not!"

"Impossible is a big word, Princess," said the official. "There may have been ways of leakage. Did you exchange any correspondence on the matter?"

"Not a line!" replied the Princess. "There was no need. We met three times and arranged everything. The only correspondence there was—if you could call it correspondence—was the exchange of cablegrams between Mr. James Allerdyke and Mr. Fullaway. I saw those cablegrams—of course the jewels were mentioned. But I don't believe Mr. James Allerdyke was the sort of man to leave his cablegrams lying around for somebody else to see. I know he had them in his pocket-book. No!" she went on, with added emphasis and conviction. "The thing did not start over there, I'm sure. It's been put up here, in London."

"Well," observed the official, after a pause, "there's only one thing more I want to ask you just now, Princess.

You gave these immensely valuable jewels to Mr. James Allerdyke? Did he hand you any receipt for them?"

"A receipt which I've got here," answered the Princess, tapping her hand-bag. "And it's all in his handwriting, and made out in the form of an inventory—all that was at his suggestion."

"And how," asked the official, "were the jewels packed when given to him?"

"Very simply," said the Princess. "That was his suggestion, too. They were wrapped up in soft paper and chamois leather, and put into an old cigar-box which he placed in his small travelling-bag. That bag, he said, would never go out of his sight until he reached London, where, when he'd exhibited the jewels to Mr. Fullaway's client, he was to lodge them in a bank. It seemed to him that the cigar-box was a good notion—the jewels themselves didn't take up so much room as you might think, and he laid some very ordinary things over the top of the package—a cake or two of soap, a sponge, and things like that—so that, supposing the cigar-box had been opened, its contents would have seemed very ordinary, you understand?"

"And yet," said the official softly, "the thieves evidently went straight for that cigar-box when the critical moment came. Well," he continued, looking round at his visitors, "I don't know that we can do more to-night. Is there anything any of you ladies or gentlemen wish to suggest?"

"Yes!" said Allerdyke. "In my opinion a most important thing. It's my decided conviction that in this case we've got to offer a reward—no mere trifling sum, but one that'll set a few fingers tingling. And it's my concern, and the Princess's, and Miss Lennard's. And if you'll permit us three to have a quiet talk in yon corner of your room, I'll tell you its result when we've finished."

The result of that quiet talk—chiefly conducted by Allerdyke with masculine force and vigour—was that by noon of next day the exterior of every London police-station attracted vast attention by reason of a freshly-posted bill. It was a long bill, and it set out the surface particulars of three murders, and of two robberies in connection therewith. The particulars made interesting reading enough—but the real fascination of the bill was in its big, staring headline—

FIFTY THOUSAND POUNDS REWARD.

15. THE BAYSWATER BOARDING-HOUSE

Some time previous to these remarkable events, Marshall Allerdyke, being constantly in London, and having to spend much time on business in the Mansion House region, had sought and obtained membership of the City Carlton Club, in St. Swithin's Lane, and at noon of the day following the arrival of the Princess Nastirsevitch, he stood in a window of the smoking-room, looking out for Appleyard, whom he had asked to lunch. In one hand he carried a folded copy of the reward bill, which Blindway had left at the Waldorf Hotel for him, and while he waited—the room being empty just then save for an old gentleman who read *The Times* in a far corner—he unfolded and took a surreptitious glance at it, chuckling to himself at the thought of the cupidity which its contents and promises would arouse in the breasts of the many thousands of folk who would read it.

"Fifty thousand pounds!" he thought, with high amusement. "Egad, some of 'em 'ud feel like Rothschild himself if they could shove that bit in their pockets— they'd take on all the airs of a Croesus!"

The thought of the Rothschild wealth made him lift his eyes and glance through the window at the gate of the quiet, ultra-respectable establishment across the way. Allerdyke, like all men of considerable means, had a mighty respect for wealth in its colossal forms, and he never visited the City Carlton, nor looked out of its smoking-room windows, without glancing with interest and admiration at the famous Rothschild offices, immediately opposite. It amused him to speculate and theorize about the vast amounts of money which must needs be turned over in theory and practice within those soberly quiet walls, to indulge in fancies about the secrets, financial and political, which must be discussed and locked up in human breasts there—to him the magic address, New Court, St. Swithin's Lane, was as full of potential mystery as the Sphinx is to an imaginative traveller. He glanced at its gates and at its sign now with an almost youthful awe and reverence—the reverence of the man of considerable wealth for the men of enormous wealth—and while his eyes were thus busy a taxi-cab came along the Lane, stopped by the entrance to New Court, and set down Mrs. Marlow.

Allerdyke instinctively shrank back within the curtains of the smoking-room window. There was no reason why he should have done so. He had no objection to Franklin Fullaway's secretary seeing him standing in a window of the City Carlton Club; he knew no reason why Mrs. Marlow should object to be seen getting out of a cab in St. Swithin's Lane. Yet, he drew back, and, from his concealed position, watched. Not that there was anything out of the ordinary to watch. Mrs. Marlow, who looked daintier, prettier, more charming than ever, paid her driver, gave him a smiling nod, and tripped into New Court, a bundle of papers in her well-gloved hand.

"Business with Rothschild's, eh?" mused Allerdyke.

"Well, I daresay there's a vast lot of folk in this city who do business across there. Um!—smart little woman that, and no doubt as clever as she's smart. I'd like to know—"

Just then the ancient hall-porter of the club (who surely missed his vocation in life, and should have been a bishop, or at least a dean) ushered in Appleyard, whom Allerdyke immediately beckoned to join him amongst the window-curtains.

"I say!" he whispered, with a side glance at *The Times*-reading old gentleman, "you remember me telling you yesterday about the lady-secretary of Fullaway's—Mrs. Marlow?—what a smart bit she looked to be. Eh?"

"Well?" replied Appleyard. "Of course, what about her?"

"She's just gone into Rothschild's across there," answered Allerdyke. "Come here, this corner; she'll be coming out before long, no doubt, and then you'll see her. As I told you about her, I want you to take a look at her—she's worth seeing for more reasons than one."

Appleyard allowed himself to be drawn into the embrasure. He waited patiently and in silence—presently Allerdyke dug a finger into his ribs.

"She's coming!" he whispered. "Now!"

Appleyard looked half-carelessly across the street—the next instant he was devoutly thanking his stars that since boyhood he had sedulously trained himself to control his countenance. He made no sign, gave no indication of previous acquaintance, as he watched Mrs. Marlow's svelt figure trip out of New Court and away up St. Swithin's Lane; his face was as calm and unemotional, his eyes as steady as ever when he turned to his employer.

"Pretty woman," he said. "Looks a sharp 'un, too, Mr. Allerdyke. Well," he went on, turning away into the room as if Mrs. Marlow no longer interested him. "I got those two reports for you—shall I tell you about them now?"

"Aye, for sure," replied Allerdyke. "Come into this corner—we'll have a glass of sherry—it's early for lunch yet. Those reports, eh? About Fullaway and Delkin, you mean?"

"Just so," said Appleyard, settling himself in the corner of a lounge and lighting the cigarette which Allerdyke offered him. "They're ordinary business reports, you know, got through the usual channels. Fullaway's all right, so far as the various commercial agencies know—nothing ever been heard against him, anyhow. The account of himself and his business which he gave to you is quite correct. To sum up—he's a sound man—quite straight—on the business surface, which is, of course, all we can get at. As for Delkin, that's a straight story, too—anyway, there's a Chicago millionaire of that name been in town some weeks—he's stopping at the Hotel Cecil—has a palatial suite there—and his daughter's about to marry Lord Hexwater. All correct there, Mr. Allerdyke, too—I mean as regards all that Fullaway told you."

"Well, there's something in knowing all that, Ambler, my lad," answered Allerdyke. "You can't get to know too much about the folks you're dealing with, you know. Very good—we'll leave that now. What d'ye think o' this?"

He unfolded and held up the reward bill, first looking as fondly at it as a youthful author looks at his first printed performance, and then glancing at his manager to see what effect it had upon him. And he saw Ambler Appleyard's sandy eyebrows go up in a definite arch.

"Fifty thousand!" muttered Appleyard. "Whew! It's a stiff figure, Mr. Allerdyke. You've put a thick finger in that pie, I'm thinking!"

"One half from the Princess; twenty thousand from me; five thousand from the singing lady," whispered Allerdyke. "That's how it's made up, my lad. And naught'll please me better than to see it paid out—that's a fact!"

"You'll have some triers," said Appleyard, with an emphatic wag of the head. "Make no mistake about that! Fifty thousand! Gosh!—why, anybody that's got the least clue, the slightest idea—and there must be somebody—'ll have a go in for all he or she's worth!"

"Let 'em try!" exclaimed Allerdyke. "The welcome man's the chap that enables us to recover and convict. Here, shove that bill in your pocket, and read it at your leisure—there's something to think about in what it says, I promise you."

Appleyard went away from the club an hour and a half later, thinking hard enough. But he was not thinking about the reward bill. What he was thinking about, had been thinking about from the moment in which Allerdyke had drawn him into the smoking-room window and pointed her out to him, was—Mrs. Marlow. For

Appleyard knew Mrs. Marlow well enough, but (always those buts in life, he reflected with a cynical laugh as he threaded his way back to Gresham Street) he knew her by another name—Miss Slade. And now he was wondering why Miss Slade or Mrs. Marlow had two names, and why she appeared to be one person as he knew her in private life, and another as he had seen her that very morning.

On Appleyard's first coming to town in the capacity of sole manager of the London warehouse of Allerdyke and Partners, Limited, he had set himself up in two rooms in a Bloomsbury lodging-house. He knew little of London life at that time, or he would have known that he was thus condemning himself to a drab and dreary existence. As it was, he quickly learnt by experience, and within six months, having picked up a comfortable knowledge of things, he transferred himself to one of those well-equipped boarding establishments in the best part of Bayswater, wherein bachelors, old maids, young women, widowers, and married couples without encumbrance, can live together in as much or as little friendship and intercourse as pleases their individual tastes. Ambler Appleyard took his time and selected the likeliest place he could find after much inspection of many similar places. His salary of a thousand a year (to which was to be added a handsome, if varying commission) enabled him to pick and choose; the house which he did choose, in the immediate neighbourhood of Lancaster Gate, was of the luxurious order; its private rooms were models of the last thing in comfort, its public rooms were equal to those of the best modern hotels. If you wanted male society, you could find it in the smoking-room and the billiard-room; if you desired feminine influences there was a pleasing variety in the drawing-room and the lounges. You could be just as much alone, and just as much in company as you pleased—anyway, the place suited Ambler Appleyard, and there he had lived for two and a half years. And during a good two of them, the young lady whom he knew as Miss Slade had lived there too.

With Miss Slade, Appleyard, as fellow-resident in the same house, was on quite friendly terms. He sometimes talked to her in one of the drawing-rooms. He knew her for a clever, rather brilliant young woman, with ideas, and the power to express them. It was evident to him that she had travelled and had seen a good deal of the world and its men and women; she could talk politics with far more knowledge and insight than most women; she knew more than a little of economic matters, and was inclined, like Appleyard himself, to utilitarianism in all things affecting government and society. But of herself she never spoke directly; all Appleyard knew of her concerns was that she was engaged in business of some nature, and went to it every morning as regularly and punctually as he went to his. He judged that whatever her business was she must be well paid for it, or must possess means of her own; nobody, man or woman, could possibly live at that boarding-house, or private hotel, as its proprietors preferred to call it, for anything less than four guineas a week. Well—here was the explanation of Miss Slade's business; she was evidently private secretary to Mr. Franklin Fullaway, and competent to do business at a place like Rothschild's. And why not?—yet ... why did she call herself Miss Slade at the boarding-house and Mrs. Marlow in her business capacity?

"And yet why shouldn't she?" asked Appleyard of himself. "A woman's a right to do what she likes in that way, and she isn't necessarily deceitful because she passes as a single woman in one place and a widow in another. I daresay she could give a very good reason for all this—but who's got any right to ask her for one? Not me, certainly!"

He had no intention of asking Miss Slade anything when he left the City for Bayswater that evening, but chance threw him into her immediate company in one of the lounges, where, after dinner, they met at a table on which the evening newspapers were laid out. As Miss Slade picked up one, Appleyard picked up another—certain big, strong letters on the front sheets of both gave him an opening.

"Have you read anything about this affair?" he asked, with apparent carelessness, pointing to a row of capitals. "This extraordinary murder-robbery business which is becoming the talk of the town? Murders of three people—theft of nearly three hundred thousand pounds' worth of jewels—and fifty thousand pounds reward! It's colossal!"

Miss Slade, without showing the slightest shade of interest, shook her head.

"I don't read murders," she answered. "Fifty thousand pounds reward! That's an awful lot, isn't it?"

"Worth trying for, anyway!" replied Appleyard. He gave her a sly look, and smiled grimly. "I think I'll try for it," he said. "Fifty thousand!"

"How could any one try unless he or she's some clue?" she asked. "If you don't know anything about it, or any of the persons concerned, where would you begin?"

"There are plenty of persons named in these accounts about whom one could find something out, at any rate," replied Appleyard, tapping the newspaper with his finger. "There's a Russian Princess with a sneezy sort of name; a Yorkshire manufacturer named Allerdyke; an American man called Franklin Fullaway—all seem to be well-known people in town. You ever hear of any of them?"

Miss Slade turned a face of absolute indifference on him and the paper to which he was pointing.

"Never," she answered calmly. "But I daresay I shall hear of them now—for nine days."

Then she went off, with her own newspaper, and Appleyard carried his to a corner and sat down.

"That's a lie!" he said to himself. "And a woman who will tell a lie as calmly and quietly as that will tell a thousand with equal assurance and cleverness. She—"

There he stopped. In the doorway Miss Slade had also stopped—stopped to speak to another resident, a man, about whom Ambler Appleyard had often wondered as keenly as he was now wondering about Miss Slade herself.

16. MR. GERALD RAYNER

There were various reasons why Ambler Appleyard's wonder had often been aroused by the man to whom Miss Slade had stopped to speak. He wondered about him, first of all, because of his personal appearance. That was striking enough to excite wonder in anybody, for he was one of those remarkable men who possess great beauty of countenance allied to unfortunate deformity of body. The face was that of a poet and a dreamer, the body that of a hunchback and a cripple. Painter or sculptor alike would have rejoiced to depict the face on canvas or carve it in marble—its perfect shape, fine tinting, the lines of the features, the beauty of the eyes, the wealth of the dark, clustering hair, were all as near artistic perfection as could be. But all else spoke of deformity—the badly bent back, the twisted body, the short leg, the misshapen foot. It was as if Nature had endeavoured in some wickedly mischievous freak to show how beauty and ugliness can be combined in one creature.

That was one reason for wonder in Appleyard's mind—he had never come across quite this type before, though he knew that hunchbacks and cripples are often gifted with unusual strength, and more than usual good looks, as if in ironic compensation for their other disadvantages. But there were others. Mr. Gerald Rayner—everybody knew everybody else's name in that private hotel, for they were all more or less permanent residents—was something of a mystery man. In spite of his deformity, he was the best-dressed man in the house—they were all smart men there, but none of them came up to him in the way of clothes, linen, and personal adornment, always in the best and most cultured taste. Also it was easy to gather that he was a young man of large means. Although he made full use of the public rooms, and was always in and about them of an evening, from dinner-time to a late hour, he tenanted a private suite of apartments in the hotel—those residents, few in number, who had been privileged to obtain entrance to them spoke with almost awed admiration of their occupant's books, pictures, and objects of art. Mr. Gerald Rayner, it was evident, was a man of culture—that, indeed, was shown by his conversation. And at first Appleyard had set him down as a poet, or an artist, or a writing man of some sort—a dilettante who possessed private means. Then, being a sharp observer of all that went on around his own centre, he began to perceive that he must be mistaken in that—Rayner was obviously a business man, like himself. For every morning, at precisely half-past nine, a smart motor-brougham arrived at the door of the private hotel and carried Rayner off Citywards; every afternoon at exactly half-past five the same conveyance brought him back. Only business men, said Appleyard, are so regular, so punctual; therefore Rayner must be a business man.

But nobody in that hotel knew anything whatever of Rayner, beyond what they saw of him within its walls. Nobody knew whither the motor-brougham carried him, what he did when he reached his destination, nobody knew what or who he was. Appleyard, who was always knocking about the heart of the City, who was for ever in its business streets, who knew all the City clubs, all the best City restaurants, and was familiar with all sorts and shades of life in the City, never saw Rayner in any of his own purlieus. Accordingly, he came to the conclusion that Rayner's business, whatever it was, did not take him to the City. Nevertheless, it was certain, in Appleyard's opinion, that he was in business, and paid scrupulous attention to his daily duties.

Over the edge of his newspaper he watched Rayner and Miss Slade meet, exchange a word or two, and retire to a corner of an inner lounge in which they often sat talking together. He had often seen them talking together, and it had struck him that they seemed to talk with more than ordinary confidence. The hunchback was on terms of easy familiarity with everybody in the house, and he had a remarkable range of topics. He could talk sport, books, finance, politics, art, science, history, theology—the variety of his conversation was astonishing. But Appleyard had begun to notice that he rarely talked to any single person with the exception of Miss Slade—he would join a group in smoking-room or drawing-room and enter gaily into whatever was being discussed, but he seemed to have no desire to hold a *tete-a-tete* talk with any one except this young woman, who was now as much an object of mystery and speculation to Appleyard as he himself was. They were often seen talking together in quiet corners—and some of the old maids and eligible widows were already saying that Miss Slade was setting her cap at Mr. Rayner's evident deep purse.

Ambler Appleyard went to bed that night wondering greatly about two matters—first, why Miss Slade was Miss Slade in Bayswater and Mrs. Marlow at Fullaway's office; second, if Miss Slade or Mrs. Marlow, whichever she really was, had any secrets with the mysterious Mr. Rayner. From that he got to wondering who Rayner really was, and what his business was. And this process of speculation began again next morning, and continued all the way to the Gresham Street warehouse, and by the time he had arrived there he had half-determined to find out more about Miss Slade than was known to him up to then—and also, since he appeared to be such great friends with Miss Slade, about Mr. Gerald Rayner.

"But how?" he mused as he ran up the steps to the warehouse. "I'm not a private detective, and I don't propose to employ one. If I knew some sharp fellow—"

Just then he caught sight of Gaffney, who sat on a bale of goods within the warehouse door, holding a note in his hand. He stood up with a grin of friendly recognition when he saw Appleyard.

"Morning, sir," he said. "Letter from Mr. Allerdyke for you. No answer, but I was to wait till you'd read it."

Appleyard opened the note there and then. It was a mere hurried scrawl, saying that Allerdyke was just setting off for Hull, in obedience to a call from the police; as Gaffney had nothing to do, would Appleyard make use of him during Allerdyke's absence?

Appleyard bade Gaffney wait a while, went into his office, ran through his correspondence, gave the morning's orders out to the warehouseman, and called the chauffeur inside.

"Gaffney," he said as he carefully closed the door on them, "you're a Londoner, aren't you?"

Gaffney smiled widely.

"Ought to be, Mr. Appleyard," he answered. "I was born within sound of Bow Bells, anyhow. Off Aldersgate Street, sir. Yes, I'm a Cockney, right enough."

"Then you know London well, of course," suggested Appleyard.

"Never went out of it much, sir, till I went down to Bradford to this present job," replied Gaffney. "I shouldn't have left it if Mr. Allerdyke hadn't given me extra good wages and a real good place."

Appleyard tossed Allerdyke's note across his desk.

"You see what Mr. Allerdyke says," he remarked. "Wants me to find you something to do while he's off. How long is he likely to be off?"

"He said he might be back to-morrow night, sir," answered Gaffney, glancing at the note. "But possibly not till the day after to-morrow."

"Well, I don't know that there's anything you can do here," said Appleyard. "We're not particularly busy, and we've a full staff. But," he continued, with a sharp glance at the chauffeur, "there's something you can do for me, privately, to-morrow morning—a quite private matter—a matter entirely between ourselves. I'll account to Mr.

Allerdyke for your time, but I don't want even him to know about this job that you can do for me—I'll pay you for doing it out of my own pocket."

"Just as you think right, sir," answered Gaffney. "So long as you make it right with the guv'nor, I'm willing."

"Very well," said Appleyard. He paused a moment, and then lowered his voice. "You've seen about this tremendous reward that's being offered in Mr. James Allerdyke's case?" he asked, with another sharp look. "You know what I mean?"

Gaffney's shrewd face grew shrewder, and he nodded knowingly.

"I know!" he said. "Fifty thousand! A fortune, sir!"

"What I want you to do," continued Appleyard, "may lead to something relating to that, and it mayn't. Anyway, I'll make you all right. Now, listen carefully. Do you think you could get hold of a private motor to-morrow morning? A smart, private cab in which you could put a friend of yours—well dressed—would be the thing. Early."

"Easy as winking, sir," answered Gaffney. "Know the cab, and know a friend o'mine who'd sit in it—as long as you like."

"Very good," said Appleyard. "Now, then, do you know Lancaster Gate?"

"Do I know St. Paul's?" exclaimed Gaffney, half-derisively. "Used to drive for an old gent who lived in Porchester Terrace."

"Oh!" replied Appleyard. "Then I daresay you know the Pompadour Private Hotel?"

"As well as I know my own fingers," responded Gaffney. "Driven to and from it many a hundred times."

"Just the man I want, then," continued Appleyard. "Now, to-morrow morning, get your cab early—put your friend in it—dressed up, of course—and at half-past nine to the very minute drive slowly past the front door of the Pompadour. You'll see a private motor-brougham there—

dark green—you'll also see a hunchbacked gentleman enter it—you can't mistake him. Follow him! Never mind where he goes, or how long it takes to get there—or how few minutes it takes to get there, for that matter!—follow him and find out where that private cab puts him down. Then—come and report to me. Is that all clear?"

"Clear as noonday, sir," answered Gaffney. "I understand—I've been at that sort of game more than once."

"All right," said Appleyard. "I leave it to you. Take every care—I don't want this man to get the least suspicion that he's followed. And—" He hesitated, considering his plans over again. "Yes," he went on, "there's just another detail that I may mention—it'll save time. This hunchback gentleman's name is Rayner—Mr. Gerald Rayner. Can you remember it?"

"As well as my own," answered Gaffney. "Mr. Gerald Rayner. I've got it."

"Very good. Now, then, can you trust this friend of yours?" asked Appleyard. "Is he a chap of common sense?"

"It's my own brother," replied Gaffney. "Some people say I'm the sharper of the two, some say he is. There's a pair of us, anyhow."

"That'll do," said Appleyard. "Now, wherever you see this Mr. Rayner set down, let your brother get out of your cab and take particular notice if he goes into any shop, office, flats, buildings, anything of that sort which bears his name—Rayner. D'you see? I want to know what his business is. And now that you know what I want, you and your brother put your heads together and try to find it out, and come to me when you've done, and I'll make it worth your while. You'd better go now and make your arrangements."

Gaffney went away, evidently delighted with his commission, and Appleyard turned to his business of the day, wondering if he was not going to waste the chauffer's time and his own money. Next morning he purposely hung about the Pompadour until the time for Rayner's departure arrived; from one of the front windows he saw the hunchback enter his brougham and drive away; at the same moment he saw a neat private cab, driven by Gaffney, and occupied by a smart-looking young gentleman in a silk hat, come along and follow in quite an ordinary and usual manner. And on that he himself went to Gresham Street and waited.

Gaffney and his brother turned in during the morning, both evidently primed with news. Appleyard shut himself into his office with them.

"Well?" he asked.

"Easy job, Mr. Appleyard," replied Gaffney. "Drove straight through the Park, Constitution Hill, the Mall, Strand, to top of Arundel Street. There he got out; brougham went off—back—he walked down street. So my brother here he got out too, and strolled down street after him. He'll tell you the rest, sir."

"Just as plain as what he's told," said the other Gaffney. "I followed him down the street; he walked one side, I t'other side. He went into Clytemnestra House— one of those big houses of business flats and offices— almost at the bottom. I waited some time to see if he was settled like, or if it was only a call he was making. Then I went into the hall of Clytemnestra House, as if I was looking for somebody. There are two boards in that hall with the names of tenants painted on 'em. But there's not that name—Gerald Rayner. Still, I'll tell you what there is, sir—there's a name that begins with the same initials—G.R."

"What name?" asked Appleyard.

"The name," replied the second Gaffney, "is Gavin Ramsay—Agent."

17. THE PHOTOGRAPH

Allerdyke went off to Hull, post-haste, because of a telephone call which roused him out of bed an hour before his usual time. It came from Chettle, the New Scotland Yard man who had been sent down to Hull as soon as the news of Lydenberg's murder arrived. Chettle asked Allerdyke to join him by the very next express, and to come alone; he asked him, moreover, not to tell Mr. Franklin Fullaway whither he was bound. And Allerdyke, having taken a quick glance at a time-table, summoned Gaffney, told him of his journey, bade him keep his tongue quiet at the Waldorf, wrote his hasty note to Appleyard, dressed, and hurried away to King's Cross. He breakfasted on the train, and was in Hull by one o'clock, and Chettle hailed him as he set foot on the platform, and immediately led him off to a cab which awaited them outside the station.

"Much obliged to you for coming so promptly, Mr. Allerdyke," said the detective. "And for coming by yourself—that was just what I wanted."

"Aye, and why?" asked Allerdyke. "Why by myself? I've been wondering about that all the way down."

Chettle, a sleek, comfortable-looking man, with a quiet manner and a sly glance, laughed knowingly, twiddling his fat thumbs as he leaned back in the cab. "Oh, well, it doesn't do—in my opinion—to spread information amongst too many people, Mr. Allerdyke," he said. "That's my notion of things, anyway. I just wanted to go into a few matters with you, alone, d'ye see? I didn't want that American gentleman along with you. Eh?"

"Now, why?" asked Allerdyke. "Out with it!"

"Well, you see, Mr. Allerdyke," answered the detective, "we know you. You're a man of substance, you've got a big stake in the country—you're Allerdyke, of Allerdyke and Partners, Limited, Bradford and London. But we don't know Fullaway. He may be all right, but you could only call him a bird of passage, like. He can close down his business and be away out of England to-morrow, and, personally, I don't believe in letting him into every secret about all this affair until we know more about him. You see, Mr. Allerdyke, there's one thing very certain—so far as we've ascertained at present, nobody but Fullaway, and possibly whoever's in his employ, was acquainted with the fact that your cousin was carrying those jewels from Russia to England. Nobody in this country, at any rate. And—it's a thing of serious importance, sir."

Just what Appleyard had said!—what, indeed, no one of discernment could help saying, thought Allerdyke. The sole knowledge, of course, was with Fullaway and his lady clerk—so far as was known. Therefore—

"Just so," he said aloud. "I see your point—of course, I've already seen it. Well, what are we going to do—now? You've brought me down here for something special, no doubt."

"Quite so, sir," answered Chettle composedly. "I want to draw your attention to some very special features and to ask you certain questions arising out of 'em. We'll take things in order, Mr. Allerdyke. We're driving now to the High Street—I want to show you the exact spot where Lydenberg was shot dead. After that we'll go to the police-station and I'll show you two or three little matters, and we'll have a talk about them. And now, before we get to the High Street, I may as well tell you that on examining Lydenberg's body very little was found in the way of papers—scarcely anything, and nothing connecting him with your cousin's affair—in fact, the police here say they never saw a foreign gentleman with less on him in that way. But in the inside pocket of his overcoat there was a postcard, which had been posted here in Hull. Here it is—

and you'll see that it was the cause of taking him to the spot where he was shot."

Chettle took from an old letter-case an innocent-looking postcard, on one corner of which was a stain.

"His blood," he remarked laconically. "He was shot clean through the heart. Well, you see, it's a mere line."

Allerdyke took the card and looked at it with a mingled feeling of repulsion and fascination. The writing on it was thin, angular, upright, and it suggested foreign origin. And the communication was brief—and unsigned—

"High Street morning eleven sharp left-hand side old houses."

"You don't recognize that handwriting, of course, Mr. Allerdyke?" asked Chettle. "Never seen it before, I suppose?"

"No!" replied Allerdyke. "Never. But I should say it's a foreigner's."

"Very likely," assented Chettle. "Aye, well, sir, it lured the man to his death. And now I'll show you where he died, and how easy it was for the murderer to kill him and get away unobserved."

He pulled the cab up at the corner of the High Street, and turned southward towards the river, looking round at his companion with one of his sly smiles.

"I daresay that you, being a Yorkshireman, Mr. Allerdyke, know all about this old street," he remarked as they walked forward. "I never saw it, never heard of it, until the other day, when I was sent down on this Lydenberg business, but it struck me at once. I should think it's one of the oldest streets left in England."

"It is," answered Allerdyke. "I know it well enough, and I've seen it changed. It used to be the street of the old Hull merchants—they had their houses and warehouses all combined, with gardens at the back running down to the river Hull. Queer old places there used to be in this street, I can tell you when I was a lad!—of late years they've pulled a lot of property down that had got what you might call thoroughly worm-eaten—oh, yes, the place isn't half as ancient or picturesque as it was even twenty years ago!"

"There's plenty of the ancient about it still, for all that," observed Chettle, with a dry laugh. "There was more than enough of it for Lydenberg the other day, at any rate. Now, then, you remember what it said on the postcard—he was to walk down the High Street, on the left-hand side, at eleven o'clock? Very well—down the High Street he walks, on this side which we are now—he strolls along, by these old houses, looking about him, of course, for the person he was to meet. The few people who were about down here that morning, and who saw him, said that he was looking about from side to side. And all of a sudden a shot rang out, and Lydenberg fell—just here—right on this very pavement."

He pulled Allerdyke up in a narrow part of the old street, jointed to the flags, and then to the house behind them—an ancient, ramshackle place, the doors and windows of which were boarded up, the entire fabric of which showed unmistakable readiness for the pick and shovel of the house-breaker. And he laid a hand on one of the shattered windows, close by a big hole in the decaying wood.

"There's no doubt the murderer was hidden behind this shutter, and that he fired at Lydenberg from it, through this hole," he said. "So, you see, he'd only be a few feet from his man. He was evidently a good shot, and a fellow of resolute nerve, for he made no mistake. He only fired once, but he shot Lydenberg clean through the heart, dead!"

"Anybody see it happen?" asked Allerdyke, staring about him at the scene of the tragedy, and thinking how very ordinary and commonplace everything looked. "I suppose there'd be people about, though the street, at this end, anyway, isn't as busy as it once was?"

"Several people saw him fall," answered Chettle.

"They say he jumped, spun round, and fell across the pavement. And they all thought it was a case of suicide. That, of course, gave the murderer a bigger and better chance of making off. You see, as these people saw no assailant, it never struck 'em that the shot had been fired from behind this window. When they collected their thoughts, found it wasn't suicide, and realized that it was murder, the murderer was—Lord knows where! From behind these old houses, Mr. Allerdyke, there's a perfect rabbit-warren of alleys, courts, slums, twists, and turns! The man could slip out at the back, go left or right, mix himself up with the crowd on the quays and wharves, walk into the streets, go anywhere—all in a minute or two."

"Clever—very clever! You've no clue?" asked Allerdyke.

"None; not a scrap!" replied the detective. "Bless you, there's score of foreigners knocking about Hull. Scores! Hundreds! We've done all we can, the local police and myself—we've no clue whatever. But, of course, it was done by one of the gang."

"By one of the gang!" exclaimed Allerdyke. "Ah you've got a theory of your own, then?"

Chettle laughed quietly as they turned and retraced their steps up the street.

"It 'ud be queer if I hadn't, by this time," he answered. "Oh yes, I've thought things out pretty well, and I should say our people at the Yard have come to the same conclusion that I have—I'm not conceited enough, Mr. Allerdyke, to fancy that I'm the only person who's arrived at a reasonable theory, not I?"

"Well—what is your theory?" asked Allerdyke.

"This," replied the detective. "The whole thing, the theft of the Princess Nastirsevitch's jewels from your cousin, of Miss de Longarde's or Lennard's jewels, was the work of a peculiarly clever gang—though it may be of an individual—who made use of both Lydenberg and the

French maid as instruments, and subsequently murdered those two in order to silence them forever. I say it may be the work of an individual—it's quite possible that the man who killed the Frenchwoman is also the man who shot Lydenberg—but it may be the work of one, two, or three separate persons, acting in collusion. I believe that Lydenberg was the actual thief of the Princess's jewels from your cousin; that the Frenchwoman actually stole her mistress's jewels. But as to how it was worked—as to who invented and carried out the whole thing—ah!"

"And to that—to the real secret of the whole matter—we haven't the ghost of a clue!" muttered Allerdyke. "That's about it, eh?"

Chettle laughed—a sly, suggestive laugh. He gave his companion one of his half-apologetic looks.

"I'm not so sure, Mr. Allerdyke," he said. "We may have—and that's why I wanted to see you by yourself. Come round to the police-station."

In a quiet room in the usual drab and dismal atmosphere which Allerdyke was beginning to associate with police affairs, Chettle produced the personal property of the dead man, all removed, he said, from the Station Hotel, for safe keeping.

"There's little to go on, Mr. Allerdyke," he said, pointing to one article after another. "You'll remember that the man represented himself as being a Norwegian doctor, who had come to Hull on private business. He may have been that—we're making inquiries about him in Christiania, where he hailed from. According to those who're in a position to speak, his clothing, linen, boots, and so on are all of the sort you'd get in that country. But he'd no papers on him to show his business, no private letters, no documents connecting him with Hull in any way: he hadn't even a visiting-card. He'd a return ticket—from Hull to Christiania—and he'd plenty of money, English and foreign. When I got down here, I helped the local police to go through everything—we even searched the linings of his clothing and ripped his one handbag to pieces. But we've found no more than I've said. However—I've found something. Nobody knows that I've found it. I haven't told the people here—I haven't even reported it to headquarters in London. I wanted you to see it before I spoke of it to a soul. Look here!"

Chettle opened a square cardboard box in which certain personal effects belonging to Lydenberg had been placed—one or two rings, a pocket-knife, his purse and its contents, a cigar-case, his watch and chain. He took up the watch, detached it from the chain, and held it towards Allerdyke, who was regarding these proceedings with intense curiosity.

"You see this watch, Mr. Allerdyke," he said. "It's a watch of foreign make—Swiss—and it's an old one, a good many years old, I should say. Consequently, it's a bit what we might call massive. Now, I was looking at it yesterday—late last night, in fact—and an idea suddenly struck me. In consequence of that idea, I opened the back of the watch, and discovered—that!"

He snapped open the case of the watch as he spoke and showed Allerdyke, neatly cut out to a circle, neatly fitted into the case, a photograph—the photograph of James Allerdyke! And Allerdyke started as if he had been shot, and let out a sharp exclamation.

"My God!" he cried. "James! James, by all that's holy—and in there!"

"You recognize it, of course?" said Chettle, with a grim smile. "No doubt of it, eh?"

"Doubt! Recognize!" exclaimed Allerdyke. "Lord, man—why, I took it myself, not two months ago!"

18. Definite Suspicion

Chettle laughed—a low, suggestive, satisfied chuckle. He laid the watch, its case still open, on the table at which they were standing, and tapped the photograph with the point of his finger.

"That may be the first step to the scaffold—for somebody," he said, with a meaning glance. "Ah—it's extraordinary what little, innocent-looking things help to put a bit of rope round a man's neck! So you took this, Mr. Allerdyke?—took it yourself, you say?"

"Took it myself, some eight or nine weeks ago," answered Allerdyke. "I took it in my garden one Sunday afternoon when my cousin James happened to be there. I do a bit in that way—amusement, you know. I just chanced to have a camera in my hand, and I saw James in a very favourable light and position, and I snapped him. And it was such a good 'un when developed that I printed off a few copies."

The detective's face became anxious.

"How many, now?" he asked. "How many, Mr. Allerdyke? I hope you can remember?—it's a point of the utmost seriousness."

"Naught easier," answered Allerdyke readily. "I've a good memory for little things as well as big 'uns. I printed off four copies. One of 'em I pasted into an album in which I keep particularly good photographs of my own taking; the other three I gave to him—he put 'em in his pocket-book."

"All unmounted—like this?" asked Chettle.

"All unmounted—like that," affirmed Allerdyke. "And now, then, since it seems to be a matter of importance, I can tell you what James did with at any rate two of 'em. He gave one to our cousin Grace—Mrs. Henry Mallins—a Bradford lady. He gave another to a friend of my own, another amateur photographer, Wilson Firth—gave him it in my presence at the Midland Hotel one day, when we were all three having a cigar together in the smoking-room there. Wilson Firth's a bit of a rival of mine in the amateur photographic line—we each try to beat the other, you understand. Now, then, James pulled one of these snapshots out and handed it over to Wilson with a laugh. 'There,' he says, 'that's our Marshall's latest performance—you'll have a job to do aught better than that, Wilson, my lad,' he says. So that accounts for two. And—this is the third!"

"And the question, Mr. Allerdyke, the big question—a most important question!—is, how did it come into this man Lydenberg's possession?" said the detective anxiously. "If we can find that out—"

"I've been thinking," interrupted Allerdyke. "There's this about it, you know: James and this Lydenberg came over together from Christiania to Hull in the *Perisco*. They talked to one another—that's certain. James may have given it to Lydenberg. But the thing is—is that likely?"

"No!" replied Chettle, with emphatic assurance. "No, sir! And I'll tell you why. If your cousin had given this photo to Lydenberg, as he might, of course, have given it to a mere passing acquaintance, because that acquaintance took a fancy to it, or something of that sort, Lydenberg would in all reasonable probability have just slipped in into his pocket-book, or put it loose amongst his letters and papers. But, as we see, however Lydenberg became possessed of this photo, he took unusual pains and precautions about it. You see, he cut it down, most carefully and neatly, to fit into the cover of his watch—he took the trouble to carry it where no one else would see it, but where he could see it himself at a second's notice—he'd nothing to do but to snap open that cover. No, sir, your cousin didn't give that photo to Lydenberg. That photo was sent to Lydenberg, Mr. Allerdyke—sent! And it was sent for one purpose only. What? That he should be able to identify Mr. James Allerdyke as soon as he set eyes on him!"

Allerdyke nodded his head—in complete understanding and affirmation. He was thinking the same thing—thinking, too, that here was at least a clue, a real tangible clue.

"Aye!" he said. "I agree with you. Then, of course, the one and only thing to do is—"

"To find out who the person was that your cousin gave this particular print to!" said Chettle eagerly. "Of course, it's a big field. So far as I understand things, he'd been knocking round a good bit between the time of your taking this photo and his death. He'd been in London, hadn't he? And in Russia—in two or three places. How can we find out when and how he parted with this? For give it to somebody he did, and that somebody was a person who knew of the jewel transaction, and employed Lydenberg in it, and sent the photo to Lydenberg so that he should know your cousin by sight—at once. Mr. Allerdyke, the secret of these murders and thefts is—there!"

Chettle replaced the watch in the cardboard box from which he had taken it, produced a bit of sealing-wax from his pocket, sealed up the box, and put it and the other things belonging to Lydenberg back in the small trunk from which he had withdrawn them to show his companion. And Allerdyke watched him in silence, wondering and speculating about this new development.

"What do you want me to do?" he asked suddenly. "You've got some scheme, of course, or you wouldn't have got me down here alone."

"Just so," agreed Chettle. "I have a scheme—and that's why I did get you down here alone. Mr. Allerdyke, you're a sharp, shrewd man—all you Yorkshiremen are!—at least, all that I've ever come across. You're good hands at ferreting things out. Now, Mr. Allerdyke, let's be plain—there's no two ways about it, no doubt whatever of it, the only people in England that we're aware of who knew about this Nastirsevitch jewel transaction are—Fullaway and whoever he has in his employ! We know of nobody else—unless, indeed, it's the Chicago millionaire, Delkin, and he's not very likely to have wanted to go in for a job of this sort. No, sir—Fullaway is the suspected person, in my opinion!—though I'm going to take precious good care to keep that opinion to myself yet awhile, I can tell you. Fullaway, Mr. Allerdyke, Fullaway!"

"Well?" demanded Allerdyke. "And so—"

"And so I want you to use your utmost ingenuity to find out if your cousin James gave that photo to Fullaway," continued Chettle. "We know very well that he was in touch with Fullaway before he went off to Russia—I have it in my notes that when Fullaway came to see you here in Hull, at the Station Hotel, the day of your cousin's death, he told you that he and Mr. James Allerdyke had been doing business for a couple of years, and that they'd last met in London about the end of March, just before your cousin set off on his journey to Russia. Is that correct?"

"Quite correct—to the letter," answered Allerdyke.

"Very well," said Chettle. "Now, according to you, that 'ud be not so very long after you took that snapshot of your cousin? So, he'd probably have the third print of it—the one we've just been looking at—on him when he was in London at that time?"

"Very likely," assented Allerdyke.

"Then," said Chettle with great eagerness, "try, Mr. Allerdyke, try your best and cleverest to find out if he gave it to Fullaway. You can think—you with a sharp brain!—of some cunning fashion of finding that out. What?"

"I don't know," replied Allerdyke, slowly and doubtfully. He possessed quite as much ingenuity as

Chettle credited him with, but his own resourcefulness in that direction only inclined him to credit other men with the possession of just the same faculty. "I don't know about that. If James did give that print to Fullaway, and if Fullaway made use of it as you think, Fullaway'll be far too cute ever to let on that it was given to him. See!"

"I see that—been seeing it all through," answered Chettle. "All the same, there's ways and means. Think of something—you know Fullaway a bit by this time. Try it!"

"Oh, I'll try it, you bet!" exclaimed Allerdyke. "I'll try it for all it's worth, and as cleverly as I can. In fact, I've already thought of a plan, and if you don't want me any more just now, I'll go to the post-office and send off a telegram that's something to do with it."

"Nothing more now, sir," answered Chettle. "But look here—you're not going back to town to-night?"

"Why, that's just what I meant to do," replied Allerdyke. "There's naught to stop here for, is there?"

"I'm expecting a message from the Christiania police some time this afternoon or evening," said Chettle. "I cabled to them yesterday making full inquiries about Lydenberg—he represented himself here, to Dr. Orwin and the police-surgeons especially, as being a medical man in practice in Christiania, who had come across to Hull on some entirely private family business. Now, we've made the most exhaustive inquiries here in Hull—there isn't a soul in the town knows anything whatever of Lydenberg! I'm as certain as I am that I see you that he'd no business here at all—except to kill and rob your cousin. And so, of course, we want to know if he really was what he said he was, over there. I pressed upon the Christiania police to let me know all they could within thirty-six hours. So if you'll stop the night here, I'll likely be able to show you their reply to me."

"Right!" answered Allerdyke. "I'll put up at the Station Hotel. You come and have your dinner with me there at seven o'clock."

"Much obliged, Mr. Allerdyke," replied Chettle. "I'll come."

Then Allerdyke went off to the General Post Office and sent a telegram to his housekeeper in Bradford—

"Send off at once by registered parcel post to me at Waldorf Hotel, London, the morocco-bound photograph album lying on right-hand corner of my writing-desk in the library.—MARSHALL ALLERDYKE."

He went out of the post-office laughing cynically. Bit by bit things were coming out, he said to himself as he strolled away towards the hotel; link after link the chain was being forged. But around whom, in the end, was it going to be fastened? It was the first time in his life that he had ever been brought face to face with crime, and the seeking out of the criminal was beginning to fascinate him.

"Egad, it's a queer business!" he muttered. "A thread here, a thread there!—Heaven knows what it'll all come to. But this Chettle's a good 'un—he's like to do things."

Chettle joined him in the smoking-room of the hotel at a quarter to seven, and immediately produced a telegram.

"Came half an hour ago," he said as they sat down in a corner. "Nobody but myself seen it up to now. And—it's just what I expected. Read it."

Allerdyke slowly read the message through, pondering over it—

"We have made fullest inquiries concerning Lydenberg. He was certainly not in practice here either under that or any other name. Nothing is known of him as a resident in this city. We have definitely ascertained that he came to Christiania from Copenhagen, by land, via Lund and Copenhagen, arriving Christiania May 7th, and that he left here by steamship *Perisco* for Hull, May 10th."

"You notice the dates?" observed Chettle. "May 7th and 10th. Now, it was on May 8th that your cousin wired to Fullaway from Christiania, Mr. Allerdyke—there's no doubt about it! This man, Lydenberg, whoever he is or was, was sent to waylay your cousin at Christiania—sent from London. I've worked it out—he went overland— Belgium, Holland, Germany, Denmark, Sweden, Norway. Sounds a lot—but it's a quick journey. Sir—he was sent! And the sooner we find out about that photograph the better."

"I'm at work," answered Allerdyke. "Leave it to me."

He found his morocco-bound photograph album awaiting him when he arrived at the Waldorf Hotel next day, and during the afternoon he took it in his hand and strolled quietly and casually into Franklin Fullaway's rooms. Everything there looked as he had always seen it—Mrs. Marlow, charming as ever, was tapping steadily at her typewriter: Fullaway, himself a large cigar in his mouth, was reading the American newspapers, just arrived, in his own sanctum. He greeted Allerdyke with enthusiasm.

"Been away since yesterday, eh?" he said, after warm greetings. "Home?"

"Aye, I've been down to Yorkshire," responded Allerdyke offhandedly. "One or two things I wanted to see to, and some things I wanted to get. This is one of 'em."

"Family Bible?" inquired Fullaway, eyeing the solemnly bound album.

"No. Photos," answered Allerdyke. He was going to test things at once, and he opened the book at the fateful page. "I'm a bit of an amateur photographer," he went on, with a laugh. "Here's what's probably the last photo ever taken of James. What d'ye think of it?"

Fullaway glanced at the photograph, all unconscious that his caller was watching him as he had never been watched in his life. He waved his cigar at the open page.

"Oh!" he said airily. "A remarkably good likeness—wonderful! I said so when I saw it before—excellent likeness, Allerdyke, excellent! Couldn't be beaten by a professional. Excellent!"

Marshall Allerdyke felt his heart beating like a sledgehammer as he put his next question, and for the life of him he could not tell how he managed to keep his voice under control.

"Ah!" he said. "You've seen it before, then? James show it to you?"

Fullaway nodded towards the door of the outer room, from which came the faint click of the secretary's machine.

"He gave one to Mrs. Marlow the very last time he was here." he answered. "They were talking about amateur photography, and he pulled a print of that out of his pocket and made her a present of it; said it couldn't be beaten. You're a clever hand, Allerdyke—most lifelike portrait I ever saw. Well—any news?"

19. THE LATE CALL

It was with a mighty effort of will that Allerdyke controlled himself sufficiently to be able to answer Fullaway's question with calmness. This was for him a critical moment. He knew now to whom James Allerdyke had given the photograph which Chettle had found concealed in Lydenberg's watch; knew that the recipient was sitting close by him, separated only from him by a wall and a door; knew that between her and Lydenberg, or those who had been in touch with Lydenberg, there must be some strange, secret, and sinister connection. From Mrs. Marlow to Lydenberg that photograph had somehow passed, and, as Chettle had well said, the entire problem of the murders and thefts was mixed up in its transference. All that was certain—what seemed certain, too, was that Fullaway knew nothing of these things, and was as innocent as he himself. And for the fraction of a second he was half-minded to tell all he knew to Fullaway there and then—and it was only by a still stronger effort of will that he restrained his tongue, determined to keep a stricter silence than ever, and replied to the American in an offhand, casual tone.

"News?" he said, with a half-laugh. "Nay, not that I know of. They take their time, those detective chaps. You heard aught?"

"Nothing particular," answered Fullaway. "Except that the Princess was in here this morning, and that Miss Lennard came at the same time. But neither of them had anything of importance to tell. The Princess has been ransacking her memory all about her affairs with your cousin; she's more certain than ever now that nobody in

Russia but he and she knew anything about the jewel deal. They were always in strict privacy when they discussed the matter; no one was present when she gave him the jewels; she never mentioned the affair to a soul, and she's confident from what she knew of him, that he wouldn't. So she's more convinced than ever that the news got out from this side."

"And Miss Lennard—what did she want?" asked Allerdyke.

"Oh! she's found the various references—two or three of 'em—that she had with the French maid," replied Fullaway. "I looked at them—there's nothing in them but what you'd expect to find. Two of the writers are well-known society women, the third was a French marquise. I don't think anything's to be got out of them, but, anyway, I sent her off to Scotland Yard with them—it's their work that. Fine photos there, Allerdyke," he continued, turning over the leaves of the album. "Some of your places in Bradford, eh."

Allerdyke, who was particularly anxious that he should not seem to have had an ulterior object in bringing the album up to Fullaway's office hailed this question with relief. He began to point out and explain the various pictures—photographs of his mills, warehouses, town office, his own private house, grounds, surroundings, chatting unconcernedly about each. And while the two men were thus engaged in came Mrs. Marlow, bringing letters which needed Fullaway's signature.

"Mrs. Marlow knows more about amateur photography than I do," remarked Fullaway, with a glance at his secretary. "Here, Mrs. Marlow, these are same of Mr. Allerdyke's productions—you remember that his cousin, Mr. James Allerdyke, gave you a photo which this Mr. Allerdyke had taken?"

Allerdyke, keenly watching the secretary's pretty face as she laid her papers on Fullaway's desk, saw no sign of embarrassment or confusion; Fullaway might have made the most innocent and ordinary remark in the world, and yet, according to Allerdyke's theory and positive knowledge, it must be fraught with serious meaning to this woman.

"Oh yes!" she flashed, without as much as the flicker of an eyelash. "I remember—a particularly good photo. So like him!"

Allerdyke's ingenuity immediately invented a remark; he was at that stage when, he wanted to know as much as possible.

"I wonder which print it was that he gave you?" he said. "One of them—I only did a few—had a spot in it that'll spread. If that's the one you've got, I'll give you another in its place, Mrs. Marlow. Have you got it here?"

But Mrs. Marlow shook her head and presented the same unabashed front.

"No," she answered readily enough. "I took it home, Mr. Allerdyke. But there's no spot on my print—I should have noticed it at once. May I look at your album when Mr. Fullaway's finished with it?"

Allerdyke left the album with them and went away. He was utterly astonished by Mrs. Marlow's coolness. If, as he already believed, she was mixed up in the murders and robberies, she must know that the photograph which James Allerdyke had given her was a most important factor, and yet she spoke of it as calmly and unconcernedly as if it had been a mere scrap of paper! Of course she hadn't got it at the office—nor at her home either—it was there at Hull, fitted into the cover of Lydenberg's old watch.

"A cool hand!" soliloquized Allerdyke as he went downstairs. "Cool, clever, calm, never off her guard. A damned dangerous woman!—that's the long and short of it. And—what next?"

Experience and observation of life had taught Marshall Allerdyke that good counsel is one of life's most valuable assets. He could think for himself and decide for himself at any moment, but he knew the worth and value of putting two heads together, especially at a juncture like this. And so, the afternoon being still young, he went off to his warehouse in Gresham Street, closeted himself with Ambler Appleyard, and having pledged him to secrecy, told him all that had happened since the previous morning.

Ambler Appleyard listened in silence. It was only two or three hours since he had listened to another story—the report of the two Gaffneys, and Allerdyke, all unaware of that business, had come upon him while he was still thinking it over. And while Appleyard gave full attention to all that his employer said, he was also thinking of what he himself could tell. By the time that Allerdyke had finished he, too, had decided to speak.

"So there it is, my lad!" exclaimed Allerdyke, throwing out his hands with an eloquent gesture as he made an end of his story. "I hope I've put it clearly to you. It's just as that Chap Chettle said—the whole secret is in that photograph! And isn't it plain?—that photograph must have been transferred somehow by this Mrs. Marlow to this Lydenberg. How? Why? When we can answer those questions—"

He paused at that, and, looking fixedly at his manager, shook his head half-threateningly.

"I'll tell you what it is, Ambler," he went on, after a moment's silence. "I've got a good, strong mind to go straight to the police authorities, tell 'em what I know, insist on 'em fetching Chettle up from Hull at once, and having that woman arrested. Why not?"

"No!" said Appleyard firmly. "Not yet. Too soon, Mr. Allerdyke—wait a bit. And now listen to me—I've something to tell you. I've been busy while you've been away—in this affair. Bit of detective work. I'll tell you all about it—all! You remember that day I went to lunch with you at the City Carlton, and you pointed out this Mrs. Marlow to me, going into Rothschild's? Yes, well—I recognized her."

"You did!" exclaimed Allerdyke. "Nay!"

"I recognized her," repeated Appleyard. "I said naught to you at the time, but I knew her well enough. As a matter of fact, I've known her for two years. She lives at the same boarding-house, the Pompadour Private Hotel, in Bayswater, that I live in. I see her—have been seeing her for two years—every day, morning and night. But I know her as Miss Slade."

"Miss?" ejaculated Allerdyke.

"Miss—Miss Slade," answered Appleyard. He drew his chair nearer to Allerdyke's, and went on in a lower voice. "Now, then, pay attention, and I'll tell you all about it, and what I've done since I got your note yesterday morning."

He told Allerdyke the whole story of his endeavour to find out something about Rayner merely because Rayner seemed to be in Miss Slade's confidence, and because Miss Slade was certainly a woman of mystery. And Allerdyke listened as quietly and attentively as Appleyard had listened to him, nodding his head at all the important points, and in the end he slapped his manager's shoulder with an approving hand.

"Good—good!" he said. "Good, Ambler! That was a bit of right work, and hang me if I don't believe we shall find something out. But what's to be done? You know, if these two are in at it, they may slip. That 'ud never do!"

"I don't think there's any fear of that—yet," answered Appleyard. "The probability is that neither has any suspicion of being watched—the whole thing's so clever that they probably believe themselves safe. Of course, mind you, this man Rayner may be as innocent as you or I. But against her, on the facts of that photograph affair, there's a *prima facie* case. Only—don't let's spoil things by undue haste or rashness. I've thought things out a good deal, and we can do a lot, you and me, before going to the police, though I don't think it 'ud do any harm to tell this man Chettle, supposing he were here—because his discovery of that photo is the real thing."

"What can we do, then?" asked Allerdyke.

"Make use of the two Gaffneys," answered Appleyard without hesitation. "They're smart chaps—-real keen 'uns. We want to find out who Rayner is; what his connection, if any, with Miss Slade, alias Mrs. Marlow, is; who she is, and why she goes under two names. That's all what you might call initial proceedings. What I propose is this—when you go back to your hotel, get Gaffney into your private sitting-room. You, of course, know him much better than I do, but from what bit I've seen of him I'm sure he's the sort of man one can trust. Tell him to get hold of that brother of his and bring him here at any hour you like to-morrow, and then—well, we can have a conference, and decide on some means of finding out more about Rayner and keeping an eye on him. For that sort of work I should say that other Gaffney's remarkably well cut out—he's a typical, sharp, knowing Cockney, with all his wits about him, and plenty of assurance."

"It's detective work, you know, Ambler," said Allerdyke. "It needs a bit of more than ordinary cuteness."

"From my observation, I should say both those chaps are just cut for it," answered Appleyard, with a laugh. "What's more, they enjoy it. And when men enjoy what they're doing—"

"Why, they do it well," agreed Allerdyke, finishing the sentence. "Aye, that's true enough. All right—I'll speak to Gaffney, when I go back. And look here—as you're so well known to this woman, Miss Slade or Mrs. Marlow, whichever her name is, you'd better not show up at the Waldorf at any time in my company, eh?"

"Of course," said Appleyard. "You trust me for that! What we've got to do must be done as secretly as possible."

Allerdyke rose to go, but turned before he reached the door.

"There's one thing I'm uneasy about," he said. "If—I say if, of course—if these folks—I mean the lot that's behind this woman, for I can't believe that she's worked it all herself—have got those jewels, won't they want to clear out with them? Isn't delay dangerous?"

"Not such delay as I'm thinking of," answered Appleyard firmly. "She's cute enough, this lady, and if she made herself scarce just now, she'd know very well that it would excite suspicion. Don't let's spoil things by being too previous. We've got a pretty good watch on her, you know. I should know very quickly if she cleared out of the Pompadour; you'd know if she didn't turn up at Fullaway's. Wait a bit, Mr. Allerdyke; it's the best policy. You'll come here to-morrow?"

"Eleven o'clock in the morning," replied Allerdyke. "I'll fix it with Gaffney to-night."

He went back to the Waldorf, summoned Gaffney to his private room, and sent him to arrange matters with his brother. Gaffney accepted the commission with alacrity; his brother, he said, was just then out of a job, having lost a clerkship through the sudden bankruptcy of his employers; such a bit of business as that which Mr. Appleyard had entrusted to him was so much meat and drink to one of his tastes—in more ways than one.

"It's the sort of thing he likes, sir," remarked Gaffney, confidentially. "He's always been a great hand at reading these detective tales, and to set him to watch anybody is like offering chickens to a nigger—he fair revels in it!"

"Well, there's plenty for him to revel in," observed Allerdyke grimly.

Plenty! he said to himself with a cynical laugh when Gaffney had left him—aye, plenty, and to spare. He spent the whole of that evening alone, turning every detail over in his own mind; he was still thinking, and speculating, and putting two and two together when he went to bed at eleven o'clock. And just as he was about to switch off his light a waiter knocked on his door.

"Gentleman downstairs, sir, very anxious to see you at once," he said, when Allerdyke opened it. "His card, sir."

Allerdyke gave one glance at the card—a plain bit of pasteboard on which one word had been hastily pencilled—

CHETTLE.

20. Number Fifty-Three

Chettle!—whom he had left only that morning in Hull, two hundred miles away, both of them agreed that the next step was still unseen, and that immediate action was yet problematical. Something had surely happened to bring Chettle up to town and to him.

"Show Mr. Chettle up here at once," he said to the waiter. "And here—bring a small decanter of whisky and a syphon of soda-water and glasses. Be sharp with 'em."

He pulled on a dressing-gown when the man had gone, and, tying its cord about his waist, went a step or two into the corridor to look out for his visitor. A few minutes elapsed; then the lift came up, and the waiter, killing two birds with one stone, appeared again, escorting the detective and carrying a tray. And Allerdyke, with a sly wink at Chettle, greeted him unconcernedly, ushered him into his room and chatted about nothing until the waiter had gone away. Then he turned on him eagerly.

"What is it?" he demanded. "Something, of course! Aught new?"

For answer Chettle thrust his hand inside his overcoat and brought out a small package, wrapped in cartridge paper, and sealed.

He began to break the seals and unwrap the covering.

"Well, it brought me up here—straight," he said. "I think I shall have to let our people at the yard know everything, Mr. Allerdyke. But I came to you first—-I only got to King's Cross half an hour ago, and I drove on to you at once. We'll see what you think before I decide on anything."

"What is it!" repeated Allerdyke, gazing with interest at the package. "You've found something of fresh importance, eh!"

Chettle took the lid off a small box and produced Lydenberg's watch and postcard on which the appointment in the High Street had been made. He sat down at the table, laying his hand on the watch.

"After you left me this morning," he said, "I started puzzling and puzzling over what had been discovered, what had been done, whether there was more that I could do. I kept thinking things over all the morning, and half the afternoon. Then it suddenly struck me—there was one thing—that I'd never done and that ought to have been done—I don't know why I'd never thought of it till then—but I'd never had this photograph out of the watch. And so I went back to the police-station and got the watch and opened it, and—look there, Mr. Allerdyke!"

He had snapped open the case of the watch as he talked, and he now detached the photograph and turning it over, laid the reverse side down on the table by the postcard.

"Look at it!" he went on. "Do you see?—there's writing on it! You see what it says? 'This is J.A. Burn this when made use of.' You see? And—it's the same handwriting as that on this card, making the appointment! Here, look at both for yourself—hold 'em closer to the light. Mr. Allerdyke—that was all written by the same hand, or I'm—no good!"

Allerdyke went close to the electric globe above his dressing-table, the photograph in one hand, the postcard in the other. He looked searchingly at both, brought them back, and laid them down again.

"No doubt of it, Chettle," he said. "No doubt of it! It doesn't need any expert to be certain sure of that. The same, identical fist, without a shadow of doubt. Well— what d'ye make of it? Here—have a drink."

He mixed a couple of drinks, pushed one glass to the detective, and took the other himself.

"Egad!" he muttered, after drinking. "Things are getting—hottish, anyway. As I say, what do you make of this? Of course, you've come to some conclusion?"

"Yes," answered Chettle, taking up his glass and silently bowing his acknowledgments. "I have! The only one I could come to. The man who sent this photograph to Lydenberg, to help him to identify your cousin at sight, is the man who afterwards lured Lydenberg into that part of Hull High Street, and shot him dead. In plain words, the master shot his man—when he'd done with him. Just as he poisoned the Frenchwoman—when he'd done with her. Mr. Allerdyke, I'm more than ever convinced that these two murders—Lydenberg's and the French maid's—were the work of one hand."

"Likely!" assented Allerdyke. "It's getting to look like it. But—whose? That's the problem, Chettle. Well, I've done a bit since I got back this afternoon. You've had something to tell me—now I've something to tell you. I've found out who it was that James gave the photograph to!"

Chettle showed his gratification by a start of pleased surprise.

"You have—already!" he exclaimed.

"Already!" replied Allerdyke. "Found it out within an hour of getting back in here. He gave it"—here, though the door was closed and bolted, and there was no fear of eavesdroppers, he sank his voice to a whisper—"he gave it to Fullaway's secretary, the woman we discussed, Mrs. Marlow. That's a fact. He gave it to her just before he set off for Russia."

Chettle screwed his lips up to whistle—instead of whistling he suddenly relaxed them to a comprehending smile.

"Aye, just so!" he said. "I was sure it lay somewhere—here. Fullaway himself, now—does he know?"

"James gave it to her in Fullaway's presence," replied Allerdyke. "She's a bit of a photographer, I understand—they were talking about photography, I gathered, one day when James was in Fullaway's office, and James pulled that out and gave it to her as a specimen of my work."

"All that came out in talk this afternoon?" asked Chettle.

"Just so. Ordinary, casual talk," assented Allerdyke.

"No suspicion roused?" suggested Chettle.

"I don't think so. Of course, you never can tell. I should say," continued Allerdyke, "that she's as deep and clever as ever they make 'em! But it was all so casual, and so natural, that I don't think she'd the slightest idea that I was trying to get at anything. However, I found this much out—she couldn't produce the photograph. Said she'd taken it home. Well—there we are! That's part one of my bit of news, Chettle. Now for part two. This woman's leading a double life. She's Mrs. Marlow as Fullaway's secretary and here at his rooms and on his business; where she lives she's Miss Slade. Eh?"

Chettle pricked his ears.

"When did you find that out?" he asked. "Since you left me this morning?"

"Found it out this afternoon," replied Allerdyke, with something of triumph. He had been strolling about the bedroom up to that moment, but now he drew a chair to the table at which Chettle sat and dropped into it close beside his visitor.

"I'll tell you all about it," he went on. "You said at Hull yesterday that you'd always found Yorkshiremen sharp and shrewd—well, this is a bit more Yorkshire work—work of my manager here in town—Mr. Appleyard. Listen!"

He gave the detective a clear and succinct account of all that Appleyard and his satellites had done, and Chettle listened with deep attention, nodding his head at the various points.

"Yes," he said, when Allerdyke had made an end, "yes, that's all right, so far. Good, useful work. The thing is— can you fully trust these two young men—your chauffeur and his brother?"

"I could and would trust my chauffeur with my last shilling," answered Allerdyke. "And as for his brother, I'll take my man's word for him. Besides, they both know—or Mr. Gaffney knows—that I'm a pretty generous paymaster. If a man does aught for me, and does it well, he profits to a nice penny!"

"A good argument," agreed Chettle. "I don't know that you could beat it, Mr. Allerdyke. Well, well—we're getting to something and to somewhere! Now, as you've told me all this, I'll just keep things quiet until I've met you and your manager to-morrow, with these two Gaffneys—we'll have a conference. I won't go near the Yard until after that. Eleven o'clock to-morrow, then, at your warehouse in Gresham Street."

He presently replaced the watch and the postcard in an inner pocket, and took his leave, and Allerdyke, letting him out, walked along the corridor with him as far as the lift. And as Allerdyke turned back to his own room, the third event of that day happened, and seemed to him to be the most surprising and important one of all.

What made Allerdyke pause as he retraced his steps along the corridor, pause to look over the balustrade to the floor immediately below his own, he never knew nor could explain. But, just as he was about to re-enter his room, he did so pause, leaning over the railings and looking down for a moment. In that moment he saw Mrs. Marlow.

A considerable portion of the floor immediately beneath him was fully exposed to the view of any one leaning over the balustrade as Allerdyke did. This was a quiet part of the hotel, a sort of wing cut away from the main building; the floor at which he was looking was given up to private suites of rooms, one of them, a larger one than the others, being Fullaway's, which filled one side of the corridor; the others were suites of two, in some cases of three rooms. As he looked over and down, Allerdyke suddenly saw a door open in one of these smaller suites—open silently and stealthily. Then he saw Mrs. Marlow look out, and she glanced right and left about her. The next instant, she emerged from the room with the same stealthiness, closed and locked the door with a key which she immediately pocketed, slipped along the corridor, and disappeared into Franklin Fullaway's suite. It was all over in less than a minute, and Allerdyke turned into his own door, smiling cynically to himself.

"She looked right and left, but she forgot to look up!" he muttered. "Ah! those small details. And what does that mean? Anyway, I know which door she came out of!"

He glanced at his watch—precisely half-past eleven. He made a note of the time in his pocket-book and went to bed. And next morning, rising early, as was his custom, he descended to the ground floor by means of the stairs instead of the lift, and as he passed the door from which he had seen Mrs. Marlow emerge he mentally registered the number. Fifty-three. Number fifty-three.

Allerdyke, who could not exist without fresh air and exercise, went for a stroll before breakfast when he was in London—he usually chose the Embankment, as being the nearest convenient open space, and thither he now repaired, thinking things over. There were many new features of this affair to think about, but the one of the previous night now occupied his thoughts to the exclusion of the others. What was this woman doing, coming—with evident secrecy—out of one set of rooms, and entering another at that late hour? He wanted to know—he must find out—and he would find out with ease,—and indirectly, from Fullaway.

Fullaway always took his breakfast at a certain table in a certain corner of the coffee-room at the hotel; there Allerdyke had sometimes joined him. He found the American there, steadily eating, when he returned from his walk, and he dropped into a chair at his side with a casual remark about the fine morning.

"Didn't set eyes on you last night at all," he went on, as he picked up his napkin. "Off somewhere, eh?"

"Spent the evening out," answered Fullaway. "Not often I do, but I did—for once in a way. Van Koon and I (you don't know Van Koon, do you?—he's a fellow countryman of mine, stopping here for the summer, and a very clever man) we dined at the Carlton, and then went to the Haymarket Theatre. I was going to ask you to join us, Allerdyke, but you were out and hadn't come in by the time we had to go."

"Thank you—no, I didn't get in until seven o'clock or so," answered Allerdyke. "So I'd a quiet evening."

"No news, I suppose?" asked Fullaway, going vigorously forward with his breakfast. "Heard nothing from the police authorities?"

"Nothing," replied Allerdyke. "I suppose they're doing things in their own way, as usual."

"Just so," assented Fullaway. "Well, it's an odd thing to me that nobody comes forward to make some sort of a shot at that reward! Most extraordinary that the man of the Eastbourne Terrace affair should have been able to get clean away without anybody in London having seen him—or at any rate that the people who must have seen him are unable to connect him with the murder of that woman. Extraordinary!"

"It's all extraordinary," said Allerdyke. He took up a newspaper which Fullaway had thrown down and began to talk of some subject that caught his eye, until Fullaway rose, pleaded business, and went off to his rooms upstairs. When he had gone Allerdyke reconsidered matters. So Fullaway had been out the night before, had he—dining out, and at a theatre? Then, of course, it would be quite midnight before he got in. Therefore, presumably, he did not know that his secretary was about his rooms—and entering and leaving another suite close by. No—Fullaway knew nothing—that seemed certain.

The remembrance of what he had seen sent Allerdyke, as soon as he had breakfasted, to the hall of the hotel, and to the register of guests. There was no one at the register at that moment, and he turned the pages at his leisure until he came to what he wanted. And there it was—in plain black and white—

NUMBER 53. MR. JOHN VAN KOON. NEW YORK CITY, U.S.A.

21. THE YOUNG MAN WHO LED PUGS

Allerdyke, with a gesture peculiar to him, thrust his hands in the pockets of his trousers, strolled away from the desk on which the register lay open, and going over to the hall door stood there a while, staring out on the tide of life that rolled by, and listening to the subdued rattle of the traffic in its ceaseless traverse of the Strand. And as he stood in this apparently idle and purposeless lounging attitude, he thought—thought of a certain birthday of his, a good thirty years before, whereon a kind, elderly aunt had made him a present of a box of puzzles. There were all sorts of puzzles in that box—things that you had to put together, things that had to be arranged, things that had to be adjusted. But there was one in particular which had taken his youthful fancy, and had at the same time tried his youthful temper—a shallow tray wherein were a vast quantity of all sorts and sizes of bits of wood, gaily coloured. There were quite a hundred of those bits, and you had to fit them one into the other. When, after much trying of temper, much exercise of patience, you had accomplished the task, there was a beautiful bit of mosaic work, a picture, a harmonious whole, lovely to look upon, something worthy of the admiring approbation of uncles and aunts, grandmothers and grandfathers. But—the doing of it!

"Naught, however, to this confounded thing!" mused Allerdyke, gazing at and not seeing the folk on the broad sidewalk. "When all the bits of this puzzle have been fitted into place I daresay one'll be able to look down on it as a whole and say it looks simple enough when finished, but, egad, they're of so many sorts and shapes and queer angles that they're more than a bit difficult to fit at present. Now who the deuce is this Van Koon, and what was that Mrs. Marlow, alias Miss Slade, doing in his rooms last night when he was out?"

He was exercising his brains over a possible solution of this problem when Fullaway suddenly appeared in the hall behind him, accompanied by a man whom Allerdyke at once took to be the very individual about whom he was speculating. He was a man of apparently forty years of age, of average height and build, of a full countenance, sallow in complexion, clean-shaven, wearing gold-rimmed spectacles over a pair of sapphire blue eyes—a shrewd, able-looking man, clad in the loose fitting, square-cut garments just then affected by his fellow-countrymen, and having a low-crowned, soft straw hat pulled down over his forehead. His hands were thrust into the pockets of his jacket; a long, thin, black cigar stuck out of a corner of his humorous-looking lips; he cocked an intelligent eye at Allerdyke as he and Fullaway advanced to the door.

"Hullo, Allerdyke!" said Fullaway in his usual vivacious fashion. "Viewing the prospect o'er, eh? Allow me to introduce Mr. Van Koon, whom I don't think you've met, though he's under the same roof. Van Koon, this is the Mr. Allerdyke I've mentioned to you."

The two men shook hands and stared at each other. Whoever and whatever this man may be, thought Allerdyke, he gives you a straight look and a good grip—two characteristics which in his opinion went far to establish any unknown individual's honesty.

"No," remarked Van Koon. "I haven't had the pleasure of meeting Mr. Allerdyke before. But I'm out a great deal—I don't spend much time indoors this fine weather. You gentlemen know your London well—I don't, and I'm putting in all the time I can to cultivate her acquaintance."

"Been in town long?" asked Allerdyke, wanting to say something and impelled to this apparently trite question by the New Yorker's own observations.

"Since the first week in April," answered Van Koon, "And as this is my first visit to England, I'm endeavouring to do everything well. Fullaway tells me, Mr. Allerdyke, that you come from Bradford, the big manufacturing city up north. Well, now, Bradford is one of the places on my list—hullo!" he exclaimed, breaking off short. "I guess here's a man who's wanting you, Fullaway, in a considerable bit of a hurry."

Fullaway and Allerdyke looked out on to the pavement and saw Blindway, who had just jumped out of a taxi-cab, and was advancing upon them. He came up and addressed them jointly—would they go back with him at once to New Scotland Yard?—the chief wanted to see them for a few minutes.

"Come on, Allerdyke," said Fullaway. "We'd better go at once. Van Koon," he continued, turning to his compatriot, "do me a favour—just look in at my rooms upstairs, and tell Mrs. Marlow, if she's come—she hadn't arrived when I was up there ten minutes ago—that I'm called out for an hour or so—ask her to attend to anything that turns up until I come back—shan't be long."

Van Koon nodded and walked back into the hotel, while Allerdyke and Fullaway joined the detective in the cab and set out westward.

"What is it?" asked Fullaway. "Something new?"

"Can't say, exactly," replied Blindway. "The chief's got some woman there who thinks she can tell something about the French maid, so he sent me for you, and he's sent another man for Miss Lennard. It may be something good; it mayn't. Otherwise," he concluded with a shake of the head that was almost dismal, "otherwise, I don't know of anything new. Never knew of a case in my life, gentlemen, in which less turned up than's turning up in this affair! And fifty thousand pounds going a-begging!"

"I suppose this woman's after it," remarked Fullaway. "You didn't hear of anything she had to tell?"

"Nothing," answered Blindway. "You'll hear it in a minute or two."

He took them straight up into the same room, and the same official whom they had previously seen, and who now sat at his desk with Celia Lennard on one side of him, and a middle-aged woman, evidently of the poorer classes, on the other. Allerdyke and Fullaway, after a brief interchange of salutations with the official and the prima donna, looked at the stranger—a quiet, respectably-dressed woman who united a natural shyness with an evident determination to go through with the business that had brought her there. She was just the sort of woman who can be seen by the hundred— laundress, seamstress, charwoman, caretaker, got up in her Sunday best. Odd, indeed, it would be, thought Allerdyke, if this quiet, humble-looking creature should give information which would place fifty thousand pounds at her command!

"This is Mrs. Perrigo," said the chief pleasantly, as he motioned the two men to chairs near Celia's and beckoned Blindway to his side. "Mrs. Perrigo, of—where is it, ma'am?"

"I live in Alpha Place, off Park Street, sir," announced Mrs. Perrigo, in a small, quiet voice. "Number 14, sir. I'm a clear-starcher by trade, sir."

"Put that down, Blindway," said the chief, "and take a note of what Mrs. Perrigo tells us. Now, Mrs. Perrigo, you think you've seen the dead woman, Lisette Beaurepaire, at some time or another, in company with a young man? Where and when was this?"

"Well, three times, sir. Three times that I'm certain of—there was another time that I wasn't certain about; at least, that I'm not certain about now. If I could just tell you about it in my way, sir—"

"Certainly—certainly, Mrs. Perrigo! Exactly what I wish. Tell us all about it in your own way. Take your own time."

"Well, sir, it 'ud be, as near as I can fix it, about the middle of March—two months ago, sir," began Mrs. Perrigo. "You see, I had the misfortune to burn my right hand very badly, sir, and having to put my work aside, and it being nice weather, and warm for the time of year, I used to go and sit in Kensington Gardens a good deal, which, of course, was when I see this young lady whose picture's been in the paper of late, and—"

"A moment, Mrs. Perrigo," interrupted the official. "Miss Lennard, it will simplify matters considerably if I ask you a question. Were you and your late maid in town about the time Mrs. Perrigo speaks of—the middle of March?"

"Yes," replied Celia promptly. "We were here from March 3rd, when we came back from the Continent, to March 29th, when we left for Russia."

"Continue, Mrs. Perrigo, if you please," said the official. "Take your time—tell things your own way."

"Yes, sir," said Mrs. Perrigo dutifully. "If you please, sir. Well, when I see those pictures in the papers—several papers, sir—of the young lady with the foreign name I says to myself, and to my neighbour, Mrs. Watson, which is all I ever talk much to, 'That,' I says, 'is the young woman I see in Kensington Gardens a time or two and remarks of for her elegant figure and smart air in general—I could have picked her out from a thousand,' I says. Which there was, and is a particular spot, sir, in Kensington Gardens where I used to sit, and you pays a penny for a chair, which I did, and there's other chairs about, near a fallen tree, which is still there, for I went to make sure last night, and there, on three afternoons while I was there, this young lady came at about, say, four o'clock each time, and was met by this here young man what I don't remember as clear as I remember her, me not taking so much notice of him. And—"

"Another moment, Mrs. Perrigo." The chief turned again to Celia. "Did your maid ever go out in the afternoons about that time?" he asked.

"Probably every afternoon," replied Celia. "I myself was away from London from the 11th to the 18th of March, staying with friends in the country. I didn't take her with me—so, of course, she'd nothing to do but follow her own inclinations."

The chief turned to Mrs. Perrigo again.

"Yes?" he said. "You saw the young woman whose photograph you have seen in the papers meet a young man in Kensington Gardens on three separate occasions. Yes?"

"Three separate occasions, close by—on penny chairs, sir, where they sat and talked foreign, which I didn't understand—and on another occasion, when I see 'em walking by the Round Pond, me being at some distance, but recognizing her by her elegant figure. I took particular notice of the young woman's face, sir, me being a noticing person, and I'll take my dying oath, if need be, that this here picture is hers!"

Mrs. Perrigo here produced a much worn and crumpled illustrated newspaper and laid her hand solemnly upon it. That done, she shook her head.

"But I ain't so certain about the young man as met her," she said sorrowfully. "Him I did not notice with such attention, being, as I say, more attracted to her. All the same, he was a young man—and spoke the same foreign language as what she did. Of them facts, sure I am, sir."

"They sat near you, Mrs. Perrigo?"

"As near, sir, as I am now to that lady. And paid their pennies for their chairs in my presence; leastways, the young man paid. Always the same place it was, and always the same time—three days all within a week, and then the day when I see 'em walking at a distance."

"Can't you remember anything about the young man, Mrs. Perrigo?" asked the chief. "Come!—try to think. That is the really important thing. You must have some recollection of him, you know, some idea of what he was like."

Mrs. Perrigo took a corner of her shawl between her fingers and proceeded to fold and pleat it while she thoughtfully fixed her eyes on Blindway's unmoved countenance, as if to find inspiration there. And after a time she nodded her head as though memory had stirred within her.

"Which every time I see him," she said, with an evident quickening of interest, "he had two of them dogs with him what has turned-up noses and twisted tails."

"Pugs?" suggested the chief.

"No doubt that is their name, sir, but unbeknown to me as I never kept such an animal," answered Mrs. Perrigo. "My meaning being clear, no doubt, and there being no mistaking of 'em—their tails and noses being of that order. And had 'em always on a chain—gentlemen's dogs you could see they was, and carefully looked after with blue bows at the back of their necks, same as if they was Christians. And him, I should say, speaking from memory, a dark young man—such is my recollection."

"It comes to this," remarked the chief, looking at the three listeners with a smile. "Mrs. Perrigo says that she is certain that upon three occasions about the middle of March last she witnessed meetings at a particular spot in Kensington Gardens between a young woman answering the description and photographs of Lisette Beaurepaire and a young man of whom she cannot definitely remember anything except that she thinks he was dark, spoke a foreign language, and was in charge of two pug dogs which wore blue ribbons. That's it, isn't it, Mrs. Perrigo?"

"And willing to take my solemn oath of the same whenever convenient, sir," replied Mrs. Perrigo. "And if so be as what I've told you should lead to anything, gentlemen—and lady—I can assure you that me being a poor widow, and—"

Five minutes later, Mrs. Perrigo, with some present reward in her pocket, was walking quietly up Whitehall with a composed countenance, while Allerdyke, already late for his Gresham Street appointment, sped towards the City as fast as a hastily chartered taxi-cab could carry him. And all the way thither, being alone, he repeated certain words over and over again.

"A dark young man who led two pugs—a dark young man who led two pugs! With blue ribbons on their necks—with blue ribbons on their necks, same as Christians!"

22. THICK FOG

It was half-past eleven when Allerdyke reached Gresham Street: by half-past one, so curiously and rapidly did events crowd upon each other, he was in a state of complete mental confusion. He sat down to lunch that day feeling as a man feels who has lost his way in an unknown country in the midst of a blinding mist; as a weaver might feel who is at work on an intricate pattern and suddenly finds all his threads inextricably mixed up and tangled. Instead of things getting better and clearer, that morning's work made them more hopelessly muddled.

Chettle was hanging about the door of the warehouse when Allerdyke drove up. His usually sly look was accentuated that morning, and as soon as Allerdyke stepped from his cab he drew him aside with a meaning gesture.

"A word or two before we go in, Mr. Allerdyke," he said as they walked a few steps along the street. "Look here, sir," he went on in a whisper. "I've been reflecting on things since I saw you last night. Of course, I'm supposed to be in Hull, you know. But I shall have to report myself at the Yard this morning—can't avoid that. And I shall have to tell them why I came up. Now, it's here, Mr. Allerdyke—how much or how little shall I tell 'em? What I mean sir, is this—do you want to keep any of this recently acquired knowledge to yourself? Of course, if you do—well, I needn't tell any more there—at headquarters—than you wish me to tell. I can easy make excuse for coming up. And, of course, in that case—"

"Well!" demanded Allerdyke impatiently. "What then?"

Chettle gave him another look of suggestive meaning, and taking off his square felt hat, wiped his forehead with a big coloured handkerchief.

"Well, of course, Mr. Allerdyke," he said insinuatingly. "Of course, sir, I'm a poor man, and I've a rising family that I want to do my best for. I could do with a substantial amount of that reward, you know, Mr. Allerdyke. We've all a right to do the best we can for ourselves, sir. And if you're wanting to, follow this affair out on your own, sir, independent of the police—eh?"

Allerdyke's sense of duty arose in strong protest against this very palpable suggestion. He shook his head.

"No—no!" he said. "That won't do, Chettle. You must do your duty to your superiors. You'll find that you'll be all right. If the police solve this affair, that reward'll go to the police, and you'll get your proper share. No—no underhand work. You make your report in your ordinary way. No more of that!"

"Aye, but do you understand, Mr. Allerdyke?" said the detective anxiously. "Do you comprehend what it'll mean. You know very well that there's a lot of red tape in our work—they go a great deal by rule and precedent, as you might say. Now, if I go to the Yard—as I shall have to, as soon as you've done with me—and tell the chief that I've found this photo of your cousin in Lydenberg's watch, and that you're certain that your cousin gave that particular photo to Mrs. Marlow, alias Miss Slade, do you know what'll happen?"

"What?" asked Allerdyke.

"They'll arrest her within half an hour," answered Chettle. "Dead certain!"

"Well?" said Allerdyke. "And—what then!"

"Why, it'll probably upset the whole bag of tricks!" exclaimed Chettle. "The thing'll be spoiled before we've properly worked it out. See?"

Allerdyke did see. He had sufficient knowledge of police matters to know that Chettle was right, and that a too hasty step would probably ruin everything. He turned towards the warehouse.

"Just so," he said. "I take your meaning. Now then, come in, and we'll put it before my manager, Mr. Appleyard. I've great faith in his judgment—let's see what he's got to say."

The two Gaffneys were waiting just within the packingroom of the warehouse. Allerdyke bade them wait a little longer, and took the detective straight into Appleyard's office. There, behind the closed door, he told Appleyard of everything that had happened since their last meeting, and of what Chettle had just said. The problem was, in view of all that, of the mysterious proceedings of Mrs. Marlow the night before, and of what Allerdyke had just heard at New Scotland Yard—what was best to be done, severally and collectively, by all of them?

Ambler Appleyard grasped the situation at once and solved the problem in a few direct words. There was no need whatever, he said, for Chettle to do more than his plain duty, no need for him to exceed it. He was bound, being what he was, to make his report about his discovery of the photograph and the writing on it. That he must do. But he was not bound to tell anything that Allerdyke had told him: he was not bound to give information which Allerdyke had collected. Let Chettle go and tell the plain facts about his own knowledge of the photo and leave Allerdyke, for the moment, clean out of the question. Allerdyke himself could go with his news in due course. And, wound up Appleyard, who had a keen knowledge of human nature and saw deep into Chettle's mind, Mr. Allerdyke would doubtless see that Chettle lost nothing by holding his tongue about anything that wasn't exactly ripe for discussion. At present, he repeated, let Chettle do his duty—not exceed it.

"That's it," agreed Allerdyke. "You've hit it, Ambler. You go and tell what you know of your own knowledge," he went on, turning to Chettle. "Leave me clean out for the time being. I'll come in at the right moment. Say naught about me or of what I've told you. And if you're sent back to Hull, just contrive to see me before you go. And, as Mr. Appleyard says, I'll see you're all right, anyhow."

When Chettle had gone, Allerdyke closed the door on him and turned to his manager with a knowing look.

"That chap's right, you know, Ambler," he said. "A false move, a too hasty step'll ruin everything. If that woman's startled—if she gets a suspicion—egad, it's all mixed up about as badly as can be! Now, about these Gaffneys?"

"Wait a while," said Appleyard. "I don't know that we want their services just yet. I've found out a thing or two that may be useful. About this man Rayner now, who's in evident close touch with Miss Slade (by the by, you saw her at the Waldorf at half-past eleven last night, and I saw her come into the Pompadour at half-past twelve, with Rayner), and about whom we accordingly want to know something—I've found out, through ordinary business channels, that he does carry on a business at Clytemnestra House, in Arundel Street, under the name of Gavin Ramsay. And—if we want to know more of him—I've an idea. You go and see him, Mr. Allerdyke—on business."

"I? Business?" exclaimed Allerdyke. "What sort of business?"

"He's an inventor's agent," replied Appleyard. "It's a profession I never heard of before, but he seems to act as a go-between. Folks that have got an invention go to him—he helps 'em about it—helps 'em to perfect it, patent it, get it on the market. You've a good excuse— there's that patent railway chair of your man Gankrodgers, been lying there in that corner for the past year, and you promised Gankrodgers you'd help him about it. Put it in a cab and go to this Rayner, or Ramsay—there's your excuse, and you can say you heard of him in the City, from Wilmingtons—it was they who told me what he was. It's a good notion, Mr. Allerdyke."

"What object?" asked Allerdyke.

"Simply to get a look at him," replied Appleyard. "Look here—you know very well that there's a strong suspicion against Miss Slade. Miss Slade, to my knowledge, is in close touch, with Rayner. Therefore, let's know what we can about Rayner. You're the man to go and see him at his own place. Do it—and we'll consider the question of having him watched by the two Gaffneys when you've seen and talked to him."

Allerdyke considered this somewhat strange proposal in silence for a while. At last he rose with a look of decision.

"Well, I've certainly a good excuse," he said. "Here, have that thing packed up and put in a cab—I'll go."

Half an hour later he found himself shown into a smartly furnished office where Mr. Gavin Ramsay sat at a handsome desk surrounded by shelves and cabinets whereon and wherein were set out the products of the brains of many inventors—models of machines, mechanical toys, labour-saving notions, things plainly useful, things obviously extravagant. The occupant of this museum glanced at Allerdyke and the box which he carried with an amused smile, and Allerdyke said to himself that Appleyard was right in his description—if the man was crippled and deformed he certainly possessed a beautiful face.

"Mr. Marshall Allerdyke," said the hope of inventors, glancing at the card which his visitor had sent in.

"The same, sir," replied Allerdyke, setting down his box. "Mr. Ramsay, I presume? I heard of you, Mr. Ramsay, through Wilmingtons, in the City; heard you can be of great use to inventors. I have here," he continued, opening the box, "a railway chair, invented by one of my workmen, a clever fellow. You see, it 'ud do away with the present system of putting wooden blocks in the chairs now used—this would fasten the sleepers and rails together automatically. It is patented—provisionally protected, anyhow—but my man's never got a railway company to try it, so far. Think you can do anything, Mr. Ramsay?"

The hunchback got up from his desk, took the invention out of its box, and carefully inspected it, asking Allerdyke a few shrewd questions about the thing's possibilities which showed the caller that he knew what he was talking about. Then he sat down again and went into business details in a way which impressed Allerdyke—clearly this man, whoever he was, and whatever mystery might attach to him, was a smart individual. Also he had a frank, direct way of talking which gave his visitor a very good first opinion of him.

"Very well, Mr. Allerdyke," he said, in conclusion. "Leave the thing with me, and I will see what I can do. As I say, the proper course will be to get it tried on one of the smaller railway lines—if it answers there, we can, perhaps, induce one of the bigger companies to take it up. I'll do my best."

Allerdyke thanked him and rose. He had certainly done something for his man Gankrodgers, and he had seen Ramsay, or Rayner, at close quarters, but—Ramsay was speaking again. He had picked up Allerdyke's card, and glanced from it to its presenter, half shyly.

"You're the cousin of the Mr. Allerdyke whose name's been in the papers so much in connection with this murder and robbery affair, I suppose?" he said. "I've seen your own name, of course, in the various accounts."

"I am," replied Allerdyke. He had moved towards the door, but he turned and looked at his questioner. "You followed it, then?" he asked.

"Yes," assented Ramsay. "Closely. A curiously intricate case."

"Any solution of it present itself to your mind?" asked Allerdyke in his brusque, downright fashion. "Got any theory?"

Ramsay smiled and shook his finely shaped head. He, too, rose, walking towards the door.

"It's a little early for that, isn't it?" he said. "I've studied these affairs—criminology, you know—for many years. In my opinion, it's a mistake to be too hasty in trying to arrive at solutions. But," he added, with a shrug of his misshapen shoulders, "it's always the way of the police, and of most folk who try to get at the truth. Things that are deep down need some deep digging for!"

"There's the question of the present whereabouts of nearly three hundred thousand pounds' worth of jewels," remarked Allerdyke grimly. "Remember that!"

"Quite so," agreed Ramsay. "But—your own particular and personal desire, as I gather from the newspapers, is to find the murderer of your cousin?"

"Ah!" said Allerdyke. "And it is! Got any ideas on that point?"

Ramsay smiled as he opened the door.

"I think," he said, with a quiet significance. "I think that you'll be having all this mystery explained and cleared up all of a sudden, Mr. Allerdyke, in a way that'll surprise you. These things are like warfare—there's a sudden turn of events, a sudden big event just when you're not expecting it. Well, good-bye—thank you for giving me a chance with your man's invention."

Allerdyke found himself walking up Arundel Street before he had quite realized that this curious interview was over. At the top he paused, staring vacantly at the folk who passed and repassed along the Strand.

"I'd lay a pound to a penny that chap's all right," he muttered to himself. "He's not a wrong 'un—unless he's damned deceitful! All the same, he knows something! What? My conscience!—was there ever such a confounded muddle in this world as this is!"

But the muddle was a deeper one within the next few minutes. He crossed over to his hotel, and as he was entering he met Mrs. Marlow coming out, fresh, dainty, charming, as usual. She stopped at sight of him and held up the little hand-bag which hung from her wrist.

"Oh, Mr. Allerdyke!" she said, opening the bag and taking an envelope from it. "I've something for you. See— here's the photograph your cousin gave me. You were wrong, you see—there's no spot in it—it's a particularly clear print. Look!"

In Allerdyke's big palm she laid the very photograph which, according to all his reckoning, was that which Chettle had found within the cover of Lydenberg's watch.

23. THE POSSIBLE DEATH WARRANT

"Quite a clear print, you see," repeated Mrs. Marlow brightly. "No spot there. You must have been thinking of another."

"Aye, just so," replied Allerdyke absentmindedly. "Another, yes, of course. Aye, to be sure—you're right. No spot on that, certainly."

He was talking aimlessly, confusedly, as he turned the print over in his hand, examining it back and front. And having no excuse for keeping it, he handed it back with a keen look at its owner. What the devil, he asked himself, was this mysterious woman playing at?

"I'm going to have this mounted and framed," said Mrs. Marlow, as she put the photograph back in her bag and turned to go. "I misplaced it some time ago and couldn't lay hands on it, but I came across it by accident this morning, so now I'll take care of it."

She nodded, smiled, and went off into the sunlight outside, and Allerdyke, more puzzled than ever, walked forward into the hotel and towards the restaurant. At its door he met Fullaway, coming out, and in his usual hurry.

Fullaway started at sight of Allerdyke, button-holed him, and led him into a corner.

"Oh, I say, Allerdyke!" he said, in his bustling fashion. "Look here, a word with you. You've no objection, have you?" he went on in subdued tones, "if Van Koon and I have a try for that reward? It doesn't matter to you, or to the Princess, or to Miss Lennard, who gets the reward so long as the criminals are brought to justice and the goods found—eh? And you know fifty thousand is—what it is."

"You've got an idea?" asked Allerdyke, regarding his questioner steadily.

"Frankly, yes—an idea—a notion," answered Fullaway. "Van Koon and I have been discussing the whole affair—just now. He's a smart man, and has had experience in these things on the other side. But, of course, we don't want to give our idea away. We want to work in entire independence of the police, for instance. What we're thinking of requires patience and deep investigation. So we want to work on our own methods. See?"

"It doesn't matter to me who gets the reward—as you say," said Allerdyke slowly. "I want justice. I'm not so much concerned about the jewels as about who killed my cousin. I believe that man Lydenberg did the actual killing—but who was at Lydenberg's back? Find that out, and—"

"Exactly—exactly!" broke in Fullaway. "The very thing! Well—you understand, Allerdyke. Van Koon and I will want to keep our operations to ourselves. We don't want police interference. So, if any of these Scotland Yard chaps come to you here for talk or information, don't bring me into it. And don't expect me to tell what we're doing until we've carried out our investigations. No interim reports, you know, Allerdyke. Personally, I believe we're on the track."

"Do just what you please," replied Allerdyke. "You're not the only two who are after that reward. Go ahead—your own way."

He turned into the restaurant and ordered his lunch, and while it was being brought sat drumming his fingers on the table, staring vacantly at the people about him and wondering over the events of the morning. Rayner's, or Ramsay's, vague hint that something might suddenly clear everything up; Fullaway's announcement that he and Van Koon had put their heads together; Mrs. Perrigo's story of the French maid and the young man who led blue-ribboned pug-dogs—but all these were as nothing compared to the fact that Mrs. Marlow had actually shown him the photograph which he had until then firmly believed to lie hidden in the case of Lydenberg's watch. That beat him.

"Is my blessed memory going wrong?" he said to himself. "Did I actually print more than four copies of that thing! No—no!—I'm shot if I did. My memory never fails. I did not print off more than four. James had three; I had one. Mine's in my album upstairs. I know what James did with his. Cousin Grace has one; Wilson Firth has another; he gave the third to this Mrs. Marlow—and she's got it! Then—how the devil did that photograph, which looks to be of my taking, which I'd swear is of my taking, come to be in Lydenberg's watch? Gad—it's enough to make a man's brain turn to pap!"

He was moodily finishing his lunch when Chettle came in to find him. Allerdyke, who was in a quiet corner, beckoned the detective to a seat, and offered him a drink.

"Well?" he asked. "What's been done?"

"It's all right," answered Chettle. "I've told no more than was necessary—just what we agreed upon. To tell you the truth, our folks don't attach such tremendous importance to it—they will, of course, when you tell them your story about the photo. Just at present they merely see the obvious fact—that Lydenberg was furnished with the photo as a means of ready identification of your brother. No—at this moment they're full of the Perrigo woman's story—they think that's a sure clue—a good beginning. Somebody, they say, must own, or have owned, those pugs! Therefore they're going strong on that. Meanwhile, I'm going back to Hull for at any rate a few days."

"You've still got that watch on you?" asked Allerdyke.

"Certainly," answered Chettle, clapping his hand to his breast-pocket. "Technically speaking, it's in charge of the Hull police—it'll have to be produced there. Did you want to see it again, Mr. Allerdyke?"

"Finish your drink and come up to my sitting-room," said Allerdyke. "I'll give you a cigar up there. Yes," he added, as they left the restaurant and went upstairs. "I do want to see it again—or, rather, the photograph. You're in no hurry?"

"A good hour to spare yet," replied Chettle.

Allerdyke locked the door of the sitting-room when they were once inside it, and that done he placed a decanter, a syphon, and a glass on his table, and flanked them with a box of cigars. He waved a hospitable hand towards these comforts.

"Sit down and help yourself, Chettle," he said. "A drop of my whisky'll do you no harm—that's some I got down from home, and you'll not find its like everywhere. Light a cigar—and put a couple in your pocket to smoke in the train. Now then, let's see that photograph once more."

Chettle handed over the watch, and Allerdyke, opening the case, delicately removed the print. He sat down at the table with his back to the light, and carefully examined the thing back and front, while the detective, glass in hand, cigar in lips, and thumb in the armhole of his waistcoat, watched him appreciatively and inquisitively.

"Make aught new out of it, sir?" he asked after a while.

Instead of answering, Allerdyke laid the photograph down, went across to another table, and took from it his album. He turned its leaves over until he came to a few loose prints. He picked them up one after another and examined them. And suddenly he knew the secret. There was no longer any problem, any difficulty about that photograph. He knew—now! And with a sharp exclamation, he flung the album back to the side-table, and turned to the detective.

"Chettle!" he said. "You know me well enough to know that I can make it well worth any man's while to keep a secret until I tell him he can speak about it! What!"

"I should think so, Mr. Allerdyke," responded Chettle, readily enough. "And if you want me to keep a secret—"

"I do—for the time being," answered Allerdyke. He sat down again and picked up the photograph which had exercised his thoughts so intensely. "I've found out the truth concerning this," he said, tapping it with his finger. "Yes, I've hit it! Listen, now—I told you I'd only made four prints of this photo, and that I knew exactly where they all were—one in my own album there, two given by James to friends in Bradford, one—as we more recently found out—given by James to Mrs. Marlow. That one— the Mrs. Marlow one—we believed to be—this—this!"

"And isn't it, Mr. Allerdyke?" asked Chettle wonderingly.

Allerdyke laughed—a laugh of relief and satisfaction.

"Less than an hour ago," he replied, "in fact, just before you came in, Mrs. Marlow showed me the photo which James gave her—showed it to me, out below there in the hall. No mistaking it! And so—when you came, I was racking my brains to rags trying to settle what this photo—this!—was. And now I know what it is—and damn me if I know whether the discovery makes things plainer or more mixed up! But—I know what this is, anyway."

"And—what is it, sir?" asked Chettle eagerly, eyeing the photo as if it were some fearful living curiosity. "What, Mr. Allerdyke?"

"Why, it's a photograph of my photograph!" almost shouted Allerdyke, with a thump of his big hand on the table. "That's the truth. This has been reproduced from mine, d'ye see? Look here—happen you don't know much about photography, but you'll follow me—I always use a certain sort of printing-out paper; I've stuck to one particular sort for years—all the photos in that album are done on that particular sort. The four prints I made of James's last photo were done on that paper. Now then— this photo, this print that you found in Lydenberg's watch, is not done on that paper—it's a totally different paper. Therefore—this is a reproduction! It is not my original print at all—it's been copied from it. See?"

Chettle, who had followed all this with concentrated attention, nodded his head several times.

"Clever—clever—clever!" he said with undisguised admiration. "Clever, indeed! That's a smart bit of work, sir. I see—I understand! Bless my soul! And what do you gather from that, Mr. Allerdyke?"

"This!" answered Allerdyke. "Just now, Mrs. Marlow said to me, speaking of her photo—the fourth print, you know—'I misplaced it some time ago,' she said, 'and couldn't lay hands on it, but I came across it accidentally this morning.' Now then, Chettle, here's the thing— somebody took that fourth print from Mrs. Marlow, reproduced it—and that—that print which you found in Lydenberg's watch is the reproduction!"

"So that," began Chettle suggestively, "so that—"

"So that the thing now is to find who it is that made the reproduction," said Allerdyke. "When we've found him—or her—I reckon we shall have found the man who's at the heart of all this. Leave that to me! Keep this a dead secret until I tell you to speak—we shall have to tell all this, and a bonny sight more, to your bosses at headquarters—off you go to Hull, and do what you have to do, and I'll get on with my work here. I said I didn't know whether this discovery makes things thicker or clearer, but, by George, it's a step forward anyway!"

Chettle put the reproduction back into the case of the watch and bestowed it safely in his pocket.

"One step forward's a good deal in a case like this, Mr. Allerdyke," he said. "What are you going to do about the next step, now?"

"Try to find out who made that reproduction," replied Allerdyke bluntly. "No easy job, either! The ground's continually shifting and changing under one's very feet. But I don't mind telling you my present theory— somebody's got information of that jewel deal from Fullaway's office, somebody who had access to his papers, somebody who managed to steal that photo of mine from Mrs. Marlow for a few days or until they could reproduce it. What I want to find now is—an idea of that somebody. And—I'll get it!—I'll move heaven and earth to get it! But—other matters. You say your folks at the Yard are going to follow up that Perrigo woman's clue? They think it important, then?"

"In the case of the Frenchwoman, yes," answered Chettle. He thrust his hand into a side-pocket and brought out a crumpled paper. "Here's a proof of the bill they're getting out," he said. "They set to work on that as soon as they'd got the information. That'll be up outside every police-station in a few hours, and it's gone out to the Press, too."

Allerdyke took the proof, still damp from the machine, and looked it over. It asked, in the usual formal language, for any information about a young man, dark, presumably a foreigner, who, about the middle of March, was in the habit of taking two pug dogs, generally bedecked with blue ribbons, into Kensington Gardens.

"There ought to be some response to that, you know, Mr. Allerdyke," remarked Chettle. "Somebody must remember and know something about that young fellow. But, upon my soul, as I said to Blindway just now, I don't know whether that bill's a mere advertisement or a— death warrant!"

"Death warrant!" exclaimed Allerdyke. "What d'you mean?"

Chettle chuckled knowingly.

"Mean," he said. "Why, this—if that young fellow who led pugs about, and talked to Mamselle Lisette in Kensington Gardens, is another of the cat's paws that this gang evidently made use of, I should say that when the gang sees he's being searched for, they'll out him, just as they outed her and Lydenberg. That's what I mean, Mr. Allerdyke—they'll do him in themselves before anybody else can get at him! See?"

Allerdyke saw. And when the detective had gone, he threw himself into a chair, lighted one of his strongest cigars, drew pen, ink, and paper to him, and began to work at his problem with a grim determination to evolve at any rate a clear theory of its possible solution.

24. Concerning Carl Federman

Next morning, as Allerdyke was leaving the hotel with the intention of going down to Gresham Street, one of the hall-porters ran after and hailed him.

"You're wanted at the telephone, sir," he said. "Call for you just come through."

Allerdyke went back, to find himself hailed by Blindway. Would he drive on to the Yard at once and bring Mr. Fullaway with him?—both were wanted, particularly in connection with the Perrigo information.

Allerdyke promised for himself, and went upstairs to find Fullaway. He met him coming down, and gave him the message. Fullaway looked undecided.

"You know what I told you yesterday, Allerdyke," he said. "I didn't want to be bothered further with these police chaps. Van Koon and I are on a line of our own, and—"

"As you like," interrupted Allerdyke, "but all the same, if I were in your place I shouldn't refuse a chance of acquiring information. Even if you don't want to tell the police anything, that's no reason why you shouldn't learn something from them."

"There's that in it, certainly," assented Fullaway. "All right. You get a taxi and I'll join you in a minute or two."

As they got out of one cab at the police headquarters Celia Lennard appeared in another. She made a little grimace as the two men greeted her.

"Again!" she exclaimed, "What are we going to be treated to now? More old women with vague stories, I suppose. What good is it at all? And when am I going to hear something about my jewels?"

"You never know what you're going to hear when you visit these palatial halls," answered Fullaway. "You may be going to have the biggest surprise of your life, you know. They sent for you?"

"Rang me up in the middle of my breakfast," answered Celia. "Well—let's find out what new sensation this is. Some extraordinary creature on view again, of course."

The creature on view proved to be a little fat man, obviously French or Swiss, who sat, his rotund figure tightly enveloped in a frock-coat, the lapel of which was decorated with a bit of ribbon, on the edge of a chair facing the chief's desk. He was a nervous, alert little man; his carefully trimmed moustache and pointed beard quivered with excitement; his dark eyes blazed. And at sight of the elegantly attired lady he bounced out of his chair, swept his silk hat to the ground, and executed a deep bow of the most extreme politeness.

"This," observed the chief, with a smile at his visitors, "is Monsieur Aristide Bonnechose. M. Bonnechose believes that he can tell us something. It is a supplement to what Mrs. Perrigo told us yesterday. It relates, of course to the young man whom Mrs. Perrigo told us of— the young man who led pugs in Kensington Gardens."

"The pogs of Madame, my spouse," said M. Bonnechose, with a bow and a solemn expression. "Two pogs—Fifi and Chou-Chou."

"M. Bonnechose," continued the chief, regarding his company with yet another smile, "is the proprietor of a— what is your establishment, monsieur?"

"Cafe-restaurant, monsieur," replied M. Bonnechose, promptly and politely. "Small, but elegant. Of my name, monsieur—the Cafe Bonnechose, Oxford Street. Established nine years—I succeeded to a former proprietor, Monsieur Jules, on his lamented decease."

"I think M. Bonnechose had better tell us his history in his own fashion," remarked the chief, looking around. "You are aware, Mr. Allerdyke, and you, too, Mr. Fullaway, and so I suppose are you Miss Lennard, that after hearing what Mrs. Perrigo had to tell us I put out a bill asking for information about the young man Mrs. Perrigo described, and the matter was also mentioned in last night's and this morning's papers. M. Bonnechose read about it in his newspaper, and so he came here at once. He tells me that he knew a young man who was good enough during the early spring, to occasionally take out Madame Bonnechose's prize dogs for an airing. That seems to have been the same man referred to by Mrs. Perrigo. Now, M. Bonnechose, give us the details."

M. Bonnechose set down his tall, very Parisian hat on the edge of the chief's desk, and proceeded to use his hands in conjunction with his tongue.

"With pleasure, monsieur," he responded. "It is this way, then. You will comprehend that Madame, my spouse, and myself are of the busiest. We do not keep a great staff; accordingly we have much to do ourselves. Consequently we have not much time to go out, to take the air. Madame, my spouse, she has a love for the dogs—she keeps two, Fifi and Chou-Chou—pogs. What they call pedigree dogs—valuable. Beautiful animals—but needing exercise. It is a trouble to Madame that they cannot disport themselves more frequently. Now, about the beginning of this spring, a young man—compatriot of my own—a Swiss from the Vaud canton—he begins coming to my cafe. Sometimes he comes for his lunch—sometimes he drops in, as they say, for a cup of coffee. We find out, he and I, that we come from the same district. In the event, we become friendly."

"This young man's name, M. Bonnechose?" asked the chief.

"What we knew him by—Federman," replied M. Bonnechose. "Carl Federman. He told me he was looking out for a job as valet to a rich man. He had been a waiter—somewhere in London—some hotel, I think—I did not pay much attention. Anyway, while he was looking for his job he certainly had plenty of money— plenty! He do himself very well with his lunches—

sometimes he come and have his dinner at night. We are not expensive, you understand—nice lunch for two shillings, nice dinner for three—nothing to him, that—he always carry plenty of money in his pockets. Well, then, of course, having nothing to do, often he talks to me and Madame. One day we talk of the pogs, then walking about the establishment. He remarks that they are too fat. Madame sighs and says the poor darlings do not get sufficient exercise. He is good-natured, this Federman— he say at once 'I will exercise them—I, myself.' So he come next day, like a good friend, Madame puts blue ribbons on the pogs, and bids them behave nicely—away they go with Federman for the excursion. Many days he thus takes them—to Hyde Park, to Kensington Gardens—out of the neighbourliness, you understand. Madame is much obliged to him—she regards him as a kind young man—eh? And then, all of a sudden, we do not see Federman any more—no. Nor hear of him until monsieur asks for news of him in the papers. I see that news last night—Madame sees it! We start—we look at each other—we regard ourselves with comprehension. We both make the same exclamation—'It is Federman! He is wanted! He has done something!' Then Madame says, 'Aristide, in the morning, you will go to the police commissary,' I say 'It shall be done—we will have no mystery around the Cafe Bonnechose.' Monsieur, I am here—and I have spoken!"

"And that is all you know, M. Bonnechose?" asked the chief.

"All, monsieur, absolutely all!"

"About when was it that this young man first came to your cafe, then?"

"About the beginning of March, or end of February, monsieur—it was the beginning of the good weather, you understand."

"And he left off coming—when?"

"Beginning of April, monsieur—after that we never see him again. Often we say to ourselves, 'Where is

Federman?' The pogs, they look at the seat which he was accustomed to take, as much as to ask the same question. But," concluded M. Bonnechose, with a dismal shake of his close-cropped head, and a spreading forth of his hands, "he never visit us no more—no!"

"Now, listen, M. Bonnechose," said the chief; "did this man ever give you any particulars about himself?"

"None but what I have told you, monsieur—and which I do not now remember."

"Ever tell you where he lived in London—-at the time he was visiting you?"

"No, monsieur—never."

"Did he ever come to your place accompanied by anybody? Bring any friends there?"

M. Bonnechose put himself into an attitude of deep thought. He remained in it for a moment or two; then he exchanged it for one of joyful recollection.

"On one occasion, a lady!" he exclaimed. "A Frenchwoman. Tall—that is, taller than is usual amongst Frenchwomen—slender—elegant. Dark—dark, black eyes—not beautiful, you understand, but—engaging."

"Lisette!" muttered Celia.

"On only one occasion, you say, M. Bonnechose?" asked the chief. "When was it?"

"About the time I speak of, monsieur. They came in one night—rather late. They had a light supper—nothing much."

"He did not tell you who she was?"

"Not a word, monsieur! He was, as a rule, very secretive, this Federman, saying little about his own affairs."

"You don't remember that he ever brought any one else there! No men, for instance?"

M. Bonnechose shook his head. Then, once again, his face brightened.

"No!" he said. "But once—just once—I saw Federman talking to a man in the street—Shaftesbury Avenue. A clean-shaven man, well built, brown hair—a Frenchman, I think. But, of course, a stranger to me."

The chief exchanged a glance with Allerdyke and Fullaway—both knew what that glance meant. M. Bonnechose's description tallied remarkably with that of the man who had gone to Eastbourne Terrace Hotel with Lisette Beaurepaire.

"A clean-shaven man, with brown hair, and well built, eh?" said the chief. "And when—"

Just then an interruption came in the person of a man who entered the room and gave evident signs of a desire to tell something to his superior. The chief left his chair, went across to the door, and received a communication which was evidently of considerable moment. He turned and beckoned Blindway; the three went out of the room. Several minutes passed; then the chief came back alone, and looked at his visitors with a glance of significance.

"We have just got news of something that relates, I think, to the very subject we were discussing," he said. "A young man has been found dead in bed at a City hotel this morning under very suspicious circumstances— circumstances very similar to those of the Eastbourne Terrace affair. And," he went on, glancing at a scrap of paper which he held in his hand, "the description of him very closely resembles that of this man Federman. Of course, it's not an uncommon type, but—"

"Another of 'em!" exclaimed Allerdyke. He had suddenly remembered what Chettle had said about the new bill being a possible death-warrant, and the words started irrepressibly to his lips. "Good Lord!"

The chief gave him a quick glance; it seemed as if he instinctively divined what was passing in Allerdyke's mind.

"I'm sorry to trouble you," he said, without referring to Allerdyke's interruption, "but I'm afraid I must ask you—all of you—to run down to this City hotel with me. We mustn't leave a stone unturned, and if any of you can identify this man—"

"Oh, you don't want me, surely!" cried Celia. "Please let me off—I do so hate that sort of thing!"

"Naturally," remarked the chief. "But I'm afraid I want you more than any one, Miss Lennard—you and M. Bonnechose. Come—we'll go at once—Blindway has gone down to get two cabs for us."

Blindway, M. Bonnechose, and Fullaway rode to the City in one cab; Celia, Allerdyke, and the chief in another. Their journey came to an end in a quiet old street near the Docks, and at the door of an old-fashioned looking hotel. There was a much-worried landlord, and a detective or two, and sundry police to meet them, and inquisitive eyes looked out of doors and round corners as they went upstairs to a door which was guarded by two constables. The chief turned to Celia with a word of encouragement.

"One look will answer the purpose," he said quietly. "But—look closely!"

The next moment all six were standing round a narrow bed on which was laid out the dead body of a young man. The face, calm, composed, looked more like that of a man who lay quietly and peacefully asleep than one who had died under suspicious circumstances.

"Well?" asked the chief presently. "What do you say, Miss Lennard?"

Celia caught her breath.

"This—this is the man who came to Hull," she whispered. "The man, you know, who called himself Lisette's brother. I knew him instantly."

"And you, M. Bonnechose?" said the chief. "Do you recognize him?"

The cafe-keeper, who had been making inarticulate murmurs of surprise and grief, nodded.

"Federman!" he said. "Oh, yes, monsieur—Federman, without doubt. Poor fellow!"

The chief turned to leave the room, saying quietly that that was all he wished. But Fullaway, who had been staring moodily at the dead man, suddenly stopped him. "Look here!" he said. "I know this man, too—but not as Federman. I'm not mistaken about him, and I don't think Miss Lennard or M. Bonnechose are, either. But I knew him as Fritz Ebers. He acted as my valet at the Waldorf from the beginning of April to about the end of the first week in May last. And—since we now know what we do— it's my opinion that there—there in that dead man—is the last of the puppets! The Frenchwoman—Lydenberg— now this fellow—all three got rid of! Now, then—where's the man who pulled the strings! Where's the arch-murderer!"

25. The Card On The Door

The chief made no immediate reply to Fullaway's somewhat excited outburst; he led his little party from the room, and in the corridor turned to Celia and the cafe keeper.

"That's all, Miss Lennard, thank you," he said. "Sorry to have to ask you to take part in these painful affairs, but it can't be helped. M. Bonnechose, I'm obliged to you—you'll hear from me again very soon. In the meantime, keep counsel—don't talk to anybody except Madame—no gossiping with customers, you know. Mr. Allerdyke, will you see Miss Lennard downstairs and into a cab, and then join Mr. Fullaway and me again?—we must have a talk with the police and the hotel people."

When Allerdyke went back into the hotel he found Blindway waiting for him at the door of a ground-floor room in which the chief, Fullaway, a City police-inspector and a detective were already closeted with the landlord and landlady. The landlord, a somewhat sullen individual, who appeared to be greatly vexed and disconcerted by these events, was already being questioned by the chief as to what he knew of the young man whose body they had just seen, and he was replying somewhat testily.

"I know no more about him than I know of any chance customer," he was saying when Allerdyke was ushered in by Blindway, who immediately closed the door on this informal conclave. "You see what this house is?—a second-class house for gentlemen having business in this part, round about the Docks. We get a lot of commercial gentlemen, sea-faring men, such-like. Lots of our customers are people who are going to foreign places—Antwerp, Rotterdam, Hamburg, and so on—they put up here just for the night, before sailing. I took this young man for one of that sort—in fact, I think he made some inquiry about one of the boats."

"He did," affirmed the landlady. "He asked William, the head-waiter, what time the Rotterdam steamer sailed this morning."

"And that's about all we know," continued the landlord. "I never took any particular notice of him, and—"

"Just answer a few questions," said the chief, interrupting him quietly. "We shall get at what we want to know more easily that way. What time did this young man come to the hotel yesterday?"

The landlord turned to his wife with an expressive gesture.

"Ask her," he answered. "She looks after all that—I'm not so much in the office."

"He came at seven o'clock last night," said the landlady. "I was in the office, and I booked him and gave him his room—27."

"Was he alone?"

"Quite alone. He'd the suit-case that's upstairs in the room now, and an overcoat and an umbrella."

"Of course," said the chief, "he gave you some name—some address?"

"He gave the name and address of Frank Herman, Walthamstow," replied the landlady, opening a ledger which she had brought into the room. "There you are—that's his writing."

The chief drew the book to him, glanced at the entry, and closed the book again, keeping a finger in it.

"Well, what was seen of him during the evening!" he asked.

"Nothing much," replied the landlady. "He had his supper in the coffee-room—a couple of chops and coffee. He was reading the papers in the smoking-room until about half-past ten; I saw him myself going upstairs between that and eleven. As I didn't see him about next morning and as his breakfast wasn't booked, I asked where he was, and the chambermaid said there was a card on his door saying that he wasn't to be called till eleven."

"Where is that card?" asked the chief.

"It's here in this envelope," answered the landlady, who seemed to be much more alert and much sharper of intellect than her husband. "I took care of it when we found out what had happened. I suppose you'll take charge of it?"

"If you please," answered the chief. He took the envelope, looked inside it to make sure that the card was there, and turned to the landlady again.

"Yes?" he said. "When you found out what had happened. Now, who did find out what had happened?"

"Well," answered the landlady, "the chambermaid came down soon after eleven, and said she couldn't get 27 to answer her knock. Of course, I understood that he wanted to catch the Rotterdam boat which sailed about noon, so I sent my husband up. And as he couldn't get any answer—"

"I went in with the chambermaid's key," broke in the landlord, "and there he was—just as you've seen him—dead. And if you ask me, he was cold, too—been dead some time, in my opinion."

"The surgeon said several hours—six or seven," remarked the inspector in an aside to the chief. "Thought he'd been dead since four o'clock."

"No signs of anything in the room, I suppose?" asked the chief. "Nothing disturbed, eh?"

"Nothing!" replied the landlord stolidly. "The room was as you'd expect to find it; tidy enough. And nothing touched—as the police that were called in at first can testify. They can swear as his money was all right and his watch and chain all right—there'd been no robbery. And," he added with resentful emphasis, "I don't care what you nor nobody says!—'tain't no case of murder, this! It's suicide, that's what it is. I don't want my house to get the name and character of a murder place! I can't help it if a quiet-looking, apparently respectable young fellow comes and suicides himself in my house—there's nobody can avoid that, as I know of, but when it comes to murder—"

"No one has said anything about murder so far," interrupted the chief quietly. "But since you suggest it, perhaps we'd better ask who you'd got in the house last night." He opened the register at the page in which he had kept his finger, and looked at the last entries. "I see that three—no, four—people came in after this young man who called himself Frank Herman. You booked them, I suppose?" he went on, turning to the landlady. "Were they known to you?"

"Only one—that one, Mr. Peter Donaldson, Dundee," answered the landlady. "He's the representative of a jute firm—he often comes here. He's in the house now, or he was, an hour ago—he'll be here for two or three days. Those two, Mr. and Mrs. Nielsen—they appeared to be foreigners. They were here for the night, had breakfast early, and went away by some boat—our porter carried their things to it. Quiet, elderly folks, they were."

"And the fourth—John Barcombe, Manchester—you didn't know him?" asked the chief, pointing to the last entry. "I see you gave him Number 29—two doors from Herman."

"Yes," said the landlady. "No—I didn't know him. He came in about nine o'clock and had some supper before he went up. He'd his breakfast at eight o'clock this morning, and went away at once. Lots of our customers do that— they're just in for bed and breakfast, and we scarcely notice them."

"Did you notice this man—Barcombe?" asked the chief.

"Well, not particularly. But I've a fair recollection of him. A rather pale, stiffish-built man, lightish brown hair and moustache, dressed in a dark suit. He'd no luggage, and he paid me for supper, bed, and breakfast when he booked his room," replied the landlady. "Quite a quiet, respectable man—he said something about being unexpectedly obliged to stop for the night, but I didn't pay any great attention."

The chief looked attentively at the open page of the register. Then he drew the attention of those around him to the signature of John Barcombe. It was a big, sprawling signature, all the letters sloping downward from left to right, and being of an unusual size for a man.

"That looks to me like a feigned handwriting," he said. "However, note this. You see that entry of Frank Herman? Observe his handwriting. Now compare it with the writing on the card which was fixed on the door of 27—Herman's room. Look!"

He drew the card out of its envelope as he spoke and laid it beside the entry in the register. And Marshall Allerdyke, bending over his shoulder to look, almost cried out with astonishment, for the writing on the card was certainly the same as that which Chettle had shown him on the post-card found on Lydenberg, and on the back of the photograph of James Allerdyke discovered in Lydenberg's watch. It was only by a big effort that he checked the exclamation which was springing to his lips, and stopped himself from snatching up the card from the table.

"You observe," said the chief quietly, "you can't fail to observe that the writing in the register, is not the writing of the card pinned on the door of Number 27. They are quite different. The writing of Frank Herman in the register is in thick, stunted strokes; the writing on the card is in thin, angular, what are commonly called crabbed strokes. Yet it is supposed that Herman put that card outside his bedroom door. How is it, then, that Herman's handwriting was thick and stunted when he registered at seven o'clock and slender and a bit shaky when he wrote this card at, say, half-past ten or eleven? Of course, Herman, or whatever his real name is, never wrote the line on that card, and never pinned that card on his door!"

The landlord opened his heavy lips and gasped: the landlady sighed with a gradually awakening interest. Amidst a dead silence the chief went on with his critical inspection of the handwriting.

"But now look at the signature of the man who called himself John Barcombe, of Manchester. You will observe that he signed that name in a great, sprawling hand across the page, and that the letters slope from left to right, downward, instead of in the usually accepted fashion of left to right, upward. Now at first sight there is no great similarity in the writing of that entry in the register and that on the card—one is rounded and sprawling, and the other is thin and precise. But there is one remarkable and striking similarity. In the entry in the register there are two a's—the a in Barcombe, the a in Manchester. On the one line on the card found pinned to the door there are also two a's—the a in please; the a in call. Now observe—whether the writing is big, sprawling, thin, precise; feigned, obviously, in one case, natural, I think, in the other, all those four a's are the same! This man has grown so accustomed to making his a's after the Greek fashion—a—done in one turn of the pen—that he has made them even in his feigned handwriting! There's not a doubt, to my mind, that the card found on Herman's door was written, and put on that door, by the man who registered as John Barcombe. And," he added in an undertone to Allerdyke, "I've no doubt, either, that he's the man of the Eastbourne Terrace affair."

The landlord had risen to his feet, and was scowling gloomily at everybody.

"Then you are making it out to be murder?" he exclaimed sulkily. "Just what I expected! Never had police called in yet without 'em making mountains out of molehills! Murder, indeed!—nothing but a case of suicide, that's what I say. And as this is a temperance hotel, and not a licensed house, I'll be obliged to you if you'll have that body taken away to the mortuary—I shall be having the character of my place taken away next, and then where shall I be I should like to know!"

He swung indignantly out of the room, and his wife, murmuring that it was certainly very hard on innocent people that these things went on, followed him. The police, giving no heed to these protests, proceeded to examine the articles taken from the dead man's clothing. Whatever had been the object of the murderer, it was certainly not robbery. There was a purse and a pocket-book, containing a considerable amount of money in gold and notes; a good watch and chain, and a ring or two of some value.

"Just the same circumstances as in the Eastbourne Terrace affair," said the chief as he rose. "Well—the thing is to find that man. You've no doubt whatever, Mr. Fullaway, that this dead man upstairs is the man you knew as Ebers, a valet at your hotel?"

"None!" answered Fullaway emphatically. "None whatever. Lots of people will be able to identify him."

"That's good, at any rate," remarked the chief. "It's a long step towards—something. Well, I must go."

Allerdyke was in more than half a mind to draw the chief aside and tell him about Chettle's discoveries as regards the handwriting, but while he hesitated Fullaway tugged earnestly at his sleeve.

"Come away!" whispered Fullaway. "Come! We're going to cut in at this ourselves!"

26. Participants In The Secret

Allerdyke was scarcely prepared for the feverish energy with which Fullaway dragged him out of the hotel, forced him into the first taxi-cab they met, and bade the driver make haste to the Waldorf. He knew by that time that the American was a nervous, excitable individual who now and then took on tremendous fits of work in which he hustled and bustled everybody around him, but he had never seen him quite so excited and eager as now. The discovery at that shabby hotel which they had just quitted seemed to have acted on him like the smell of powder on an old war-horse; he appeared to be positively panting for action.

"Allerdyke!" he almost shouted as the cab moved away, and he himself smote one clenched fist upon the other. "Allerdyke—this thing has got to go through! I resign all claim to that reward. Allerdyke!—this affair is too serious for any hole-and-corner work. I shall tell Van Koon that what we know, or fancy, must be thrown into the common stock of knowledge! The thing is to get at the people who've been behind this poor chap Ebers, or Federman, or Herman, or whatever his name is. Allerdyke!—we must go right into things."

Allerdyke laughed sardonically. When Fullaway developed excitement, he developed coolness, and his voice became as dry and hard as the other's was fervid and eloquent.

"Aye!" he said in his most phlegmatic tones. "Aye, just so! And where d'ye intend to cut in, now, like? Is it a sort of Gordian knot affair that you're thinking of? Going to solve this difficulty at one blow?"

"Don't be sarcastic," retorted Fullaway. "I'm going to take things clean up from this Federman or Ebers affair. I'm going deep—deep! You'll see in a few minutes."

"Willing to see—and to hear—aught," remarked Allerdyke laconically. "I've been doing naught else since I got that wireless telegram."

Then they relapsed into silence until the Waldorf was reached. There Fullaway raced his companion upstairs to his rooms and burst in upon Mrs. Marlow like a whirlwind. The pretty secretary, busied with her typewriter, looked up, glanced at both men, and calmly resumed her labours.

"Mrs. Marlow!" exclaimed Fullaway. "Just step to Mr. Van Koon's rooms and beg him to come back here to my sitting-room with you—important business, Mrs. Marlow—I want you, too."

Allerdyke, closely watching the woman around whom so much mystery centred, saw that she did not move so much as an eyelash. She laid her work aside, left the room, and within a minute returned with Van Koon, who gazed at Fullaway with an air of half-amused inquiry.

"Something happened?" he asked, nodding to Allerdyke. "Town on fire?"

"Van Koon, sit down," commanded Fullaway, pushing his compatriot into the inner room. "Mrs. Marlow, fasten that outer door and come in here. We're going to have a stiff conference. Sit down, please, all of you. Now," he went on, when the other three had ranged themselves about the centre table, "There is news, Van Koon. Allerdyke and I have just come away from an hotel in the Docks where we've seen the dead body of a young man who's been found dead there under precisely similar circumstances to those which attended the death of the French maid in Eastbourne Terrace. We've also heard a description of a man who was at this hotel in the Docks last night—it corresponds to that of the fellow who accompanied Lisette Beaurepaire. I, personally, have no doubt that this man, whoever he is, is the murderer of

Lisette and of this youngster whose body we've just seen. Mrs. Marlow, this dead young fellow, from whose death-chamber we've just come, is that valet I used to have here—Ebers. You remember him?"

"Sure!" answered Mrs. Marlow, quite calmly and unconcernedly. "Very well indeed."

"This Ebers," continued Fullaway, turning to Van Koon, "was a young fellow, Swiss, German, something of that sort, who acted as valet to me and to some other men here in this hotel for a time. I needn't go into too many details now, but there's no doubt that he knew, and was in touch with, Lisette Beaurepaire, and Miss Lennard positively identifies him as the man who met her and Lisette at Hull, and represented himself as Lisette's brother. Now then, Ebers—we'll stick to that name for the sake of clearness—was in and out of my rooms a good deal, of course. And what I want to know now, Mrs. Marlow, is—do you think he got access to our letters, papers, books? Could he find out, for instance, that I was engaged in this deal between the Princess Nastirsevitch and Mr. Delkin, and that Miss Lennard had bought the Pinkie Pell pearls? Think!"

Mrs. Marlow had evidently done her thinking; she replied without hesitation.

"If he did, or could, it would be through your own carelessness, Mr. Fullaway," she said. "You know that I am ridiculously careful about that sort of thing! From the time I come here in the morning—ten-o'clock—until I leave at five, no one has any chance of seeing our papers, or our letter book, or our telegram-copies book. They are always on my desk while I am in the office, and when I go downstairs to lunch I lock them up in the safe. But—you're not careful! How many times have I come in the morning, and found that you've taken these things out of the safe over-night and left them lying about for anybody to see? Dozens of times!"

"I know—I know!" admitted Fullaway with a groan. "I'm frightfully careless—always was. I quite admit it, Mrs. Marlow, quite!"

"Of course," continued Mrs. Marlow, in precise, even tones, "of course if you left the letter-book lying round, and the book in which the duplicates of all our telegrams and cablegrams are kept, too—why, this Ebers man could easily read what he liked for himself when he was in here of a morning before you got up. He was in and out a great deal, that's certain. And as regards those two affairs, the documents we have about them are pretty plain, Mr. Fullaway. Anybody of average intelligence could find out in ten minutes from our letter-book and telegram-book that we negotiated the sale of the Pinkie Pell pearls to Miss Lennard, and that Mr. James Allerdyke was bringing here a valuable parcel of jewels from Russia. And," concluded Mrs. Marlow quietly, "from what I saw of him, Ebers was a smart man."

Van Koon, who had been listening attentively to all this, turned a half-whimsical, half-reproving glance on Fullaway, who sat in a contrite attitude, drumming his fingers on the polished table.

"I guess you're a very careless individual, my friend," he said, shaking his head. "If you will leave your important papers lying about, as this lady says you're in the habit of doing, what do you expect? Now, you've been wondering who got wind of this jewel deal, and here's the very proof that you gave every chance to this Ebers to acquaint himself with it! And what I'd like to know now, Fullaway, is this—what use do you suppose this young fellow made of the information he acquired? That seems to me to be the point."

"Yes!" exclaimed Allerdyke suddenly. "That is the point!"

Fullaway smote the table.

"The thing's obvious!" he cried. "He sold his information to a gang. There must have been—I mean must be—a gang. It's utterly impossible that all this could have been worked by one man. The man we've heard of in connection with the deaths of Lisette Beaurepaire and of Ebers himself is only one of the combination. I'm as sure of that as I am that I see you. But—who are they?"

Nobody answered this question. Allerdyke plunged his hands in his pockets and stared at Fullaway; Mrs. Marlow began to trace imaginary patterns on the surface of the table; Van Koon produced a penknife and began to scrape the edges of his filbert nails with a preoccupied air.

"There's the thing I've insisted on all along, Fullaway, you know," he said at last, finding that no one seemed inclined to speak. "I've insisted on it, but you've always put it off. I don't care what you say—it'll have to come to it. Let me suggest it, now, to our friends here—they're both cute enough, I reckon!"

"Oh, as you please, as you please!" replied Fullaway, with a wave of his hands. "Say anything you like, Van Koon—it seems as if too much couldn't be said at this juncture."

"All right," answered Van Koon. He turned to Allerdyke and Mrs. Marlow. "Ever since this affair was brought under my notice," he said, "I've pointed out to Fullaway certain features in connection with it. First—there's no evidence whatever that this plot originated in or was worked from Russia. Second—there is evidence that it began here in London and was carried out from London. And following on that second proposition comes another. Fullaway knew that these jewels were coming—"

He paused and gave the secretary a keen look. And Allerdyke, watching her just as keenly, saw her face and eyes as calm and inscrutable as ever; it was absolutely evident that nothing could move this woman, no chance word or allusion take her unawares. Van Koon smiled, and leaned nearer.

"But," he said, tapping the table in emphasis of his words, "there was somebody else who knew of this deal, somebody whose name Fullaway there steadfastly refuses to bring in. Delkin!"

Fullaway suddenly laughed, throwing up his arms.

"Delkin!" he exclaimed satirically. "A millionaire several times over! The thing's ridiculous, Van Koon! Delkin would kick me out if I went and asked him—"

"Delkin will have to be asked," interrupted Van Koon. "You will not face the facts, Fullaway. Millionaire, multimillionaire, Delkin was the third person (I'm leaving this valet, Ebers, clean out, though I've not the slightest doubt he was one of the pieces of the machine) who knew that James Allerdyke was bringing two hundred and fifty thousand pounds' worth of jewels for his, Delkin's approval! That's a fact, Fullaway, which cannot be got over."

"Psha!" exclaimed Fullaway. "I suppose you think Delkin, who could buy up the best jeweller's shop in London or Paris and throw its contents to the street children to play with—"

"What is it that's in your mind, Mr. Van Koon?" asked Allerdyke, interrupting Fullaway's eloquence. "You've some theory?"

"Well, I don't know about theory," answered Van Koon, "but I guess I've got some natural common sense. If Fullaway there thinks I'm suggesting that Delkin organized a grand conspiracy to rob James Allerdyke, Fullaway's wrong—I'm not. What I am suggesting, and have been suggesting this last three days, is that Delkin should be asked a plain and simple question, which is this—did he ever tell anybody of this proposed deal? If so—whom did he tell? And if that isn't business," concluded Van Koon, "then I don't know business when I see it!"

"What's your objection?" asked Allerdyke, looking across at Fullaway. "What objection can you have?"

Fullaway shook his head.

"Oh, I don't know!" he said. "Except that it seems immaterial, and that I don't want to bother Delkin. I'm hoping that these jewels will be found, and that I'll be able to complete the transaction, and—besides, I don't believe for one instant that Delkin would tell anybody. I only had two interviews with Delkin—one at his hotel, one here. He understood the affair was an entirely private and secret transaction."

Mrs. Marlow suddenly raised her head, and spoke quickly.

"You're forgetting something, Mr. Fullaway," she said. "You had a letter from Mr. Delkin confirming the provisional agreement, which was that he should have the first option of buying the Princess Nastirsevitch's jewels, then being brought by Mr. James Allerdyke from Russia."

"True—true!" exclaimed Fullaway, clapping a hand to his forehead. "So I had! I'd forgotten that. But, after all, it was purely a private letter from Delkin, and—"

"No," interrupted Mrs. Marlow. "It was written and signed by Mr. Delkin's secretary. So that the secretary knew of the transaction."

Van Koon shook his head and glanced at Allerdyke.

"There you are!" he said. "The secretary knew—Delkin's secretary! How do we know that Delkin's secretary—?"

"Oh, that's all rot, Van Koon!" exclaimed Fullaway testily. "Delkin's secretary, Merrifield, has been with him for years to my knowledge, and—"

But Allerdyke had suddenly risen and was picking up his hat from a side table. He turned to Fullaway as he put it on.

"I quite agree with Mr. Van Koon," he said, "and as I'm James Allerdyke's cousin and his executor, I'm going to step round and see this Mr. Delkin at his hotel—the Cecil, you said. It's no use trifling, Fullaway—Delkin knew, and Mrs. Marlow now tells us his secretary knew.

All right!—my job is to see, in person, anybody who knew. Then, maybe, I myself shall get to know."

Van Koon, too, rose.

"I know Delkin, slightly," he said. "I'll go with you."

At that, Fullaway jumped up, evidently annoyed and unwilling, but prepared to act against his own wishes.

"Oh, all right, all right!" he exclaimed. "In that case we'll all go. Come on—it's only across the Strand. Back after lunch, Mrs. Marlow, if anybody wants me."

The three men marched out, and left the pretty secretary standing by the table from which they had all risen. She stood there for a few minutes in deep thought—stood until a single stroke from the clock on the mantelpiece roused her. At that she walked into the outer office, put on her coat and hat, and, leaving the hotel, went sharply off in the direction of Arundel Street.

27. THE MILLIONAIRE, THE STRANGER, AND THE PRINCESS

As the three men threaded their way through the crowded Strand and approached the Hotel Cecil, Fullaway suddenly drew their attention to a private automobile which was turning in at the entrance to the courtyard.

"There's Delkin, in his car," he exclaimed, "and, great Scott, there's our Princess with him—Nastirsevitch! But who's the other man? Looks like a compatriot of ours, Van Koon, eh?"

Van Koon, who had been staring about him as they crossed over from the corner of Wellington Street, turned and glanced at the occupants of the car. Allerdyke was looking there, too. He had never seen Delkin as yet, and he was curious to set eyes on a man who had made several millions out of canning meat. He had no very clear conception of American millionaires, and he scarcely knew what he expected to see. But there were two men in the car with the Princess Nastirsevitch, and they were both middle-aged. One man was a tall, handsome, military-looking fellow, dressed in grey tweeds and wearing a Homburg hat of light grey with a darker band; his upturned, grizzled moustache gave him a smart, rather aggressive appearance; the monocle in his eye added to his general impressiveness. The other man was not particularly impressive—a medium sized, rather plump little man, with a bland, smiling countenance and mild eyes beaming through gold-rimmed spectacles; he sat with his back to the driver, and was just then leaning forward to tell something to the Princess and the man in the Homburg hat who were bending towards him and, smiling at what he said.

"Which of 'em is Delkin, then?" asked Allerdyke as the automobile swept into the courtyard. "Big or little?"

"The little fellow with the spectacles," replied Fullaway. "Quiet, unobtrusive man, Delkin—but cute as they're made. Know the other man, Van Koon?"

Van Koon had twisted round and was staring back in the direction from which they had come, he shook his head, a little absent-mindedly.

"Not from Adam," he answered, "but there's a man— Bostonian—just gone along there that I do know and want to see badly. Wait a bit for me in the courtyard there, Fullaway—shan't be long."

He turned as he spoke, and darted off through the crowd, unusually dense at that moment because of the luncheon hour. Fullaway, making no comment, walked forward into the courtyard and looked about him. Suddenly he nodded his head towards a far corner.

"There's Delkin and the Princess, and the man who was with them, sitting at a table over there," he said. "I didn't know that Delkin and the Princess were acquainted. But then, of course, they're both staying in this hotel, and they're both American. Well, shall we go to them now, Allerdyke, or shall we sit down here and wait a bit for Van Koon?"

"We'll wait," replied Allerdyke. He dropped into a chair and drew out his cigarette-case. "Have a drink while we're waiting?" he suggested, beckoning a waiter who was passing. "What's it to be?"

"Oh—something small, then," said Fullaway. "Dry sherry. Better bring three—Van Koon won't be long."

But the minutes passed and Van Koon was still absent. Ten minutes more went, and still he did not come. And Fullaway pulled out his watch with an air of annoyance.

"Too bad of Van Koon," he said. "Time's going, and I know Delkin lunches at two o'clock. Come on, Allerdyke," he continued, rising, "we'll go over to Delkin. If Van Koon comes, he'll find us. He's probably gone off with that other man, though—he's an absent-minded chap in some things, and too much given to the affair of the moment. Come on—I'll introduce you."

The Chicago millionaire, once put in possession of Allerdyke's name, looked at him with manifest curiosity, and motioned him and Fullaway to take seats with himself and his two companions.

"We were just talking of your case, Mr. Allerdyke," he said quietly. "The Princess, of course, has told me about you. Fullaway, I don't know if you know this gentleman— his name's well enough known, anyway. This gentleman is Mr. Chilverton, the famous New York detective. Chilverton—Mr. Fullaway, Mr. Allerdyke."

Fullaway and Allerdyke both looked at the man in the Homburg hat with great interest as they shook hands with him. Fullaway at any rate knew of his world-wide reputation; Allerdyke faintly remembered that he had heard of him in connection with some great criminal affair.

"Been telling Mr. Chilverton about our business, Mr. Delkin?" asked Fullaway pleasantly. "Asking his expert advice?"

"I've told him no more than what he could read for himself in the newspapers," answered Delkin. "He's got stuff of his own to attend to, here in London. About our affair now, as you call it, Fullaway. It's not my affair, or I guess I'd have been more into it by this time. The Princess here thinks things are going real slow, and so do I. What do you think, Mr. Allerdyke!"

"It's a case in which things go slow of sheer necessity," replied Allerdyke. "It's a case of widespread ramifications—to use a long word. But—we keep having developments, Mr. Delkin. There's been one this morning. We came to see you about it—and perhaps you'll let

Fullaway tell!—he'll put things into fewer words than I should."

"Sure!" answered the millionaire. "Go ahead, Fullaway—we're all interested."

Fullaway briefly told the story of the discovery at the hotel in the Docks that morning, and explained the deductions which had been made from it. He detailed the connection of Ebers, alias Federman or Herman, with himself, and reported the conversation which had just taken place at his own rooms. And then he turned to Allerdyke, with an expressive gesture.

"I'll let Allerdyke say why we came here," he said. "It was his idea and Van Koon's—not mine. Your turn, Allerdyke."

"I shan't be slow to take it," responded Allerdyke, stirring himself. "I'm one business man—Mr. Delkin's another. I only want to ask you, Mr. Delkin, if you ever talked of this jewel transaction to anybody beyond your own secretary? It's a plain question, and you'll understand why I ask it."

"Of course," replied Delkin genially. "Quite right to ask. I can answer it in one word. No! As to telling my secretary, Merrifield, who's been with me twelve years, and is a thoroughly trustworthy man, I merely told him sufficient for him to write and send that formal letter—he knew, and knows (at least, not from me) no details. No, sir!—never a word from me got about—not even to my own daughter. Of course, the Princess here and myself have discussed matters—since she came. And now that you're here, Fullaway, I'll tell you what I think—straight out. I think this affair has all been planned from your own office!"

Fullaway flushed and sat up in an attitude of sudden indignation.

"Oh, come, Mr. Delkin!" he exclaimed. "I—"

"Go softly, young man." said Delkin. "I mean no harm to you, and no reflections on you. But you know, I've been in your office a few times, and I have eyes in my head.

What do you know about that fascinating young woman you have there? I'm a pretty good judge of human nature and character, and I should say that young lady is as clever and deep as they make 'em. Who is she? There's one thing sure from what you've just told us, Fullaway— you let her know all your business secrets."

Fullaway made no attempt to conceal his chagrin and vexation.

"I've had Mrs. Marlow in my employ for three years," he answered. "She came to me with excellent testimonials and references. I've just as much reason to trust her as you have to trust Merrifield. If she'd been untrustworthy, she could have robbed or defrauded me many a time over; she—"

"Did she ever have the chance of getting hold of a quarter of a million's worth of jewels before?" asked Delkin with a shrewd glance at Allerdyke. "Come, now! Even the most trusted people fall before a very big temptation. All business folk know that. What's Mr. Allerdyke think?"

Allerdyke was not going to say what he thought. He was wondering if Fullaway knew what he knew—that Mrs. Marlow was also Miss Slade, that she had some relations with a man who also bore two different names, that her actions were somewhat suspicious. But that was not the time to say all this—he said something non-committal instead.

"There seems to be no doubt that the knowledge that my cousin was carrying the jewels leaked out here—and from Fullaway's office," he answered.

"Through this fellow Ebers!" broke in Fullaway excitedly. "It's all rot to think that Mrs. Marlow had anything to do with it! Great Scott!—do any of you mean to suggest that she engineered several murders, and—"

Delkin laughed—a soft, cynical laugh.

"You're lumping a lot of big stuff altogether, Fullaway," he remarked drily. "Do you know what I think

of all this business? I think that everybody's jumping at
conclusions. There are lots of questions, problems,
difficulties that want solving and answering before I come
to any conclusion. I'll tell you what they are," he went on
bending forward in his lounge chair and looking from one
to the other of the faces around him and beginning to tick
off his points on the tips of his fingers. "Listen! One—Was
James Allerdyke really murdered, or did he die a natural
death? Two—Had James Allerdyke those jewels in his
possession when he entered that S—— Hotel at Hull!
Three—Has the robbery, or disappearance, of the
Princess Nastirsevitch's jewels anything whatever to do
with the theft of Mademoiselle de Longarde's property?
Four—Was that man Lydenberg shot in Hull as a result
of some connection with either, or both, of these affairs, or
was he murdered for private or political reasons? Let me
get a clear understanding of everything that's behind all
these problems," he concluded, with a knowing smile,
"and I'll tell you something!"

"You think it possible that the Nastirsevitch affair is
the work of one lot, and the Lennard affair the work of
another?" asked Allerdyke, thoughtfully. "In that case, I'll
ask you a question, Mr. Delkin. How do you account for
the fact that my cousin James, the Frenchwoman, Lisette
Beaurepaire, and his valet, Ebers, or Federman, or
Herman, were all found dead under similar
circumstances? Come, now!"

"Aye, but were they?" demanded Delkin, clapping his
hands together with a smile of triumphantly suggestive
doubt. "Were they? You don't know—and the expert
analysts don't know yet, and perhaps never will. I'll grant
you that there's a strong probability that Ebers and the
French maid were victims of the same murderer; but that
doesn't prove that your cousin was. No, sir!—my
impression is that everybody is taking too much for
granted. And whether it offends you or not, Fullaway—
and my intention's good—you ought to make drastic

researches into your office procedure—you know what I mean. The leakage of the secret, sir, came from—there!"

Fullaway rose.

"Well, I shan't do any good by sitting here," he said, a little huffily. "If I'm going to begin those drastic researches I'd better begin. Coming, Allerdyke?"

The two men walked away together after taking leave of the millionaire and the Princess. But before they were clear of the courtyard, Chilverton caught them and tapped Fullaway on the elbow.

"Say!" he said confidentially. "You won't mind my asking you—who's this Van Koon that you mentioned?"

"Man from our side who's been here in London all this spring," answered Fullaway promptly. "He was coming with Allerdyke and me just now, but he turned back—just when you and Delkin drove in here."

Chilverton gave Fullaway a quick look.

"Did he see me?" he asked.

"Sure!" replied Fullaway. "Asked who you were—or I did."

"You did," remarked Allerdyke. "Then he went off."

"Describe him," said Chilverton. He listened attentively while Fullaway gave him a sketch of Van Koon's appearance. "Um!" he continued. "Do you mind my walking to your hotel with you? I believe I know that man, and I'd like to see him."

A hall-porter was standing at the door of the Waldorf who had been there when the three men went out together at one o'clock. Fullaway beckoned him.

"Seen anything of Mr. Van Koon?" he asked.

"Mr. Van Koon?—yes, sir. He came back a few minutes after you and Mr. Allerdyke and he had gone out, got a suit-case from upstairs, left word that he'd be away for the night, and went off in a taxi, sir," answered the man. "Seemed to be in a great hurry, sir!"

Before Fullaway could speak, Chilverton seized the hall-porter's arm. "Did you hear him give the cab-driver any direction?"

"Yes, sir," replied the man promptly. "St. Pancras Station, sir."

Without a word, Chilverton turned, hurried out to the pavement, and leapt into a taxi-cab that was standing there unengaged. In another instant the taxi-cab was off, and Allerdyke and Fullaway turned to each other. Then Allerdyke laughed.

"That's why Van Koon turned back, Fullaway," he said in a low voice. "He recognized Chilverton. Now, then—why did that recognition make him run? And—who is he?"

28. The First Pursuit

For a moment Fullaway stood in the doorway of the hotel, staring towards the mouth of Kingsway, around the corner of which Chilverton's cab had already disappeared. Then he turned, gave Allerdyke a look of absolute non-comprehension, and with a sudden gesture, as of surrender to circumstances, walked into the hotel and made for the stairs.

"That licks everything!" he muttered, as he and Allerdyke went up to the first floor. "Tell you what it is, Allerdyke—my poor brain is getting into a whirl! We've had quite enough excitement this morning in all conscience, and now this comes on top of it. Now, how in creation do you explain this last occurrence?"

Allerdyke laughed cynically.

"I don't know so much of the world as you do, Fullaway," he said, "but I don't think this needs much explanation. When a man makes himself suddenly scarce at sight of a well-known detective, I should say that man knows the detective wants him—badly! My impression is that at this moment your friend Van Koon is running away from Chilverton, and Chilverton's going hot-foot after him. And—"

They were at that moment passing the room which Van Koon had occupied, and Allerdyke suddenly remembered the occasion on which he had seen Mrs. Marlow steal out of it, suspiciously and furtively, and when its proper tenant was away. He had carefully abstained from telling Fullaway about that little incident, preferring to wait until events had further developed. Should he tell him now—now that there seemed to be evidence that Van Koon himself was a doubtful character? He hesitated—and while he hesitated

Fullaway strode on, flung open his office door, turned to the letter-box at the back, and took out some letters and a telegram. He tore the telegram open, and the next instant flung it on the table with a fierce exclamation.

"Damn it all, Allerdyke!" he said, waving an indignant hand at the bit of pink paper. "What in the name of all that's wicked is the meaning of that? Read it—read!"

Allerdyke picked the telegram up and read it aloud.

"Regret shall be unable to return to office for day or two; called away on extremely urgent private business.— MARLOW."

He laughed again as he put the telegram back and turned to Fullaway, who, hands plunged deep in pockets and black of countenance, was stamping up and down the room.

"Um!" said Allerdyke. "Um! Now, in my humble opinion, Fullaway, that's a good deal queerer than the Van Koon incident. For look you here—your secretary was talking to us in your room there at less than five minutes to one, and we left her here when we went out on the stroke of one. And yet—look at the wire!—she handed that in at the East Strand post office within ten minutes after we'd left her! What do you make of that?"

"Damnation!" exclaimed Fullaway. "How the blazes do I know what to make of it! I seem to be surrounded with—God knows what hellish mysteries! Allerdyke, is there a regular devil's conspiracy, or—what is there?"

Allerdyke made a show of looking at the telegram again. In reality, he was considering matters. Should he tell Fullaway what he knew? He was more than a little tempted to do so. But his natural sense of caution and reserve stopped the words before they reached his tongue, and he took another tack.

"You said just now, in talking to Delkin, that you'd the greatest confidence in this Mrs. Marlow, and had the best references with her, Fullaway," he remarked. "What references?"

"Good business references!" answered Fullaway excitedly. "The best! Firms of high standing in the City. Couldn't have had better. Go and ask any of them about her—I'll lay my last dollar they will say the same. Capital secretary—clever woman—thoroughly trustworthy!"

"What do you know about her private life?" asked Allerdyke.

"What the deuce has the woman's private life to do with me?" snapped Fullaway. "I know nothing. So long as she comes here at ten, stops till five, and does her duty— hang her private life!"

"Do you know where she lives?" asked Allerdyke imperturbably. "But of course you do."

"Then I don't!" retorted Fullaway. "Somewhere up town, I believe—West End somewhere. I don't know. I've nothing to do with her private affairs. I never have had anything to do with the private affairs of any employee of mine."

"She makes her private affairs have something to do with you though," said Allerdyke, tapping the telegram significantly. "But, in my opinion, that wire's nothing but an excuse. What're you going to do?"

"Oh, I don't know!" exclaimed Fullaway. "I'm about sick of the whole thing."

Allerdyke pulled out his watch.

"I must go," he said. "I've a business appointment. I'll see you later."

Fullaway made no reply, and Allerdyke left him, went downstairs and sought Gaffney, whom, having found, he led outside to the street.

"How soon can you lay hands on that brother of yours?" he asked.

"Twenty minutes—in a cab, sir," replied Gaffney.

"Get a cab, then, find him, and drive, both of you, to the warehouse," commanded Allerdyke. "You'll find me there."

He himself got a cab, too, and went off to Gresham Street, more puzzled and doubtful than ever. He closeted himself with Ambler Appleyard and told him all the details of the eventful morning, and the manager listened in silence, taking everything in and making his own mental notes. And with his usual acuteness of perception he quickly separated the important from the momentarily unimportant.

"You don't want to bother your head about what Mr. Delkin says just now, Mr. Allerdyke," he said, when Allerdyke had brought this story to an end. "Never mind his theories—there may be a lot in 'em, and there mayn't be any more than his personal opinion in 'em. Never mind, too, what Chilverton wants with Van Koon. Nor if there's any connection between Van Koon and Miss Slade, or Mrs. Marlow. The thing to do is to find—her!"

"You think she's hooked it?" said Allerdyke.

"I should say that something said by some of you at that talk this morning in Fullaway's room has startled her into action," answered Appleyard. "Now let's get at facts. You say she sent that wire from the East Strand post Office within ten minutes of your leaving her? Very well—I should say she was on her way to Arundel Street to see Rayner, alias Ramsay. I wish we'd had a constant watch kept on him. But we'll soon repair that if you've sent for young Gaffney."

The two Gaffneys arrived at that moment and Appleyard, after some further talk, assigned them their duties. Gaffney, the chauffeur, was to go at once and get himself a room at an inn in close proximity to the Pompadour Hotel, so that he would be at Appleyard's disposal at any hour of the coming evening and night. Albert Gaffney, the clerk, was to devote himself to watching Rayner. He was to follow Rayner wherever Rayner went from the time of his leaving Clytemnestra House that afternoon—even if Rayner should leave town by motor or by train he was to follow. For, as Appleyard sagely observed, it was not likely that Mrs. Marlow, alias

Miss Slade, would return to the Pompadour Hotel that night if her fears had been aroused by what had taken place that morning, and it was a reasonable presumption that if she and Rayner were in league she would have communicated with him on leaving Fullaway's office, and that they would meet again somewhere before the day was over.

"The only thing now," said Appleyard, when the two Gaffneys had been presented with funds sufficient to carry each through all possible immediate emergencies, "is to arrange for a meeting to-night. There are two matters we want to be certain about. First, if Albert Gaffney witnesses any meeting between Rayner and Miss Slade, and, in that case, if he can tell us where they go and what they do. Second, if they both return, or either of them returns to the Pompadour to-night. So it had better be near the Pompadour—somewhere in that district, anyhow. Can you suggest any place?" he continued, turning to the chauffeur. "You know that district well, don't you?"

"Tell you the very spot, sir," answered Gaffney promptly. "Lancaster Gate itself, sir. Close by there, convenient pub, sir—stands back a bit from the road. Bar-parlour, sir—quiet corners. What time, sir?"

Appleyard fixed half-past eleven. By that time, he said, he should know if Mr. Rayner and Miss Slade had returned to the Pompadour; by that time, too, Albert Gaffney would be in a position to report his own doings and progress. And so the two Gaffneys went off on their respective missions, and Allerdyke looked at his manager and made a grimace.

"It's like a lot of blind men seeking for something they couldn't see if it was shoved under their very noses, Ambler!" he said cynically. "Is it any good?"

"Maybe," replied Appleyard. "That Albert Gaffney's a smart chap—he'll not lose sight of Rayner once he begins to track him. And I'm certain as certain can be that if

Miss Slade's in a hole it's Rayner she'll turn to. Well—we can only wait now. What're you going to do, Mr. Allerdyke?"

"Let's have a bit of a relief," answered, Allerdyke suddenly. "Let's dine together somewhere and go to a theatre or something until it's time to keep this appointment. And not a word more of the whole thing till then!"

"You forget that I've got to look in at the Pompadour last thing to see if those two are there as usual," remarked Appleyard. "But that'll only take a few minutes—I can call there on our way to the rendezvous. All right—no more of it until half-past eleven, then."

Albert Gaffney was already in a quiet corner of the bar-parlour of the appointed meeting-place when the other three arrived there. Appleyard had already ascertained that neither Rayner nor Miss Slade had returned to the Pompadour; Gaffney, the chauffeur, who had been keeping an eye on the exterior of that establishment, had nothing to tell. And Albert's face was somewhat dismal, and his eye inclined to something like an aggrieved surliness, as he joined the new-comers and answered their first question.

"It's not my fault, gentlemen," he whispered, bending towards the others over the little table at which they were all seated. "But the truth is—I've been baulked! At the last moment as you may term it. Just when things were getting really interesting!"

"Have you seen—anything?" asked Appleyard.

"I'll give you it in proper order, sir," replied Albert Gaffney. "I've seen both of 'em—followed 'em, until this confounded accident happened. This is the story of it. I kept watch there, outside C. House—you know where I mean—till near on to six o'clock. Then he came out. But he didn't get into his motor, though it was waiting for him. He sent it away. Then he walked to the Temple Station, and I heard him book for Cannon Street. So did I, and followed him. He got out at Cannon Street and went up into the main line station and to the bookstall. There he met her—she was waiting. They talked a bit, walking about; then they went into the hotel. I had an idea that perhaps they were going to dine there, so as I was togged up for any eventualities, I followed 'em in. They did dine there—so did I, keeping an eye on 'em. They sat some time over and after their dinner, as if they were waiting for something or somebody. At last a man—better-class commercial traveller-looking sort of man—came in and went up to them. He sat down and had a glass of wine, and they all three talked—very confidential talk, you could see. At last they all left and went down to the yard outside the station and got into a taxi-cab—all three. I got another, gave the driver a quiet hint as to what I was after, and told him to keep the other cab in view. So he did—for a time. They went first to a little restaurant near Liverpool Street Station—she and the commercial-looking chap got out and went in; R. stopped in the cab. The other two came back after a bit with another man—similar sort—and all three joined R. Then they went off towards Aldgate way—and we were keeping nicely behind 'em when all of a sudden a blooming 'bus came to grief right between us and them, and blocked the traffic! And though I nearly broke my neck in trying to get through and spot them, it was no use. They'd clean disappeared. But!—I've got the number of the cab they took from Cannon Street."

Appleyard nodded approval.

"Good!" he said. "That's something, Gaffney—a good deal. We can work on from that."

"Well?" he continued, turning to Allerdyke. "I think there's nothing else we can do to-night? We'd better meet, all of us, at Gresham Street, at, say, ten to-morrow morning; then I shall be able to say if they return to the Pompadour to-night. It's my impression they won't—but we shall see."

Allerdyke presently drove him to his hotel, wondering all the way what these last doings might really mean.

They were surprising enough, but there was another surprise awaiting him. As he walked into the Waldorf the hall-porter stopped him.

"There's a gentleman for you, sir, in the waiting-room," he said. "Been waiting a good hour. Name of Chettle."

29. The Parcel From Hull

Chettle sat alone in the waiting-room, a monument of patient resignation to his fate. His hands were bunched on the head of his walking-stick, his chin propped on his hands; his eyes were bent on a certain spot on the carpet with a fixed stare. And when Allerdyke entered he sprang up as if roused from a fitful slumber.

"I should ha' been asleep in another minute, Mr. Allerdyke," he said apologetically. "Been waiting over an hour, sir—and I'm dog-tired. I've been at it, hard at it! every minute since I left you. And—I had to come. I've news."

"Come up," said Allerdyke. "I've news, too—it's been naught else but news all day. You haven't seen Fullaway while you've been waiting?"

"Seen nobody but the hotel folks," answered the detective. He followed Allerdyke up to his private sitting-room and sighed wearily as he dropped into a chair. "I'm dog-tired," he repeated. "Fair weary!"

"Have a drink," said Allerdyke, setting out his decanter and a syphon. "Take a stiff 'un—I'll have one myself. I'm tired, too. I wouldn't like this game to be on long, Chettle—it's too exhausting. But, by the Lord Harry!—I believe it's coming to an end at last!"

The detective, who had gladly helped himself to Allerdyke's whisky, took a long pull at his glass and sighed with relief.

"I believe so myself, Mr. Allerdyke," he said. "I do, indeed!—things are clearing, sir, though Heaven knows they're thick enough still. You say you've fresh news!"

Allerdyke lighted a cigar and pushed the box to his guest.

"Your news first," he said. "I daresay it's a bit out of the complete web—let's see if we can fit it in."

"It's this," answered Chettle, pulling his chair nearer to the table at which he and his host sat. "When I got back to Hull they told me at the police headquarters that a young man had been in two or three times, while I was away, asking if he could see the London detective who was down about the Station Hotel affair. They told him I'd gone up to town again, and tried to find out what he wanted, but he wouldn't tell them anything—said he'd either see me or go up to London himself. So then they let him know I was coming back, and told him he'd probably find me there at noon to-day. And at noon to-day he turns up at the police-station—a young fellow about twenty-five or so, who looked like what he was, a clerk. A very cute, sharp chap he was, the sort that's naturally keen about his own interests—name of Martindale—and before he'd say a word he wanted to see my credentials, and made me swear to treat what he said as private, and then he pulled out a copy of that reward bill of yours, and wanted to know a rare lot about that, all of which amounted to wanting to find out what chance he had of getting hold of some of the fifty thousand, if not all. And," continued Chettle with a laugh, "I'd a lot of talking and explaining and wheedling to do before he'd tell anything."

"Had he aught to tell?" asked Allerdyke. "So many of 'em think they have, and then they haven't."

"Oh, he'd something to tell!" replied Chettle. "Right enough, he'd a good deal to tell. This—he told me at last, as if every word he let out was worth a ransom, that he was a parcels office clerk in the North Eastern Railway Station at Hull, and that since the 13th of May until the day before yesterday he'd been away in the North of Scotland on his holidays—been home to his people, in fact—he is a Scotsman, which, of course, accounts for his keenness about the money. Now, then—on the night of May 12th—the night, as you know, Mr. Allerdyke, of your cousin's supposed murder, but anyway, of his arrival at

Hull—this young man Martindale was on duty in the parcels office till a very late hour. About ten to a quarter past ten, as near as he could recollect, a gentleman came into the parcels office, carrying a small, square parcel, done up in brown paper and sealed in several places with black wax. He wanted to know when the next express would be leaving for London, and if he could send the parcel by it. Martindale told him there would be an express leaving for Selby very shortly, and there would be a connection there for a Great Northern express to King's Cross. The gentleman then wanted to know what time his parcel would be likely to be delivered in London if he sent it by that train. Martindale told him that as near as he could say it would be delivered by noon on the next morning, and added that he could, by paying an extra fee, have it specially registered and delivered. The gentleman at once acceded to this, handed the parcel over, paid for it, and left. And in a few minutes after that, Martindale himself gave the parcel to the guard of the outgoing train."

Chettle paused for a moment, and took a reflective pull at his glass.

"Now, then," he went on, after an evident recollecting of his facts, "Martindale, of course, never saw the gentleman again, and dismissed such a very ordinary matter from his mind. Early next morning he went off on his holiday—where he went, right away up in Sutherland, papers were few and far between. He only heard mere bits of news about all this affair. But when he got back he turned up the Hull newspapers, and became convinced that the man who sent that parcel was—your cousin!"

"Aye!" said Allerdyke, nodding his head. "Aye! I expected that."

"He was sure it was your cousin," continued Chettle, "from the description of him in the papers, and from one or two photos of him that had appeared, though, as you

know, Mr. Allerdyke, those were poor things. But to make
sure, I showed him the photo which is inside Lydenberg's
watch-case. 'That's the man!' he said at once. 'I should
have known him again anywhere—I'd a particularly good
look at him.' Very well—that established who the sender
of the parcel was. Now then, the next thing was—to
whom was it sent. Well, this Martindale had copied down
the name and address from the station books, and he
handed me the slip of paper. Can you make any guess at
it, Mr. Allerdyke?"

"Damn guess-work!" replied Allerdyke. "Speak out!"

Chettle leaned nearer, with an instinctive glance at
the door. He lowered his voice to a whisper.

"That parcel was addressed to Franklin Fullaway,
Esq., The Waldorf Hotel, Aldwych, London," he said.
"There!"

Allerdyke slowly rose from his seat, stared at his
visitor, half-moved across the floor, as if he had some
instinctive notion of going somewhere—and then
suddenly sat down again.

"Aye!" he said. "Aye!—but was it ever delivered?"

"I'm coming to that," replied Chettle. "That, of course,
is the big thing—the prime consideration. I heard all this
young fellow Martindale had to tell—nothing much more
than that, except small details as to what would be the
likely progress of the parcel, and then I gave him strict
instructions to keep his own counsel until I saw him
again—after which I caught the afternoon train to town.
Martindale had told me where the parcel would be
delivered from, so as soon as I arrived at King's Cross I
went to the proper place. I had to tell 'em, of course, who I
was, and what I was after, and to produce my credentials
before they turned up their books and papers to trace the
delivery of the parcel. That, of course, wasn't a long or
difficult matter, as I had the exact date—May 13th. They
soon put the delivery sheet of that particular morning
before me. And there it all was—"

"And—it was delivered to and received by—who?" broke in Allerdyke eagerly. "Who, man?"

"Signed for by Mary Marlow for Franklin Fullaway," answered Chettle in the same low tones. "Delivered—here—about half-past twelve. So—there you are! That is—if you know where we are!"

Allerdyke, whose cigar had gone out, relighted it with a trembling hand.

"My God!" he said in a fierce, concentrated voice as he flung the match away. "This is getting—you're sure there was no mistaking the signature?" he went on, interrupting himself. "No mistake about it?"

"It was a woman's writing, and an educated woman's writing, anyway," said Chettle. "And plain enough. But there was one thing that rather struck me and that they couldn't explain, though they said I could have it explained by inquiry of the clerk who had the books in charge on May 13th and the boy who actually delivered the parcel—neither of 'em was about this evening."

"What?" demanded Allerdyke.

"Why, this," answered Chettle. "The parcel had evidently been signed for twice. The line on which the signatures were placed had two initials in pencil on it—scribbled hurriedly. The initials were 'F.F.' Over that was the other in ink—what I tell you: Mary Marlow for Frank Fullaway."

Allerdyke let his mind go back to the events of May 13th.

"You say the parcel was delivered here at twelve-thirty noon on May 13th?" he said presently. "Of course, Fullaway wasn't here then. He'd set off to me at Hull two or three hours before that. He joined me at Hull soon after two that day. And what I'm wondering is—does he know of that parcel's arrival here in his absence. Did he ever get it? If he did, why has he never mentioned it to me? Coming, as it did, from—James!"

"There's a much more important question than that, Mr. Allerdyke," said Chettle. "This—what was in that parcel?"

Allerdyke started. So far he had been concentrating on the facts given him by the detective—further he had not yet gone.

"Why!" he asked, a sudden suspicion beginning to dawn on him. "Good God!—you don't suggest—"

"My belief, Mr. Allerdyke," said Chettle, quietly and emphatically, "is that the parcel contained the Russian lady's jewels! I do believe it—and I'll lay anything I'm right, too."

Allerdyke shook his head.

"Nay, nay!" he said incredulously. "I can't think that James would send a quarter of a million pounds' worth of jewels in a brown paper parcel by train! Come, now!"

Chettle shook his head, too—but in contradiction, "I've known of much stranger things than that, Mr. Allerdyke," he said confidently. "Very much stranger things. Your cousin, according to your account of him, was an uncommonly sharp man. He was quick at sizing up things and people. He was the sort—as you've represented him to me—that was what's termed fertile in resource. Now, I've been theorizing a bit as I came up in the train; one's got to in my line, you know. Supposing your cousin got an idea that thieves were on his track?—supposing he himself fancied that there was danger in that hotel at Hull? What would occur to him but to get rid of his valuable consignment, as we'll call it? And what particular danger was there in sending a very ordinary-looking parcel as he did? The thing's done every day—by train or post every day valuable parcels of diamonds, for instance, are sent between London and Paris. The chances of that parcel being lost between Hull and this hotel were—infinitesimal! I honestly believe, sir, that those jewels were in that parcel—sent to be safe."

"In that case you'd have thought he'd have wired Fullaway of their dispatch," said Allerdyke.

"How do we know that he didn't intend to, first thing in the morning?" asked Chettle. "He probably did intend to—but he wasn't there to do it in the morning, poor gentleman! No—and now the thing is, Mr. Allerdyke—prompt action! What do you think, sir?"

"You mean—go and tell everything to your people at headquarters?" asked Allerdyke.

"I shall have to," answered Chettle. "There's no option for me—now. What I meant was—are you prepared to tell them all you know?"

"Yes!" replied Allerdyke. "At least, I will be in the morning—first thing. I'll just tell you how things have gone to-day. Now," he continued, when he had given Chettle a full account of the recent happenings, "you stay here to-night—you can have my chauffeur's room, next to mine—and in the morning I'll telephone to Appleyard to meet us outside of New Scotland Yard, and after a word or two with him, we'll see your chief, and then—"

Chettle shook his head.

"If that woman got a night's start, Mr. Allerdyke—" he began.

"Can't help it now," said Allerdyke decisively. "Besides, you don't know what Appleyard mayn't have learned during the night."

But when Appleyard met them in Whitehall next morning, in response to Allerdyke's telephone summons, his only news was that neither Rayner nor Miss Slade had returned to the Pompadour, and without another word Allerdyke motioned Chettle to lead the way to the man in authority.

30.. THE PACKET IN THE SAFE

It was to a hastily called together gathering of high police officials that the three visitors told all they knew. One after another they related their various stories— Chettle of his doings and discoveries at Hull, Allerdyke of what had gone on at the hotel, Appleyard of the mysterious double identity of the woman who was Miss Slade in one place and Mrs. Marlow in another. The officials listened quietly and absorbedly, rarely interrupting the narrators except to ask a searching question. And in the end they talked together apart, after which all went away except the man who had kept his hands on the reins from the beginning. He turned to his visitors with an air of decision.

"Well, of course, there's but one thing to be done, now," he said. "We must get a warrant for this woman's arrest at once. We must also get a search warrant and examine her belongings at that private hotel you've told us of, Mr. Appleyard. All that shall be done immediately. But first I want you to tell me one or two things. What are those two men you spoke of doing—the Gaffneys?"

"One of them, the chauffeur, is hanging about the Pompadour," replied Appleyard. "The other—Albert—has gone down to Cannon Street to see if he can trace the driver of the taxi-cab in which Rayner and Miss Slade drove away from there last night."

"He'll do no harm in trying to find that out," observed the chief. "But I should like to see him—I want to ask some questions about the man who joined those two after dinner at Cannon Street last night, and the other man whom he saw them take up near Liverpool Street Station. Will he keep himself in touch with your warehouse in Gresham Street?"

"Sure to," answered Appleyard.

"Then just telephone to your people there, and tell them to tell him, if he comes in asking for you, to come along and seek you here," said the chief. "I'm afraid I can't spare either you or Mr. Allerdyke, for your joint information'll be wanted presently for these warrants, and when we've got them I want you to go with me—both of you—to the Pompadour."

"You're going to search?" asked Allerdyke when Appleyard had gone to the telephone. "You think you may find something—there?"

"There's enough evidence to justify a search," answered the chief. "Naturally we want to know all we can. But I should say that if she's mixed up with a gang, and if they've got those jewels through her—as seems uncommonly likely—she'll have been ready for a start at any minute, and the probability is we'll find nothing to help us. The great thing, of course, will be to get hold of the woman herself. It's a most unfortunate thing that Albert Gaffney was stopped from following that cab, last night—I've no opinion, Mr. Allerdyke, of your amateur detective as a rule, but from Mr. Appleyard's account of him, this one seems to have done very well. If we only knew where those two went—"

Appleyard presently came back from the telephone with a face alive with fresh news.

"Albert Gaffney's at the warehouse now," he announced. "I've just had a word with him. He found the taxi-cab driver an hour ago, and he got the information he wanted. And I'm afraid it's—nothing!"

"What is it, anyhow?" asked the chief, with a smile. "Perhaps Albert Gaffney doesn't know its value."

"The man drove them, all four, to the corner of Whitechapel Church," said Appleyard. "There he set them down, and there he left them. That's all."

"Well, that's something, anyway," remarked the chief. "It carries the thing on another stage. Now we'll leave that and attend to our own business."

The Pompadour Private Hotel, like most establishments of its class in Bayswater, was a place of peace and of comparative solitude during the greater part of the day. It was busy enough up to ten o'clock in the morning, and it began to be busy enough again by six o'clock in the evening, but from ten to six more than two-thirds of its denizens were not to be found within its walls. The business man had gone to the City; the professional women had departed to their offices; nothing of humanity but a few elderly widows and spinsters, and an old gentleman or two were left in the various rooms. Everything, therefore, was quiet enough when the chief, accompanied by Chettle, drove up, entered the hall, and asked to see the manager and manageress. As for Allerdyke and Appleyard, who naturally felt considerable dislike to appearing on this particular scene of operations, they were a few hundred yards away, walking about just within the confines of Kensington Gardens, and waiting with more or less patience until the police officials came to them with news of the result of the search.

The manageress of the hotel, a smart lady who wore dignified black gowns all day long—stuff in the morning, and silk at night as if she were a barrister, gradually advancing in grandeur—gazed at the two callers with some suspicion as she ushered them into a private room at the back of her office. The chief, an irreproachably attired man, might have been an army gentleman, she thought; an instinctive wonder rose in her mind as to whether he was not some elderly man of standing who, accompanied by his valet, desired to arrange about a suite of rooms. But his first words gave her an unpleasant shock—she felt for all the world as if somebody had suddenly turned a shower of ice-cold water on her.

"Now, ma'am," said the chief, "your husband the manager is out, and you are in sole and responsible charge, I understand? Pray don't be alarmed—this is nothing that concerns you or your affairs, personally, and we will endeavor to arrange everything so that you have no annoyance. The fact of the case is, we are police officers from the Criminal Investigation Department at New Scotland Yard, and I hold two warrants, just granted by a justice of peace, which are in relation to an inmate of your hotel."

The manageress dropped into a chair and stared at her visitors. Police officers? Warrants? Justices? It was the first time in her highly respectable Bayswater existence that she had ever been brought into contact with these dreadful things. And—an inmate of her establishment!

"Oh, you must be mistaken!" she exclaimed in horror-stricken accents. "A warrant?—that means you want to arrest somebody. An inmate—surely none of my servants—"

"Nothing to do with servants," interrupted the chief. "I said an inmate. Pray don't be alarmed. We want a young lady who is known to you as Miss Mary Slade."

The manageress got up as quickly as she had sat down. For one moment she gazed at her visitor as if he had demanded her very life—the next her lip curled in scorn.

"Miss Slade!" she exclaimed. "Impossible, sir! Miss Slade is a young lady of the very highest respectability— she has resided in this hotel for three years!"

"I am quite prepared to believe that a residence of three months under your roof is enough to confer an irreproachable character on any one, ma'am," replied the chief with a polite smile. "But the fact remains, I have here a warrant for Miss Slade's arrest—never mind on what charge—and here another empowering me to search her room or rooms, her trunk, any property she has in this house. And as time presses I must ask you to give us every facility in the performance of our unpleasant duty. But first a question or two. Miss Slade is not at home?"

"She is not!" replied the manageress emphatically.

"And I think she did not return home last night?" suggested the chief.

"No—she didn't," assented the much perplexed woman. "That's quite true."

"Was that unusual?" asked the chief.

The manageress bit her lip. She did not want to talk, but she had a vague idea that the law compelled speech.

"Well, I don't know what it's all about," she said, "and I don't want to say anything that would bring trouble to Miss Slade, but—it was unusual. For two reasons. I've never known Miss Slade to be away from here for a night except when she went for her usual month's holiday, and I'm surprised that she should stop away without giving me word or sending a telephone message."

"Then her absence was unusual," said the chief smiling. "Now, was there anything else that was unusual, last night—in connection with it?"

The manageress started and looked at her visitor as if she half suspected him of possessing the power of seeing through brick walls.

"Well," she said, a little reluctantly, "there was certainly another of our guests away last night, too—one who scarcely ever is away, and certainly never without letting us know that he's going away. And it's quite true he's a very great friend of Miss Slade's—somebody did say, jokingly, this morning, that perhaps they'd run away and got married."

"Ah!" said the chief, with another smile. "I scarcely think Miss Slade would contract such an important engagement at this moment, she has evidently much else to think about. But now let us see Miss Slade's apartment, if you please, and I shall be obliged to you, ma'am, if you will accompany us."

Not only did the manageress accompany them, but the manager also, who just then arrived and was filled with proper horror to hear that such things were happening. But, being a man, he knew that it is every citizen's duty to assist the police, and he accepted his fate cheerfully, and bade his wife give the gentlemen every help that lay in her power. After which both conducted the two visitors to Miss Slade's room, and became fascinated in acting as spectators.

Miss Slade's apartment was precisely that of any other young lady of refined taste. It was a good-sized, roomy apartment, half bedroom, half sitting-room, and it was bright and gay with books and pictures, and evidences of literary and artistic fancies and leanings. And Chettle, taking a first comprehensive look round, went straight to the mantelpiece and pointed out a certain neatly framed photograph to his superior.

"That's it, sir," he said in a low voice. "That's what the other was taken from. You know, sir—Mr. James A. Mr. Marshall A. said she said she was going to have it framed. Odd, ain't it, sir?—if she really is implicated."

The chief agreed with his man. It was certainly a very odd thing that Miss Slade, alias Mrs. Marlow, if she really had any concern with the murder of James Allerdyke, should put his photograph in a fairly expensive silver frame, and hang it where she could look at it every day. But, as Chettle sagely remarked, you never can tell, and you never can account, and you never know, and meanwhile there was the urgent business on hand.

The business on hand came to nothing. Manager and manageress watched with interested amazement while the two searchers went through everything in that room with a thoroughness and rapidity produced by long practice. They were astounded at the deftness with which the heavy-looking Mr. Chettle explored drawers and trunks, and the military-looking chief peered into wardrobes and cupboards and examined desks and tables. But they were not so much astonished as the two detectives themselves were. For in all that room—always excepting the photograph of James Allerdyke—there was not a single object, a scrap of paper, anything whatever, which connected the Miss Slade of the Pompadour with the Mrs. Marlow of Fullaway's or bore reference to the matter in hand. The searchers finally retired utterly baffled.

"Drawn blank," murmured the chief good-humouredly. He turned to the lookers-on. "I suppose you have nothing of Miss Slade's?" he said. "Nothing confined to your care, eh?"

The manageress glanced at her husband, with whom she had kept up a whispered conversation. The manager nodded.

"Better tell them," he said. "No good keeping anything back."

"Ah!" said the chief. "You have something?"

"A small parcel," admitted the manageress, "which she gave me a few days ago to lock up in our safe. She said it contained something valuable, and she hadn't anything to lock it up in. It's in the safe now."

"I'm afraid we must see it," said the chief.

At the foot of the stairs the hall-porter accosted the party and looked at the chief narrowly.

"Name of Chettle, sir?" he asked. "You're wanted at our telephone—urgent."

The chief motioned to Chettle, who went off with the hall-porter; he himself followed the manageress into her office. She unlocked a safe, rummaged amongst its contents, and handed him a small square parcel, done up in brown paper and sealed with black wax. Before he could open it, Chettle returned, serious and puzzled, and whispered to him. Then, with the shortest of leave-takings, the two officers hurried away from the Pompadour, the chief carrying the little parcel tightly grasped in his right hand.

31. The Hyde Park Tea-House

Once outside the Pompadour Hotel the chief and his subordinate hurried at a great pace towards the Lancaster Gate entrance to Kensington Gardens. And when they had crossed Bayswater Road the superior pulled himself up, took a breath, and looked around him.

"No sign of them yet, Chettle," he observed. "Did he say at once?"

"Said they'd be on their way in two minutes, sir," answered Chettle. "And it wouldn't take them many minutes to run up here."

"I wonder what it's all about?" mused the chief. "Some new development since we left the Yard, of course. Well— I think we may probably find something in this parcel, Chettle, that will surprise us as much as any new development can possibly do. It strikes me—"

"Here they are, sir!" interrupted Chettle. He had lingered on the kerb, looking towards the rise of the road going towards the Marble Arch, and his quick eyes had spotted a closed taxi-cab which came out of the Marlborough Gate at full speed and turned down in their direction. "Blindway and two others," he announced. "Seems to be in force, sir, anyhow!"

The taxi-cab pulled up at the little gate leading into Kensington Gardens by the pumping-station, and Blindway, followed by two other men, hurriedly descended and joined his superior.

"Well, what is it?" demanded the chief. "Something new? And about this affair?"

Blindway made a gesture suggesting that they should enter the Gardens; once within he drew the chief aside, leaving his companions with Chettle.

"About half an hour ago," he said, "a telephone message came on from the City police. They said they'd received some queerish information about this affair, but only particularly about the death of that man down at the hotel in the Docks. Their information ran to this—that the actual murderer has an appointment with some of his associates this afternoon at that tea-house in Hyde Park, and that if the City police would send some plain-clothes men up there he'll be pointed out. So the City lot want us to join them, and I was sent along to meet you here, sir— I've brought those two men and of course there's Chettle. We're all to go along to this tea-house, not in a body, naturally, but to sort of drop in, and to wait events. Of course, sir, that last murder occurred in the City, and so the City police want to come in at it, and—"

"No further details?" asked the chief, obviously puzzled. "Nothing as to who's going to point out the murderer, and so on?"

"Nothing!" replied Blindway. "At least, nothing reported to us. All we've got to do is to be there, on the spot, and to keep our eyes open for the critical moment."

"And what time is the critical moment to be?" asked the chief, a little superciliously. "It all seems remarkably vague, Blindway—why couldn't they give us more news?"

"Don't know, sir—they seemed purposely vague," replied the detective. "However, the time fixed is two o'clock. To be there about two—that was the request—at least four of us."

The chief turned and summoned the other three men.

"You'd better break up," he said. "Two of you approach the place from one way—two from another. It's now a quarter-past one—you've plenty of time. Stroll across the park to this spot—I'll join you by two o'clock. I believe you can get light refreshments at this tea-house; get yourselves something, so as to look like mere loungers— but keep your eyes open."

"Do you want me, sir?" asked Chettle, eyeing the parcel with evident desire to know what mystery it concealed.

"No—you go with Blindway," answered the chief. "He'll tell you what's happened. I must join Mr. Allerdyke and Mr. Appleyard—then we'll come over to you. Don't take any notice of us."

The four detectives went off into Hyde Park, and there separated in couples; the chief turned and went along the straight path which runs parallel with Bayswater Road just within the shrubberies of Kensington Gardens. Presently he caught sight of Allerdyke and Appleyard, who occupied two chairs under a shady hawthorn tree, and he laid hold of another, dragged it to them, and sat down. Each looked a silent inquiry, and the chief, with a smile, held up the parcel.

"Chettle and I," he said, "have, in the presence of the manager and manageress of the Pompadour, made a thorough examination of the room and the belongings of the young lady who resides there under the name of Miss Slade. There is not a jot or tittle of anything there to show that she is also Mrs. Marlow—except one thing. That, Mr. Allerdyke, is the all-important photograph of your cousin James, which is hanging, in a neat silver frame, over her mantelpiece. What do you think of that, gentlemen?"

"Odd!" said Appleyard, after a moment's reflective silence.

"Very queer!" said Allerdyke frowning. "Very queer, indeed—considering."

"Queer and odd!" assented the chief. "As to considering—well, I don't quite know what it is that we are considering. If Miss Slade, alias Mrs. Marlow, is a member of the gang—if there is one—which killed and robbed James Allerdyke, it's a decidedly odd and queer thing that she should frame the victim's portrait and hang it where she'll see it last thing at night and first thing in the morning. Most extraordinary! And it's made me think a good deal. I believe you once said, Mr. Allerdyke, that your cousin was a bit of a ladies' man?"

"Bit that way inclined, was James," replied Allerdyke laconically. "Yes—he fancied the ladies a bit, no doubt. In

quite a proper way, you know—liked their society, and so
on."

"Just so!" assented the chief. "Well, I wonder if he and
Miss Slade, alias Mrs. Marlow, knew each other at all—
outside business? But it's not much use to speculate on
that just now—we've more urgent matters to attend to.
And first—this!"

He had put a copy of a morning newspaper round the
small brown paper parcel, and now took it off and showed
the parcel itself to the two wondering men. One of them
at any rate uttered a sharp exclamation.

"Brown paper, sealed with black wax!" said Allerdyke,
remembering what Chettle had told him. "Good Lord—
what—"

"I don't suppose this is the original brown paper, nor
these the original dabs of black wax," remarked the chief
as he produced a pocket pen-knife. "But this parcel,
gentlemen, was recently confided by Miss Slade to the
care of the manageress of the Pompadour, to be put in the
hotel safe—from which it was produced to me twenty
minutes ago. And—I am now going to see what it
contains."

The others sat in absorbed silence while the chief
delicately removed the wrappings of the mysterious
parcel. A sheet of brown paper, a sheet of cartridge paper
beneath it—and within these very ordinary envelopings
an old cigar-box, loosely tied about with a bit of knotted
string.

"Now for it!" said the chief. "The box contains—"

He raised the lid as the other two leaned nearer. A
stray ray of sunlight, filtering through the swaying
boughs of the hawthorn, shot down on the box as the chief
lifted a wad of soft paper and revealed a glittering mass
of pearls and diamonds.

"The Princess Nastirsevitch's jewels!" said the chief
softly. "That's just what I expected ever since the
manageress gave me this parcel. This, of course, is the
parcel which your cousin sent that night from Hull, Mr.

Allerdyke. It fell into Mrs. Marlow's hands—alias Miss Slade—and here it is! That's all right."

The other two men stared at the contents of the cigar-box, then at the chief, then at each other. A deep silence had fallen—it was some minutes before Allerdyke broke it.

"All wrong, I should say!" he muttered. "However, if those are the things—I only say if, mind—I suppose we're a step nearer to something else. But—what?"

The chief, who appeared to both of them to be strangely phlegmatic about the whole affair, proceeded to close the box, re-invest it in its wrappings, and tie it about with the original string.

"We are certainly a step nearer to a good deal," he said, making a neat job of his parcel and patting it affectionately as if he had been a milliner's apprentice doing up a choice confection. "And the next thing we do is to take a walk together into Hyde Park. On the way I will tell you why we are going there—that is, I will tell you what I know of the reason for such an expedition. It isn't much—but it has certain possibilities."

The two North-countrymen listened with great curiosity as they marched across the grass towards the tea-house. Each possessed the North-country love of the mysterious and the bizarre—this last development tickled their fancy and stirred their imagination.

"What on earth d'ye make out of it all?" asked Allerdyke. "Gad!—it's more like a children's game of hide-and-seek in an old house of nooks and corners than what I should have imagined police proceedings would be. What say you, Ambler?"

"I don't know how much romance and adventure there usually are in police proceedings," replied Appleyard cautiously.

"A good answer, Mr. Appleyard," said the chief laughing. "Ah, there's a lot more of both than civilians would think, in addition to all the sordid and dismal details. What do I make out of it, Mr. Appleyard? Why—I think somebody has all this time been making a special investigation of this mystery for himself, and that at last he's going to wind it up with a sensational revelation to— us! Don't you be surprised if you've an application for that fifty thousand pound reward before to-night!"

"You really think that?" exclaimed Allerdyke incredulously.

"I shouldn't be surprised," answered the chief, "Something considerable is certainly at hand. Now let us settle our plan of campaign. This tea-garden, I remember, is a biggish place. We will sit down at one of the tables— we will appear to be three quiet gentlemen disposed to take a cup of coffee with our cigars or cigarettes—we will be absorbed in our own conversation and company, but at the same time we will look about us. Therefore, use your eyes, gentlemen, as much as you like—but don't appear to take any particular interest in anything you see, and don't openly recognize any person you set eyes on."

It was a very warm and summer-like day, and the lawns around the tea-house were filled with people, young and old. Some were drinking tea, some coffee; some were indulging in iced drinks. Nursemaids and children were much in evidence under the surrounding trees; waitresses were flitting about hither and thither: there was nothing to suggest that this eminently London park scene was likely to prove the setting of the last act of a drama.

"You're much more likely to see and to recognize than we are," remarked Allerdyke, as the three gathered round a table on the edge of the crowd. "For my part I see nothing but men, women, and children—except that I also see Chettle, sitting across yonder with another man who's no doubt one of your lot."

"Just so," assented the chief. He gave an order for coffee to a passing waitress, lighted a cigar which Allerdyke offered him, and glanced round as if he were looking at nothing in particular. "Just so. Well, I see my own four men—I also see at least six detectives who belong to the City police, and there may be more. But I know those six personally. They are spread about, all over the place, and I daresay that every man is very much on the stretch, innocent enough as he looks."

"Six!" exclaimed Appleyard. "And four of yours! That looks as if they expected to have to tackle a small army!"

"You never know what you may have to tackle in affairs like this," replied the chief. "Nothing like having reserves in hand, you know. Now let me give you a tip. It is almost exactly two o'clock. Never mind the people who are already here, gentlemen. Keep your eyes open on any new-comers. Look out—quietly—for folk who seem to drop in as casually as we do. Look, for example, at those two well-dressed men who are coming across the sward there, swinging their sticks. They—"

Allerdyke suddenly bent his head towards the table.

"Careful!" he said. "Gad!—I know one of 'em, anyhow. Van Koon, as I live!"

32. The Chilverton Anti-Climax

The chief allowed himself to take a quick searching glance at the two men he had indicated. He had already heard of Van Koon and of his sudden disappearance from the hotel after the chance encounter with Chilverton, and he now regarded him with professional interest.

"The tall man, you mean?" he asked.

"Just so," answered Allerdyke. "The other man I don't know. But that's Van Koon. What's he here for, now? Is he in this, after all?"

The chief made no reply. He was furtively watching the two men, who had dropped into chairs at a vacant table beneath the shade of the trees and were talking to a waitress. Having taken a good look at Van Koon, he turned his attention to Van Koon's companion, a little, dapper man, smartly dressed in bright blue serge, and finished off with great care in all his appointments. He seemed to be approaching middle age; there were faint traces of grey in his pointed beard and upward-twisted moustaches; he carried his years, however, in very jaunty fashion, and his white Homburg hat, ornamented with a blue ribbon, was set at a rakish angle on the side of his close-cropped head. In his right eye he wore a gold-rimmed monocle; just then he was bringing it to bear an the waitress who stood between himself and his companion.

"You don't know the other man, either of you?" asked the chief suddenly.

Allerdyke shook his head, but Appleyard nodded.

"I know that chap by sight," he said. "I've seen him in the City—about Threadneedle Street—two or three times of late. He's always very smartly dressed—I took him for a foreigner of some sort."

The chief turned to his coffee.

"Well—never mind him," he said. "Pay no attention—so long as that man is Van Koon, I'll watch him quietly. But you may be sure he has come here on the same business that has brought us here. I—"

Allerdyke, whose sharp eyes were perpetually moving round the crowded enclosure and the little groups which mingled outside it, suddenly nudged the chief's elbow.

"Miss Slade!" he whispered. "And—Rayner!"

Appleyard had caught sight of his two fellow inmates of the Pompadour at the very moment in which Allerdyke espied them. He slightly turned away and bent his head; Allerdyke followed his example.

"You can't mistake them," he said to the chief. "I've described the man to you—a hunchback. They're crossing through the crowd towards the tea-house door."

"And they've gone in there," replied the chief in another minute. "Um!—this is getting more mysterious than ever. I wish I could get a word with some of our men who really know something! It seems to me—"

But at that moment Blindway came strolling along, his nose in the air, his eyes fixed on the roofs of the houses outside the park, and he quietly dropped a twisted scrap of paper at his superior's feet as he passed. The chief picked it up, spread it out on the marble-topped table, and read its message aloud to his companions.

"City men say the informant is here and will indicate the men to be arrested in a few minutes."

The chief tore the scrap of paper into minute shreds and dropped them on the grass.

"Things are almost at the crisis," he murmured with a smile. "It seems that we, gentlemen, are to play the part of spectators. The next thing to turn up—"

"Is Fullaway!" suddenly exclaimed Allerdyke, thrown off his guard and speaking aloud. "And, by Gad!—he's got that man Chilverton with him. This—by the Lord Harry, he's caught sight of us, too!"

Fullaway was coming quickly up the lawn from the direction of the Serpentine; he looked unusually alert, vigorous, and bustling; by his side, hurrying to keep pace with him, was the New York detective. And Fullaway's keen eyes, roving about, fell on Allerdyke and the chief and he made through the crowd in their direction, beckoning Chilverton to follow.

"Hullo—hullo!" he exclaimed, clapping a hand on Allerdyke's shoulder, nodding to the chief, and staring inquisitively at Appleyard. "So you're here, too, eh, Allerdyke? It wasn't you who sent me that mysterious message, was it?"

"What message?" growled Allerdyke. "Be careful! Don't attract attention—there are things going on here, I promise you! Drop into that chair, man—tell Chilverton to sit down. What message are you talking about?"

Fullaway, quick to grasp the situation, sat down in a chair which Appleyard pulled forward and motioned his companion to follow his example.

"I got a queer message—typewritten—on a sheet of notepaper which bore no address, about an hour ago," he said. "It told me that if I came here, to this Hyde Park tea-house, at two o'clock, I'd have this confounded mystery explained. No signature—nothing to show who or where it came from. So I set out. And just as I was stepping into a taxi to come on here, I met Chilverton, so he came along with me. What brings you, then? Similar message, eh? And what—"

"Hush!" whispered Appleyard. "Miss Slade's coming out of the tea-house! And who's the man that's with her?"

All five men glanced covertly over their shoulders at the open door of the tea-house, some twenty to thirty yards away. Down its steps came Miss Slade, accompanied by a man whom none of them had ever seen before—a well-built, light-complexioned, fair-haired man, certainly not an Englishman, but very evidently of Teutonic extraction, who was talking volubly to his companion and making free use of his hands to point or illustrate his conversation. And when he saw this man, the chief turned quickly to Allerdyke and intercepted a look which Allerdyke was about to give him—the same thought occurred to both. Here was the man described by the hotel-keeper of Eastbourne Terrace and the shabby establishment away in the Docks!

"Miss Slade!" exclaimed Fullaway. "What on earth are you talking about? That's my secretary, Mrs. Mar—"

"Sh!" interrupted the chief. "That's one of your surprises, Mr. Fullaway! Quiet, now, quiet. Our job is to watch. Something'll happen in a minute."

Miss Slade and her talkative companion edged their way through the crowd and passed out to an open patch of grass whereon a few children were playing. And as they went, two or three men also separated themselves from the idlers around the tables and strolled quietly and casually in the same direction. Also, Van Koon and the man with him left their table, and, as if they had no object in life but mere aimless chatter and saunter, wandered away towards the couple who had first emerged from the enclosure. And thereupon, Fullaway, not to be repressed, burst out with another exclamation.

"My God, Chilverton!" he cried. "There is Van Koon! And, by all that's wonderful, Merrifield with him. Now what—"

The New York detective, who was under no orders, and knew no reason why he should restrain himself, wasted no time in words. Like a flash, he had leapt from his chair, threaded his way through the surrounding people, and was after his quarry. And with a muttered exclamation of anger, the chief rose and followed—and it seemed to Allerdyke that almost at the same instant a score of men, up to that moment innocently idling and lounging, rose in company.

"Damn it!" he growled, as he and Appleyard got up. "That chap's going to spoil everything. What is he after?

Confound you, Fullaway!—why couldn't you keep quiet for a minute? Look there!"

Van Koon had turned and seen Chilverton. So, too, had Van Koon's companion. So, also, had Miss Slade and the man she was walking with. That man, too, saw the apparent idlers closing in upon him. For a second he, and Van Koon, and the other man stared at each other across the grass; then, as with a common instinct, each turned to flee—and at that instant Miss Slade, with a truly feminine cry, threw herself upon her companion and got an undeniably firm grip on his struggling arms.

"This is the Eastbourne Terrace man!" she panted as Allerdyke and half-a-dozen detectives relieved her. "Get the other two—Van Koon and Merrifield. Quick!"

But Van Koon was already in the secure grip of Chilverton, and the person in the light blue suit was being safely rounded up by a posse of grim-faced men.

33. The Smart Miss Slade

In no city of the world is a crowd so quickly collected as in London; in none is one so easily satisfied and dispersed. Within five minutes the detectives had hurried their three captives away towards the nearest cab-rank, and the people who had left their tea and their cakes to gather round, to stare, and to listen had gone back to their tables to discuss this latest excitement. But the chief and Allerdyke, Fullaway and Appleyard, Miss Slade and Rayner stood in a little group on the grass and looked at each other. Eventually, all looks except Rayner's centred on Miss Slade, who, somewhat out of breath from her tussle, was settling her hat and otherwise composing herself. And it was Miss Slade who spoke first when the party, as a party, found itself capable of speech.

"I don't know who it was," observed Miss Slade, rather more than a little acidly, "who came interfering in my business, but whoever he was he nearly spoilt it."

She darted a much-displeased look at the chief, who hastened to exculpate himself.

"Not I!" he said with a smile. "So don't blame me, Miss Slade. I was merely a looker-on, a passive spectator—until the right moment arrived. Do I gather that the right moment had not actually arrived—for your purpose?"

"You do," answered Miss Slade. "It hadn't. If you had all waited a few moments you would have had all three men in conference round one of those tables, and they could have been taken with far less fuss and bother—and far less danger to me. It's the greatest wonder in the world that I'm not lying dead on that grass!"

"We are devoutly thankful that you are not," said the chief fervently. "But—you're not! And the main thing is that the three men are in custody, and as for interference—"

"It was Chilverton," interrupted Fullaway, who had been staring at his mysterious secretary as if she were some rare object which he had never seen before. "Chilverton!—all Chilverton's fault. As soon as he set eyes on Van Koon nothing would hold him. And what I want to know—"

"We all want to know a good deal," remarked the chief, glancing invitingly at Miss Slade. "Miss Slade has no doubt a good deal to tell. I suggest that we walk across to those very convenient chairs which I see over there by the shrubbery—then perhaps—"

"I want to know a good deal, too," said Miss Slade.

"I don't know who you are, to start with, and I don't know why Mr. Appleyard happens to be here, to end with."

Appleyard answered these two questions readily.

"I'm here because I happen to be Mr. Allerdyke's London representative," he said. "This gentleman is a very highly placed official of the Criminal Investigation Department."

Miss Slade, having composed herself, favoured the chief with a deliberate inspection.

"Oh! in that case," she remarked, "in that case, I suppose I had better satisfy your curiosity. That is," she continued, turning to Rayner, "if Mr. Rayner thinks I may?"

"I was going to suggest it," answered Rayner. "Let's sit down and tell them all about it."

The party of six went across to the quiet spot which the chief had indicated, and Fullaway and Appleyard obligingly arranged the chairs in a group. Seated in the midst and quite conscious that she was the centre of attraction in several ways, Miss Slade began her explanation of the events and mysteries which had culminated in the recent sensational event.

"I daresay," she said, looking round her, "that some of you know a great deal more about this affair than I do. What I do know, however, is this—the three men who have just been removed are without doubt the arch-spirits of the combination which robbed Miss Lennard, attempted to rob Mr. James Allerdyke, possibly murdered Mr. James Allerdyke, and certainly murdered Lydenberg, Lisette Beaurepaire, and Ebers. Van Koon is an American crook, whose real name is Vankin; Merrifield, as you know, is Mr. Delkin's secretary; the other man is one Otto Schmall, a German chemist, and a most remarkably clever person, who has a shop and a chemical manufactory in Whitechapel. He's an expert in poison—and I think you will have some interesting matters to deal with when you come to tackle his share. Well, that's plain fact; and now you want to know how I—and Mr. Rayner—found all this out."

"Chiefly you," murmured Rayner, "chiefly you!"

"You had better let your minds go back to the morning of the 13th May last," continued Miss Slade, paying no apparent heed to this interruption. "On that morning I arrived at Mr. Fullaway's office at my usual time, ten o'clock, to find that Mr. Fullaway had departed suddenly, earlier in the morning, for Hull. I at once guessed why he had gone—I knew that Mr. James Allerdyke, in charge of the Princess Nastirsevitch's jewels, was to have landed at Hull the night before, and I concluded that Mr. Fullaway had set off to meet him. But Mr. Fullaway has a bad habit of leaving letters and telegrams lying about, for any one to see, and within a few minutes I found on his desk a telegram from Mr. Marshall Allerdyke, dispatched early that morning from Hull, saying that his cousin had died suddenly during the night. That, of course, definitely explained Mr. Fullaway's departure, and it also made me wonder, knowing all I did know, if the jewels were safe.

"This, I repeat, was about ten to half-past ten o'clock. About twelve o'clock of that morning, the 13th, Mr. Van Koon, whom I knew as a resident in the hotel, and a frequent caller on Mr. Fullaway, came in. He wanted Mr. Fullaway to cash a cheque for him. I told him that I could do that, and I took his cheque, wrote out one of my own and went up town to Parr's Bank, at the bottom of St. Martin's Lane, to get the cash for him. Mr. Van Koon stayed in the office, reading a bundle of American newspapers which had just been delivered. I was away from the office perhaps forty minutes or so; when I returned he was still there. I gave him the money; he thanked me, and went away.

"Towards the end of that afternoon, just before I was leaving the office, I got a wire from Mr. Fullaway, from Hull. It was quite short—it merely informed me that Mr. James Allerdyke was dead, under mysterious circumstances, and that the Nastirsevitch property was missing. Of course, I knew what that meant, and I drew my own conclusions.

"Now I come to the 14th—a critical day, so far as I am concerned. During the morning a parcels-van boy came into the office. He said that on the previous day, about half-past twelve o'clock, he had brought a small parcel there, addressed to Mr. Fullaway, and had handed it to a gentleman who was reading newspapers, and who had answered 'Yes' when inquired of as Mr. Fullaway. This gentleman—who, of course, was Van Koon—had signed for the parcel by scribbling two initials 'F. F.' in the proper space. The boy, who said he was new to his job, told me that the clerk at the parcels office objected to this as not being a proper signature, and had told him to call next time he was passing and get the thing put right. He accordingly handed me the sheet, and I, believing that this was some small parcel which Van Koon had taken in, signed for, and placed somewhere in the office or in Mr. Fullaway's private room, signed my own name, for Franklin Fullaway, over the penciled initials. And as I did so I noticed that the parcel had been sent from Hull.

"When the boy had gone I looked for that parcel. I could not find it anywhere. It was certainly not in the office, nor in any of the rooms of Mr. Fullaway's suite. I was half minded to go to Mr. Van Koon and ask about it, but I decided that I wouldn't; I thought I would wait until Mr. Fullaway returned. But all the time I was wondering what parcel it could be that was sent from Hull, and certainly dispatched from there on the very evening before Mr. Fullaway's hurried journey.

"Nothing happened until Mr. Fullaway came back. Then a lot of things happened all at once. There was the news he brought about the Hull affair. Then there was the affair of the French maid. A great deal got into the newspapers. Mr. Rayner and I, who live at the same boarding-house, began to discuss matters. I heard, through Mr. Fullaway, that there was likelihood of a big reward, and I determined to have a try for it—in conjunction with Mr. Rayner. And so I kept my own counsel—I said nothing about the affair of the parcel."

Fullaway, who had been manifesting signs of impatience and irritation during the last few minutes, here snapped out a question.

"Why didn't you tell me at once about the parcel?" he demanded. "It was your duty!"

Miss Slade gave her employer a cool glance.

"Possibly!" she retorted. "But you are much too careless to be entrusted with secrets, Mr. Fullaway. I knew that if I told you about that parcel you'd spoil everything at once. I wanted to do things my own way. I took my own way—and it's come out all right, for everybody. Now, don't you or anybody interrupt again— I'm telling it all in order."

Fullaway made an inarticulate growling protest, but Miss Slade took no notice and continued in even, dispassionate tones, as if she had been explained a mathematical problem.

"The affair prospered. The Princess came. The reward of fifty thousand pounds was offered. Then Mr. Rayner and I put our heads together more seriously. Much, of course, depended upon me, as I was on the spot. I wanted a chance to get into Van Koon's rooms, some time when he was out. Fortunately the chance came. One afternoon, when Van Koon was in our office, he and Mr. Fullaway settled to dine out together and go to the theatre afterwards. That gave me my opportunity. I made an excuse about staying late at Mr. Fullaway's office and when both men were clear away I let myself into Van Koon's room—I'd already made preparations for that— and proceeded to search. I found the parcel. It was a small, square parcel, done up in brown paper and sealed with black wax; it had been opened, the original wrapper put on again, and the seals resealed. I took it into Mr. Fullaway's rooms and opened it, carefully. Inside I found a small cigar-box, and in it the Princess's jewels. I took them out. Then I put certain articles of corresponding weight into the box, did it up again precisely as I had found it, smeared over the seals with more black wax, went back to Van Koon's room with it, and placed it again where I had found it—in a small suit-case.

"I now knew, of course, that Mr. James Allerdyke had sent those jewels direct to Mr. Fullaway, immediately on his arrival in Hull, and that they had fallen by sheer accident into Van Koon's hands. But I wanted to know more. I wanted to know if Van Koon had any connection with this affair, and if, when he saw that the parcel was from Hull, he had immediately jumped to the conclusion that it might be from James Allerdyke, and might contain the actual valuables. Fortunately, Mr. Rayner had already made arrangements with a noted private inquiry agent to have Van Koon most carefully and closely watched. And the very day after I found and took possession of the jewels we received a report from this agent that Van Koon was in the habit of visiting the shop and manufactory of a German chemist named Schmall, in Whitechapel. Further, he had twice come away from it, after lengthy visits, in company with a man whom the agent's employees had tracked to the Hotel Cecil, and whom I knew, from their description, to be Mr. Merrifield, Mr. Delkin's private secretary.

"Naturally, having discovered this, we gave instructions for a keener watch than ever to be kept on both these men. But the name of the German chemist gave me personally a new and most important clue. There had been employed at the Waldorf Hotel, for some weeks up to the end of the first week in May, a German-Swiss young man, who then called himself Ebers. He acted as valet to several residents; amongst others, Mr. Fullaway. He was often in and out of Mr. Fullaway's rooms. Once, Mr. Fullaway being out, and I having nothing to do, I was cleaning up some photographic apparatus which I had there. This man Ebers came in with some clothes of Mr. Fullaway's. Seeing what I was doing, he got talking to me about photography, saying that he himself was an amateur. He recommended to me certain materials and things of that sort which he said he could get from a friend of his, a chemist, who was an enthusiastic photographer and manufactured chemicals and things used in photography. I gave him some money to get me a supply of things, and he brought various packets and parcels to me two or three days later. Each packet bore the name of Otto Schmall, and an address in a street which runs off Mile End Road.

"Now, when the private inquiry agent made his reports to Mr. Rayner and myself about Van Koon, and told us where he had been tracked to more than once, I, of course, remembered the name of Schmall, and Mr. Rayner and I began to put certain facts together. They were these:

"*First.*—Ebers had easy access to Mr. Fullaway's room at all hours, and was often in them when both Mr. Fullaway and I were out. Mr. Fullaway is notoriously careless in leaving papers and documents, letters and telegrams lying around. Ebers had abundant opportunities of reading lots of documents relating to (1) the Pinkie Pell pearls, and (2) the proposed Nastirsevitch deal.

"*Second.*—Ebers was a friend of Schmall. Schmall was evidently a man of great cleverness in chemistry.

"*Third.*—All the circumstances of Mr. James Allerdyke's death, and of Lisette Beaurepaire's death, pointed to unusually skillful poisoning. Who was better able to engineer that than a clever chemist?

"*Fourth.*—The jewels belonging to the Princess Nastirsevitch had undoubtedly fallen into Van Koon's hands. Van Koon was a friend of Schmall. So also, evidently, was Merrifield. Now, Merrifield, as Delkin's secretary, knew of the proposed deal.

"Obviously, then, Schmall, Van Koon, and Merrifield were in league—whether Ebers was also in league, or was a catspaw, we did not trouble to decide. But there was another fact which seemed to have some bearing, though it is one which I have never yet worked out—perhaps some of you know something of it. It was this: Just before he went to Russia, Mr. James Allerdyke, being in town, gave me a photograph of himself which Mr. Marshall Allerdyke had recently taken. I kept that photo lying on my desk at Mr. Fullaway's for some time. One day I missed it. It is such an unusual thing for me to misplace anything that I turned over every paper on my desk in searching for it. It was not to be found. Four days later I found it, exactly where it ought to have been. Now, you can draw your own conclusions from that—mine are that Ebers stole it, so that he could reproduce it in order to give his reproduction to some person who wanted to identify James Allerdyke at sight.

"However, to go forward to the discovery which we made about Schmall, Van Koon, and Merrifield. As soon as we made that discovery, Mr. Rayner was for going to the police at once, but I thought not—there was still certain evidence which I wanted, so that the case could be presented without a flaw. However, all of a sudden I saw that we should have to act. Ebers was found dead in a small hotel near the Docks, and at a conference in which Mr. Fullaway insisted I should join, in his rooms, and at which Van Koon, who had been playing a bluff game, was present, there was enough said to convince me that Van Koon and his associates would take alarm and be off with what they believed themselves to possess—the jewels in that parcel. So then Mr. Rayner and I determined on big measures. And they were risky ones—for me.

"I had already been down, more than once, into Whitechapel, and had bought things at Schmall's shop, and I was convinced that he was the man who accompanied Lisette Beaurepaire to that little hotel in Eastbourne Terrace. Now that the critical moment came, after the Ebers-Federman affair, I went there again. I got Schmall outside his premises. I took a bold step. I told him that I was a woman detective, who, for purposes of my own, had been working this case, and that I was in full possession of the facts. If I had not taken the precaution to tell him this in the thick of a crowded street, he would have killed me on the spot! Then I went on to tell him more. I said that his accomplice had led him to believe that he had the Nastirsevitch jewels in a parcel in his possession. I said that Van Koon was wrong—I had them myself—I told him how I got them. He nearly collapsed at that—I restored him by saying that the real object of my visit to him was to do a deal with him. I said that it did not matter two pins to me what he and his accomplices had done—what I was out for was money, nothing but money. How much would he and the others put up for the jewels and my silence? I reminded him of the fifty thousand pound reward. He glared at me like the devil he is, and said that he'd a mind to kill me there and then, whatever happened. Whereupon I told him that I had a revolver in my jacket pocket, that it was trained on him, and that if he moved, my finger would move just as quick, and I invited him to be sensible. It was nothing but a question of money, I said—-how much would they give? Finally, we settled it at sixty thousand pounds. He was to meet me here—to-

day at two—the other two were to be about—the money
was to be paid to me on production of the jewels, for
which purpose one of them was to go with me to my
boarding-house. And—you know the rest."

Miss Slade came to a sudden stop. She glanced at
Rayner, who had been watching the effect of her story on
the other men.

"At least," she added suddenly, "you know all that's
really important. As Ebers' affair was in the City, we
warned the City police and left things with them. I think
that's all. Except, of course, Mr. Marshall Allerdyke, that
we formally claim the reward for which you're
responsible. And—equally of course—that Mr. Rayner
and I will hand over her jewels in the course of this
afternoon to the Princess. Miss Lennard's property, I
should say, you'll find hidden away on Schmall's
premises. Yes—that's all."

"Except this," said the chief quietly. He unwrapped
the newspaper in which he had carried his small parcel
and revealed its contents to Miss Slade. "The jewels, you
see, Miss Slade, are here. It has been my painful duty to
visit your hotel, and to possess myself of them. Sorry
but—"

Miss Slade gave one glance of astonishment at the
chief and his exhibit; then she laughed in his face.

"Don't apologize, and don't trouble yourself!" she said
suavely. "But you're a bit off it, all the same. Those are
some paste things which Mr. Rayner got together for me
in case it came to being obliged to exhibit some to the
crooks. You don't think, really, that I was going to run
any risks with the genuine articles? Sakes—they're all
right! They're deposited, snug and safe, at my bankers,
and if you'll get a cab, we'll drive there and get them!"

34. Merrifield Explains

Late that afternoon Marshall Allerdyke and Fullaway, responding to an urgent telephone call, went to New Scotland Yard, and were presently ushered into the presence of the great man who had been so much in evidence that day. The great man was as self-possessed, as suave, and as calmly cheerful as ever. And on the desk in front of him he had two small and neatly made up parcels, tied and sealed in obviously official fashion.

"So we seem to have come to the end of this affair, gentlemen," he observed as he waved his visitors to chairs on either side of him. "Except, of course, for the unpleasant consequences which must necessarily result to the men we caught to-day. However, there will be no consequences—of that sort—for one of them. Schmall has—escaped us!"

"Got away!" exclaimed Fullaway. "Great Scott you don't mean that!"

"Schmall committed suicide this afternoon," replied the chief calmly. "Clever man—in his own line, which was a very bad line. He was searched most narrowly and carefully, so I've come to the conclusion that he carried some of his subtle poison in his mouth—the hollow tooth dodge, no doubt. Anyway, he's dead—they found him dead in his cell. It's a pity—for he richly deserved hanging. At least, according to Merrifield."

"Ah!" said Fullaway, with a start. "According to Merrifield, eh? Now what may that mean? To find Merrifield in this at all was, of course, a regular shock to me!"

"Merrifield—just the type of man who would!—has made a clean breast of the whole thing," answered the chief. "He made it to me—an hour ago. He thought it best. He wants—naturally enough—to save his neck."

"Will he?" growled Allerdyke. "A lot of necks ought to crack, after all this!"

"Can't say—we mustn't prejudge the case," said the chief. "But that's his desire of course. He would tell me everything—at once. I had it all taken down. But I remember every scrap of it. You want to hear? Well there's a good deal of it, but I can epitomize it. You'll find that you were much to blame, Mr. Fullaway—just as that smart young woman, your secretary, was candid enough to tell you."

"Oh, I know—I know!" asserted Fullaway. "But—this confession?"

"Very well," responded the chief. "Here it is, then but you must bear in mind that Merrifield could only tell what he knew—there'll probably be details to come out later. Anyway, Merrifield—whose chief object is, I must also remind you, the clearing of himself from any charge of murder—he doesn't mind the other charge, but he does object to the graver one!—says that though he's been playing it straight for some time, ever since he went into Delkin's service, in fact—he'd had negotiations of a questionable sort with both Schmall and Van Koon before years ago, in this city and in New York. He renewed his acquaintance with Schmall when he came over this time with Delkin—met him accidentally, and got going it with him again—and they both resumed dealings with Van Koon—who, I may say, was wanted by Chilverton on a quite different charge. Schmall had set up a business here in the East End as a small manufacturing chemist— he'd evidently a perfect and a diabolical genius for chemistry, especially in secret poisons—and down there Merrifield and Van Koon used to go. Also, there used to go there the young man Ebers, or Federman—we'll stick to Ebers—who, from Merrifield's account, seems to have been a tool of Schmall's. Ebers, a fellow of evident acute perception, used to tell Schmall of things which his calling as valet at various hotels gave him knowledge—it strikes me that from what we now know we shall be able to trace to Schmall and Ebers several robberies at hotels which have puzzled us a good deal. And there is no doubt that it was Ebers who told Schmall of the two matters of which he obtained knowledge when he used to frequent your rooms. Mr. Fullaway—the pearls belonging to Miss Lennard, and the proposed jewel deal between the Princess Nastirsevitch and Mr. Delkin. But in that last Merrifield came in. He too, knew of it, and he told Schmall and Van Koon, but Ebers supplied the detailed information of what you were doing, through access, as Miss Slade said, to your papers—which you left lying about, you know."

"I know—I know!" groaned Fullaway. "Careless—careless!"

"Very!" said the chief, with a smile at Allerdyke "Teach you a lesson, perhaps. However, there this knowledge was. Now, Schmall, according to Merrifield, was the leading spirit. He had the man Lydenberg in his employ. He sent him off to Christiania to waylay James Allerdyke: he supplied him with a photograph of James Allerdyke, which Ebers procured."

"I know that!" muttered Allerdyke. "Clever, too!"

"Exactly," agreed the chief. "Now at the same time Schmall learned of Miss Lennard's return. He sent Ebers, who already knew and had been cultivating the French maid, down to Hull to meet her and bring her away with Miss Lennard's jewel-box. That was done easily. The Lydenberg affair, however, did not come off—through Lydenberg. Because, as we now know, James Allerdyke sent the Nastirsevitch jewels off to you, Mr. Fullaway. But there, fortune favoured these fellows Van Koon, for purposes of theirs, had taken up his quarters close by you—in your absence the box came into his hands. And— we know how the ingenious Miss Slade despoiled him of it!"

The chief paused for a moment, and mechanically shifted the two parcels which stood before him. He seemed to be reflecting, and when he spoke again he prefaced his words with a shake of the head.

"Now here, from this point," he continued, "I don't know if Mr. Merrifield is telling the truth. Probably he isn't. But I confess that, at present, I don't see how we're going to prove that he isn't. He strenuously declares that neither he nor Van Koon had anything whatever to do with the murder of Lisette Beaurepaire, Lydenberg, or Ebers. He further says that he does not know if Lydenberg poisoned James Allerdyke. He declares that he does not know if it was ever intended to poison James Allerdyke, though he confesses that it was intended to rob him at Hull. Schmall, he says, was the active partner in all this—he took all that into his own hands. According to Merrifield, he does not know, nor Van Koon either, if it was Schmall who went down to Hull and shot Lydenberg, or if Lydenberg was murdered by some person who had a commission for his destruction from some secret society— Lydenberg, he believed, was mixed up with that sort of thing."

"I know that, I think!" exclaimed Allerdyke.

"I daresay we all three know what we think," observed the chief. "Schmall seems to have had a genius for putting his tools out of the way when he had done with them. It was undoubtedly Schmall who took Lisette Beaurepaire to that hotel in Paddington and poisoned her; it was just as undoubtedly Schmall who took Ebers to the hotel in London Docks and got rid of him. But, I tell you, Merrifield swears that neither he nor Van Koon knew of these things, and did not connive at them."

"Did they know of them—afterwards?" asked Fullaway.

"Ah!" replied the chief. "That's what they'll have to satisfy a judge and jury about! I think they'll find it difficult. But—that's about all. Except this—that they were all three about to clear out when the enterprising

Miss Slade turned up and told Schmall she'd got the Nastirsevitch jewels. That was a stiff proposition for them. But they were equal to it. For you see Miss Slade let him know that she was open to do a deal—for sixty thousand pounds! How were they to get sixty thousand pounds? Ah!—now came a confession from Merrifield which has already—for I've told him of it—made Mr. Delkin stare. Delkin, it appears, keeps a very big banking account here in London—so big, that his bankers think nothing of his drawing what we should call enormous cash cheques. Now Merrifield—you see what a clean breast he's made—admitted to me that he was an expert forger—so he calmly forged a cheque of Delkin's, drew sixty thousand in notes—and they had them on them—at least Merrifield had—when we took all three a few hours ago. Nice people, eh!"

There was a silence of much significance for a few minutes; then Allerdyke got up from his chair with a growl.

"I'd have given a good deal if that fellow Schmall had saved his neck for the gallows!" he muttered. "He's cheated me!"

"It's my impression," said the chief, "that if Miss Slade hadn't been so smart, Schmall would have cheated his two accomplices. He had what he believed to be the parcel containing the Nastirsevitch jewels in his possession, and he also had Miss Lennard's pearls locked up in his safe. We got those this afternoon, on searching his premises; Miss Slade gave us the real Nastirsevitch jewels from her bank. Here they are—both lots, in these parcels. And if you two gentlemen will go through the formality of signing receipts for them, you, Mr. Fullaway, can take her parcel to the Princess, and you, Mr. Allerdyke, can carry hers to Miss Lennard. And, er—" he added, with a quiet smile, as he rose and produced some papers—"you won't mind, either of you, I'm sure, if a couple of my men accompany you—just to see that you accomplish your respective missions in safety?"

35. The Allerdyke Way

With the recovered pearls in his hand, and Chettle as guardian and companion at his side, Allerdyke chartered a taxi-cab and demanded to be driven to Bedford Court Mansions. And as they glided away up Whitehall he turned to the detective with a grin that had a sardonic complexion to it.

"Well—except for the law business—I reckon this is about over, Chettle," he said. "You've had plenty to do, anyway—not much kicking your heels in idleness anywhere, while this has been going on!"

Chettle pulled a long face and sighed.

"Unfortunate for me, all the same, Mr. Allerdyke," he answered. "I'd meant to have a big cut in at that reward, sir. Now I suppose that young woman'll get it."

"Miss Slade'll doubtless get most of it," replied Allerdyke. "But I think there'll have to be a bit of a dividing-up, like. You fellows are certainly entitled to some of it—especially you—and two or three of those folks who gave some information ought to have a look in. But, of course, Miss Slade will feel herself entitled to the big lump—and she'll take care to get it, don't make any mistake!"

"She's a deal too clever, that young lady," observed Chettle. "I like 'em clever, but not quite as clever as all that. In my opinion, she's mistaken her calling, has that young woman. She ought to have been one of us—they're uncommonly bent that way, some of these modern misses—they can see right through a thing, sometimes, where we men can't see an inch above our noses."

"Intuition," said Allerdyke, with a laugh. "Aye, well perhaps Miss Slade'll have got so infected with enthusiasm for your business that She'll go in for it regularly. This reward'll do for capital, you know, Chettle."

"Ah!" responded Chettle feelingly. "Wish it was coming to me! I wouldn't put no capital into that business—not me, sir! I'd have a nice little farm in the country, and I'd grow roses, and breed sheep and pigs, and—"

"And lose all your brass in a couple of years!" laughed Allerdyke. "Stick to your own game, my lad, and when you want to grow roses, do it in your own back yard for pleasure. And here we are—and you'd best wait, Chettle, until Miss Lennard herself gives a receipt for this stuff, and then you can take it back to Scotland Yard and frame it."

He left Chettle in an anti-room of Miss Lennard's flat while he himself was shown into the prima donna's presence. She was alone, and evidently unoccupied, and her eyes suddenly sparkled when Allerdyke came in as if she was glad of a visitor.

"You!" she exclaimed. "Really!"

"It's me," said Allerdyke laconically. "Nobody else," He looked round to make sure that the door was safely closed; then he advanced to the little table at which Miss Lennard was sitting and laid down his parcel.

"Something for you," he said abruptly. "Open it."

"What is it?" she asked, glancing shyly at him. "Not chocolates—surely!"

"Never bought aught of that sort in my life," replied Allerdyke. "More respect for people's teeth. Here—I'll open it," he went on, producing a penknife and cutting the string. "I've signed one receipt for this stuff already— you'll have to sign another. There's a detective in your parlour waiting for it, just now."

"A detective!" she exclaimed. "Why—why—you don't mean to say that box has my pearls in it? Oh! you don't!"

"See if they're all right," commanded Allerdyke "Gad!—they've been through some queer hands since you lost 'em. I don't know how you feel about it, but hang me if I shouldn't feel strange wearing 'em again! I should feel—but I daresay you don't!"

"No, I don't!" she said as she drew the jewels out of their wrappings and hurriedly examined them. "Of course I don't; all I feel is that I'm delighted beyond measure to get them back. You don't understand."

"No, I don't," agreed Allerdyke. He dropped into a chair close by, and quietly regarded the owner of the fateful valuables. "I'm only a man, you see. But—I should know better how to take care of things like these than you did. Come, now!"

"I shall take better care of them—in future," said Miss Lennard.

Allerdyke shook his head,

"Not you!" he retorted. "At least—not unless you've somebody to take care of you. Eh?"

Miss Lennard, who was still examining her recovered property, set it hastily down and stared at her visitor. Her colour heightened, and her eyes became inquisitive.

"Take care of—me!" she exclaimed. "Of—whatever are you talking about, Mr. Allerdyke?"

"It's like this," replied Allerdyke, involuntarily squaring himself in his chair. "You see me?—I'm as healthy a man as ever lived!—forty, but no more than five-and-twenty in health and spirits. I've plenty of brains and a rare good temper. I'm owner of one of the best businesses in Yorkshire—I'm worth a good ten thousand a year. I've one of the best houses in our parts—I'm going to take another, a country house, if you're minded. I'll guarantee to make the best husband—"

Miss Lennard dropped back on her sofa and screamed.

"Good heavens, man?" she exclaimed. "Are you—are you really asking me to—to marry you?"

"That's it," replied Allerdyke, nodding. "You've hit it. Queer way, maybe—but it's my way. See?"

"I never heard of—of such a way in all my life!" said the lady. "You're—extraordinary!"

"I am," said Allerdyke. "Yes—we are out of the ordinary in our part of the world—we know it. Well," he went on after a moment's silence, during which they looked at each other, "you've heard what I have to say. How is it to be?"

The prima donna continued to gaze intently on this strange wooer for a full minute. Then she suddenly stretched out her hand.

"I'll marry you!" she said quietly.

Allerdyke gave the hand a firm pressure, and stood up, unconsciously pulling himself to his full height.

"Thank you," he said. "You shan't regret it. And now, then—a pen, if you please. Sign that."

He handed his betrothed a paper, watched her sign it, and then, picking up the pen as she laid it down, took a cheque-book from his pocket and quickly wrote a cheque. This he placed in an envelope taken from the writing-table. Envelope and receipt in hand, he turned to the door.

"Business first," he said, smiling over his shoulder. "I'll send Chettle off—then we'll talk about ourselves."

He went away to Chettle and put the paper and the envelope in his hand.

"That's the receipt," he said. "T'other's a bit of a present for you—naught to do with the reward—a trifle from me. Ah!—you might like to know that I've just got engaged to be married!"

Chettle glanced round and inclined his head towards the room from which Allerdyke had just emerged.

"What!—to the lady!" he exclaimed. "Deary me. Well," he went on, grasping the successful suitor's hand, and giving it a warm and sympathetic squeeze, "there's one thing I can say, Mr. Allerdyke—you'll make an uncommon good-looking pair!"

THE END

Resurrected Press Mysteries by J. S. Fletcher

The Orange-Yellow Diamond
When an elderly pawnbroker is murdered in the London parish of Paddington, a young, down on his luck writer is accused of the crime. But then it's found the pawnbroker had had in his possession an extraordinary South African diamond worth over eighty-thousand pounds — a diamond that's now missing. It falls to Melky Rubenstein to unravel the mystery and prove the young man's innocence.

The Middle Temple Murder
When an elderly man's body is found on the steps of chambers in the Midde Temple, one of the Inns of Court, it falls to newspaperman Frank Spargo and Detective-Sergeant Rathbury to solve the crime. The murdered man, for indeed it was murder, was found with no money or identification on his person except for a piece of paper with the name and address of a young barrister. Who is the victim? Why was he killed? Who is the murderer?

Scarhaven Keep
Bassett Oliver, the famed actor, has gone missing. When Oliver fails to show for a rehearsal, aspiring playwright Richard Copplestone finds himself sent to the small village of Scarhaven on the northern coast of England to track down the actors movements. What he finds is mystery. Find the answers as Copplestone unravels the mystery of Scarhaven Keep.

Visit www.resurrectedpress.com

Resurrected Press Mysteries by Fergus Hume

The Green Mummy

Professor Braddock hoped to compare the burial practices of the Egyptians with those of the ancient Peruvians with his latest acquisition, the mummy of the last Inca, Caxas. But on arrival, the packing case proved to hold not the mummy, but the body of his assistant Sidney Bolton. It falls to Archie Hope to discover the murderer if he is to marry the professors step-daughter, Lucy Kendal. Who killed Bolton and where is the mummy? Was it the sea captain Hervey? The mysterious Don Pedro? Cockatoo the Polynesian servant? The professor, himself? And what has become of the emeralds? These are the questions that Hope must answer amongst the secrets of the past in The Green Mummy.

The Mystery of a Hansom Cab

"Truth is said to be stranger than fiction, and certainly the extraordinary murder which took place in Melbourne Friday morning goes a long way towards verifying that saying." Thus opens The Mystery of a Hansom Cab, the best selling mystery of the nineteenth century. When a man is found dead in a hansom cab one of Melbourne's leading citizens is accused of the murder. He pleads his innocence, yet refuses to give an alibi. It falls to a determined lawyer and an intrepid detective to find the truth, revealing long kept secrets along the way. Fergus Hume's first and perhaps most famous mystery... The Mystery Of A Hansom Cab.

Visit www.resurrectedpress.com

Resurrected Press Mysteries from the Dr. John Thorndyke Series

Dr. John Thorndyke - Lecturer on Medical Jurisprudence and Forensic Medicine. Before Bones, before CSI, before Quincy, M.E – there was Dr. John Thorndyke solving the most baffling cases of Edwardian London using the latest tools of medical science. Read about his cases in:

The Eye of Osiris
John Bellingham, noted Egyptologist has vanished not once but twice in the same day. Now Dr, Thorndyke must unravel the tangled claims on his estate, solve the riddle of the missing man and find the "Eye of Osiris".

The Mystery of 31 New Inn
When Dr. Jervis is whisked away in a coach with no windows to an unknown location to treat a man in a coma from undivulged causes it is Dr. Thorndyke who must come up with the solution.

The Red Thumb Mark
The first of Dr. Thorndyke's cases finds him trying to prove the innocence of a young man accused of being a diamond thief despite the fact that his finger print was found at the scene of the crime.

John Thorndyke's Cases
More cases of medical mysteries as told by his trusted assistant Jervis, M.D. Eight stories of crime and deduction in Edwardian London.

Visit www.resurrectedpress.com

Resurrected Press Mysteries by John R. Watson & Arthur J. Rees

The Hampstead Mystery
High Court Justice Sir Horace Fewbanks found shot dead in his Hampstead home, a butler with a criminal past, a scorned lover and a hint of scandal. These are the elements of the Hampstead Mystery that Detective Inspector Chippenfield of Scotland Yard must unravel with the assistance of the ambitious Detective Rolfe. But will he be able to sort out the tangled threads of this case and arrest the culprit before he is upstaged by the celebrated gentleman detective Crewe. Follow the details of this amazing case at it plays out across Hampstead, London and Scotland until it reaches a stunning conclusion in the courts of the Old Bailey.

The Mystery of the Downs
When Harry Marsland was caught in a sudden down pour he sought shelter at Cliff Farm. Met at the door by a young woman clearly expecting someone else he is only too glad to get inside to wait out the storm. When they hear a noise upstairs in the deserted house they investigate only to discover the body of the farm's owner, Frank Lumsden, dead of a gunshot wound. Who then, killed Lumsden, and why? Who was the woman expecting and did she have any roll in the murder? These are the questions that private detective Crewe must answer in The Mystery of the Downs.

Visit www.resurrectedpress.com

Other Resurrected Press Mysteries

Mysteries on a Train

Before the Orient Express there was:

The Rome Express by Arthur Griffiths
A man is found dead in his first class sleeping compartment on the express from Rome to Paris. Who was his murderer? The Countess? The English General? His brother the clergy man? The maid who has disappeared? Is the French justice system up to solving the crime? Read about it in The Rome Express.

The Passenger from Calais by Arthur Griffiths
Colonel Basil Annesley finds he is the only passenger on the train from Calais to Lucerne. That is until a mysterious woman shows up at the last minute to book a compartment. Who is after her? What is her secret? Is she a criminal or a victim? Read about it in The Passenger from Calais

Visit us at www.resurrectedpress.com

About Resurrected Press

A division of Intrepid Ink, LLC, Resurrected Press is dedicated to bringing high quality, vintage books back into publication. See our entire catalogue and find out more at www.ResurrectedPress.com.

About Intrepid Ink, LLC

Intrepid Ink, LLC provides full publishing services to authors of fiction and non-fiction books, eBooks and websites. From editing to formatting, from publishing to marketing, Intrepid Ink gets your creative works into the hands of the people who want to read them. Find out more at www.IntrepidInk.com.

www.ingramcontent.com/pod-product-compliance
Lightning Source LLC
Chambersburg PA
CBHW060544180626
46817CB00002B/713